SYNOPSIS

True never guessed that life would be this hard. Being only twenty-five years old, she should have been wild, reckless, and having fun, not fighting the hardest battle of her life, alongside a husband who no longer loved her. After their divorce, True wanted to be free and enjoy every day. Falling in love was *not* in the plan. She most definitely hadn't foreseen falling in love with an arrogant, womanizing hustler like Coop. Yet, she did. However, as soon as True tells him all her truth, he'll revert to that unbearable goon that wreaked havoc on the streets of Chicago.

Coop grew up an orphan, passed from foster home to foster home. A hustler, his right-hand man, was his only family. His love was the game. His side chick was money. Then he met True. She filled gaps in his life that he didn't even know needed filling. Looking at her, being in her presence, was like the first warm, sunny day after a brutal Chicago winter. Being with her felt like being lost in the right direction. Coop had thawed out his icy heart and given it to True... just for her to break it. True was gone, unable to fix what she'd broken, but, lucky for Coop; True found a way.

Remi has been with Banks for ten years. She remained loyal through every lie and infidelity in hopes that her patience and understanding will eventually bring her "happily ever after" with her one true love. Finally, Banks gives her what she has always wanted... a ring. However, that ring came with such a devasting blow, leaving Remi unsure how she will ever recover... until she meets True and Coop. Unbeknownst to her, these two strangers will mend her broken heart and cause her life to never, ever be the same again.

* This is a heart-wrenching, yet warming, story of broken women who find love in their darkest hours from the most unexpected and hardened hearts.

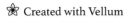 Created with Vellum

ABOUT THE AUTHOR

Jessica N. Watkins was born April 1st in Chicago, Illinois. She obtained a Bachelor of Arts with focus in Psychology from DePaul University and Masters of Applied Professional Studies with focus in Business Administration from the like institution. Working in Hospital Administration for most of her career, Watkins has also been an author of fiction literature since the young age of nine. Eventually, she used writing as an outlet during her freshmen year of high school as a single parent: "In the third grade, I entered a short story contest with a fictional tale of an apple tree that refused to grow despite the efforts of the darling main character. My writing evolved from apple trees to my seventh and eighth-grade classmates paying me to read novels I wrote about kids our age living the lives our parents wouldn't dare let us". At the age of twenty-eight, Watkins' chronicles have matured into steamy, humorous, and realistic tales of African American Romance and Urban Fiction.

In September 2013, Jessica's most recent novel, Secrets of a Side Bitch, published by SBR Publications, reached #1 on multiple charts.

Jessica N. Watkins is available for talks, workshops or book signings. Email her at authorjwatkins@gmail.com.

JESSICA WATKINS PRESENTS

When
MY SOUL MET
A THUG

NATIONAL BEST SELLING AUTHOR
JESSICA N. WATKINS

PROLOGUE

True

"Goodnight, Mommy."

I couldn't help but smile at Joy's sweet voice. At four years old, she could have been calling me a bald-headed wench, and it still would have sounded so adorable and angelic.

I bent down and kissed her chubby, chocolate cheek. She had inherited her father's deep, chocolate skin and she was the spitting image of him. But you could see remnants of me in her smile.

"Goodnight, Mama's baby. Let's say our prayers."

Her long, dark lashes appeared as if they were fanning me as she shut her eyes. It was so cute how she squeezed her eyes closed so tightly before I began to recite our prayer.

"Now I lay me down to sleep. I pray the Lord my soul to keep." My heart melted as Joy prayed along with me in her toddler dialect that missed and oddly pronounced some of the words. After four years of saying this prayer to her almost every night, she had memorized it. "If

I should die before I wake, I pray to God my soul to take. If I should live for other days, I pray the Lord to guide my ways. Amen."

"Amen!" Joy ended.

"Okay, sleep tight, sweetie." I stood up from the bed where I was sitting beside her. I then made sure that the blanket covered her up to her chin. She had begun to drift off to sleep before I had even turned to leave.

I was grateful that Joy was such a sweet, well-behaved child. My life after having her had been a complete nightmare. Yet, having her was a ray of sunshine that pierced through my fierce and deadly storm. I had been dealt one of the worst hands that any twenty-four-year-old could imagine. However, God had looked out for me by blessing me with Joy before I knew that I would even need her in my life to make it better and give me a reason to smile.

Just as I passed the kitchen, the usual feeling of nausea hit me like a sickening wave. My stomach started to swim. I instantly felt disappointment. Since Jameel was home that night, I had hoped I wouldn't be sick so that we could spend some quality time together. It had been so long since we'd been intimate, and I was dying for his affection.

Making an about-face, I scurried into the guest bathroom towards the back of the house. I fought to keep the contents of my stomach down instead of violently regurgitating, until I could make it to that bathroom. I was trying desperately to keep any sounds of my vomiting from yet again ruining any chances of me pleasing him or even more so, him being turned on enough to please me.

Luckily, I made it into the bathroom just in time to close the door tightly, turn on the light and ventilation, and empty my belly into the toilet. I heaved, gripping the sides of the toilet. No matter how many times I had done this, it never got easier.

Once my stomach finished expelling, I forced myself to my feet and reached into the medicine cabinet for toothpaste and mouthwash. Using one of the extra toothbrushes for guests, I brushed my teeth and rinsed.

As I left the bathroom, I tried to coax myself into having the strength to go into my bedroom and seduce my man. Despite my efforts, I yawned as I padded up the hallway towards the master bedroom in my home in Morgan Park, a huge difference from the low-income housing that I had been raised in with my single mother in "The Gardens."

My mother was living in Altgeld Gardens with her parents when she got pregnant with me. My father was some hustling little boy who was too immature to claim me when my mother told him that she was pregnant. My mother had raised me in my grandparents' home until I was five. She tells me all the time how, with me in her arms, she would walk right by my father as he sold drugs in the neighborhood, and he wouldn't even look at me or acknowledge her. Eventually, his occupation got him murdered when somebody robbed him when I was five. That same year, my mother met my stepfather who had some big-time position at Metra. He fell in love with my mother's regal, modelesque looks and tan skin. He took me and my mother out of the projects and moved us to Tinley Park, a suburb outside of Chicago that looked like the lap of luxury compared to the Gardens. Mama and I never looked back after that. My mother first thought I would be raised in poverty amongst the gang and gun violence in the hood of the city, but, instead, I had ended up being a spoiled suburban girl who rarely needed for anything.

My mother had met her knight in shining armor, and years later, I made sure to meet mine too. Five years ago, I met Jameel at the Metra Christmas party and fell in love with him after just three dates. He was an engineer for the company, and once I got pregnant a year later, he gave me the same comfortable life that my stepfather had given my mama and me.

Right before entering the master bedroom, I yawned again. As usual, I was so drained and ready for bed. I couldn't wait to curl up next to my man and allow his scent to relax me to sleep. However, I first intended to please him if he were in the mood that night. So, imagine my surprise when I walked into the bedroom to see him walking towards me with luggage in his hands.

"W-where are you going?" I stuttered over my words as my eyes glanced over the luggage. Instantly, my heart started to race with fear. This wasn't like Jameel to jump up and go out of town without telling me, and it was odd that he was going anywhere at nine o'clock at night. "What's going on?" I asked, praying to God that someone in his family hadn't suddenly fallen ill or worse, had passed away.

He hesitated... and I didn't like it. I didn't like the look on his face either. It was stern, mean... uncaring.

He stood in the middle of our bedroom with the handles of the two pieces of luggage—one in each hand—and simply shrugged. That one, swift, nonchalant movement told me everything. He didn't have to say anything. I hadn't expected it, and I hadn't seen it coming, not even with binoculars, but that one nonchalant shrug told me everything.

Yet, still, he sealed my fate with, "I can't do this anymore."

Instantly, my eyes welled with tears and soon began to run like faucets. On top of everything I was going through, all my suffering, and fighting every day, I didn't need this. Not *this* too.

I raced towards him, and he stepped back like the last thing he wanted me to do was touch him. "Jameel, w-what do you mean?"

He took another step back. He shook his head as he said firmly, "I can't keep living like this with you. It's too hard."

My amber eyes bulged out of their sockets as his audacity hit me in the gut. I was floored, literally flabbergasted although I shouldn't have been.

Jameel had provided for Joy and me, but he had been an asshole for most of our marriage. He took care of the household, but he didn't give a damn about me or Joy emotionally. He had shown no signs of that before we got married, however. Otherwise, I wouldn't have walked down that aisle in that thirty-thousand-dollar dress that my stepfather had purchased.

Six months into our marriage, Jameel changed. Some days were okay. Some days, I could enjoy a smile on his face and lying beside him. Other days were torturous and full of reminders from him why he wanted more and better. However, I was willing to remain married to him and keep trying if it meant me being with him and giving Joy a father figure and comfortable life just like my mother had made sure to provide me.

Though Jameel fronted to be happy with everyone else, he had recently stopped fronting with me. He was cold and unhappy. He put on for the relatives and social media. Everybody thought that we were the perfect couple and relationship goals. Yet, behind closed doors, he took his anger out on me and even sometimes Joy for being married before he was truly ready. Jameel had married me because his mother had told him to because it was cheaper to keep his pregnant girlfriend. I prayed that his heart would change, though. I prayed that his sudden disinterest in this marriage and his child was a phase. The last thing I'd needed to add to my stress was failing to keep Jameel happy.

Last year when I received devastating news, I thought it would bring us closer. I thought it would make him want to fight for me, fight with me.

I guess not.

"I'm tired. I'm done. I can't deal with this," he said, frowning as if our marriage, his family, and I were disgusting and something he just wanted to wash his hands of as fast as he could.

My eyes bucked even wider. I glared at him, daring him to be serious. "What do you mean *you* can't deal with this, Jameel? The last time I checked, I could have sworn that *I* was the one dealing with it."

His mercenary eyes rolled to the ceiling. "That's your problem. You think this only affects you when it affects all of us."

I clutched my chest in disbelief. Even though he had been clearly unhappy, I'd never thought he would leave... not now. "So, you're leaving?"

He sucked his teeth like the immature boy that he was, the little boy that I never wanted to admit that I had married. "I didn't sign up for this." He sneered.

"*No*, you didn't sign up for marriage period," I spat. "Be honest. You married me because I was pregnant, and your mama made you be a good boy, not because you loved me or even liked me."

"Fuck you," he hissed so easily, as if he had been waiting forever to tell me that.

"Fuck you too, Jameel!" I shrieked, pointing my matte, Pink nail at him.

He shrugged again and went for the luggage. "That's the problem. *You don't*. You *don't* fuck me." He started to roll the luggage towards the door. It made me sick to my stomach to wonder where he was going or better yet, *who* he was going to.

"How can I?" I protested, on his heels. "You know—"

He waved his hand so suddenly that I instantly shut up. He had never hit me. He'd always used his words to hurt me. Yet, in this moment, he was obviously so determined to break me that I didn't know what he was capable of. "I don't wanna hear that shit. It's the same sad, tired excuse all the time."

"You act like I can help it!" I cried.

He kept heading towards the bedroom door, burying my existence and heart with every word that left his throat. "You can't help your life, but I can help mine. I'm twenty-seven. You think I gotta live my life like this? With a wife that can't please me, and that I gotta —"

"Shut up!" I couldn't take hearing it. Not from him. Not like this. I raced towards him, asking, "You think I like being like this? You think I asked for this?"

On his way out of the door, he sealed my fate. "Yeah, well... It's happening to *you*, not *me*."

I stopped dead in my tracks, his harsh words paralyzing me. He had been an asshole, and he had said some awful things to me, but I didn't know that his disgust ran this deep. "Jameel..."

He didn't even bother to turn around as he shook his head. "Don't beg," left his voice so cynically that I fell back against the wall nearby. I slid down it with tears streaming from my eyes. I couldn't believe he had chosen to walk out on me at a time like this. Jameel had been such a rock for me when my stepfather passed away four years ago. That's how I fell so deep in love with him so fast. I just knew that, no matter how he felt about this marriage, he would hold on to it so that he could be there for me through this too.

I broke down in sobs, crying into my hands and wondering what else God could possibly hit me with.

I should not have ever, *ever* asked that question.

1

TRUE

- A YEAR LATER -

♫*Ayo, I been on, bitch, you been corn*
Bentley tints on, Fendi prints on
I mean I been Storm, X-Men been formed
He keep on dialin' Nicki like the Prince song
I-I-I been on, bitch, you been corn
Bentley tints on, Fendi prints on
Ayo, I been north, Lara been Croft
Plates say Chun-Li, drop the Benz off♫

"*I* went and copped the chopsticks. Put it in my bun just to pop shit. I'm always in the top shit. Box seats. Bitch, fuck the gossip'...*" I stopped rapping along to Nicki Minaj's *Chun-Li* when my phone started to ring through the Bluetooth in the Range Rover that I'd been awarded in the divorce.

Jameel had actually done me a favor when he left me that night a year ago. I didn't have time to waste by living any more days with him miserable. Our divorce was quick, easy, and final as of three months ago. He was pissed that I had gotten the house, this truck, our condo, child support, and spousal support in the divorce, but I was happy to be free of him and his pissy attitude.

I hadn't known how much of a captive I was until he walked out of my life. I was heartbroken for weeks, but eventually, I realized Jameel leaving me was a blessing in disguise. Since he'd left, the only person who was suffering was Joy. She hadn't seen Jameel since he learned how big of a settlement I was going to receive in the divorce. He had left me because of my situation, but because of my situation, he was still responsible for me financially, and that pissed him off. He called himself punishing me by leaving me one hundred percent physically responsible for Joy even though we had joint custody. However, he had been so verbally abusive since the divorce that I was fearful of the things he would say to my daughter if he were alone with her. Therefore, I was cool with him being an absentee father if I still got those checks every month.

I smiled when I looked at the dash and saw Coop calling me. I allowed the sweetest, feminine, flirtatious voice to leave my pouty lips as I answered and greeted him. "Hey, you."

"What up, tho?" he shot.

I rolled my eyes and laughed quietly to myself. *He's so damn hood.*

"Nothing. On my way to my mother's house," I lied.

"You and your mother are always together," he complained.

I wasn't surprised at Coop's response. He was always a smart ass. He rarely had anything nice to say. "Yeah, we are. And?" I shot back.

He ignored my sass and asked, "What you doin' later? I'm tryin' to see you."

"Tryin' to *see* me?" I decided to tease him just because. It was for my entertainment.

He sucked his teeth. "Yeah, man."

I rolled my eyes as I zoomed through a yellow light. "You're a damn lie. You're trying to *have sex* with me. Be honest."

"Well, you don't like when I'm an asshole, so..."

I smiled as I said, "So, that was you being nice?"

Yet again, he sucked his teeth but even harder this time. "Man, whatever."

I shook my head as I turned right onto 43rd Street. Coop was lucky that I just wanted the D instead of an actual dating relationship with him. Otherwise, I wouldn't have wanted a damn thing to do with his mean ass. His attitude reminded me too much of Jameel's, once Jameel had turned cold. That's why I would never take Coop seriously *if* I were looking to be committed to someone. Coop was a thug to his heart. He didn't sweet talk and never wined and dined. Hell, he never even called me by my name or even "baby." I was "shorty." Lucky for him, he made up for his excessively rough approach by being sexy as hell with some *exceptional* dick.

Outside of his personality, Coop was a unicorn; gorgeous, had a mouth-watering physique, and a stroke game that every man should envy. He was tall, 6'4", with chocolate skin and a kissable mouth complemented with a big, suckable bottom lip. His mean ass had the audacity to have two, deep dimples, light brown, bedroom eyes, and a full, luscious, beard that fell at least four inches away from his chin. He was thick too. He had to weigh almost three-hundred pounds. His arms were massive, and he had the legs to match.

And the dick? Lordt! He had a big dick and knew how to use it. He didn't need to do foreplay. His dick alone made me cum multiple times in one session.

Yep, he was a freaking unicorn.

He would be even more unbelievable if he were a nice person. Therefore, I appreciated his crassness because it kept me floating up onto cloud nine when we had sex.

He had been giving me orgasms for three months, and I was loving every minute of it. We knew each other intimately, but not personally. We were strictly sex, and I was okay with that.

As I parked a few feet away from Norman's Bistro, I told him, "I'll see how I feel when I get through with my mama."

"See how you feel?" he repeated with his usual attitude.

"Yes," I pressed with taunting humor in my voice. I was messing with him on purpose. "I'll see how I feel."

"Man, whatever."

As I started to laugh, his end of the line went dead.

"He hung up on me!" I threw my head back, laughing hysterically.

I shrugged as I flipped down the sun visor and checked my appearance in the mirror. I wiped off the excess gloss from the creases of my lips and smoothed the back of my tapered cut.

Thank God my hair is growing back.

Happy with how I looked, I collected my purse and cell phone from the passenger's seat. Then I hopped out of my truck. Before walking towards the restaurant, I adjusted my high-waist jeans. I noticed they were a bit loose around the thighs. I sighed, realizing I had lost even more weight. I swallowed that disappointment and made my way towards the bistro.

Once inside, I spotted my date sitting at the bar looking up at the NBA playoff game on the TV above the bar as he sipped from what I knew was his usual drink, Patrón.

A week after Jameel walked out of my life, I decided to live the rest of my life as I wanted to. I was not going to let Jameel take away any more of my happy moments. I decided to laugh a lot, drink a lot, dance a lot, and have sex a *whole* lot. So, since then, I had been dating as much as I could. Coop was only one of the members on my team. I was walking up on one of the others.

"Hey, you," I whispered into Kane's ear from behind as I slid my arms around his waist.

He jumped a bit but relaxed as soon as he recognized my voice. I giggled, let him go, and slid in the barstool next to him.

"Hey, you," he returned. "I ordered your drink already. She's making it now."

"Thank you." I smiled.

"How you been?"

I fed him a bunch of bullshit. I told him that everything was great, that I had no worries. That was how I got through my days and maintained my happiness. There was no need to talk about my reality.

That's not what these men were for. They were for my entertainment and to make me cum.

That was it. That was all.

∿

♫We out here drippin' in finesse
It don't make no sense
Out here drippin' in finesse
You know it, you know it
We out here drippin' in finesse
It don't make no sense
Out here drippin' in finesse
You know it, you know it♫

THREE HOURS LATER, Kane and I were standing in front of our barstools, swaying back and forth drunkenly to Bruno Mars. The game had gone off, and now I finally had Kane's full attention. The small bar area had filled up with a bunch of patrons who were enjoying music being spun by the deejay WyldChyld. The bartenders were luckily pouring heavy. Two peach Long Islands in, and I was ready to go back to Kane's spot around the corner on 48th and Vincennes and get some of that good D.

Kane wasn't my usual type. He was only three inches taller than me, and I was only 5'4$^{1/2}$" barefoot. I purposely wore flat shoes whenever I was around him so I could look up to him. He had very light skin, but I had a fetish for dark-skin men. Despite this, sex with him was amazing. We had chemistry that I had rarely experienced. His foreplay was on point. I had never had a man make me so wet before penetration without even giving me oral sex. He kissed me from head to toe. He touched me as if we were madly in love. Before he even penetrated me, I was so utterly turned on that his average-size member actually felt like heaven on earth.

He was good at what he did.

Thinking about his sex game, I pressed my back against him and started to twerk against his pelvis, trying to get his mind on the same thing mine was on. I smiled to myself as I felt his dick growing harder in his jeans.

However, my smile quickly faded as my eyes fell on Coop entering the bar from the patio.

"Shit!" I cursed frantically. Luckily, the music was bumping so loudly that I knew Kane hadn't heard me. I quickly turned towards Kane and hurriedly told him, "I have to go the restroom. I'll be back."

I didn't even wait for Kane to respond. I darted towards the restrooms, my heart beating frantically.

Coop and I weren't committed to each other, and neither were Kane and me, but it wasn't their business that I was sleeping with both of them!

Just as I had arrived at the ladies' room and reached for the handle, I felt a hard grasp on my arm that I knew wasn't Kane.

I turned around to see a cocky look spread across Coop's handsome face. A taunting smile was darting out of his full, luscious beard, but those eyes... They were filled with malice and showed not one ounce of friendliness as he spat, "That ain't yo' mama."

COOP

"And?" Shorty shot back, trying to be tough, but I saw the fear in her eyes as she placed her hands on her hips.

I let her go because I could see that security was watching us. I wasn't scared at all, but I wasn't ready for my night to end. I stuffed my hands in the pockets of my jeans to refrain from putting them on True. "You didn't have to lie about being with another dude. You know I'm the last person to care."

She rolled those pretty brown eyes slightly. "Yeah, I know you don't give a care, Coop."

"Then why you lie?"

"Because it wasn't any of your business. Are we in a relationship?" she sassed as she folded her arms across those pretty titties.

This was why no matter how much shorty rubbed me the wrong way, I kept going back. She was the one chick that didn't jump at my beck and call. And, even after three months of messing around, she hadn't pressed me to be in a relationship with her. She didn't want commitment from me, and that was rare. A nigga like me was all the way with that. I wasn't trying to be tied down. But because she was a challenge, she had my stubborn attention.

"You're right," I replied, nodding slowly. "You know I'mma make you pay for that, though, right?"

I watched her expression turn to concern, but I didn't even wait for her to reply. She looked relieved when I just shrugged, turned, and headed back to the patio. That whack, little, yellow punk that she was with had his corny ass in his phone.

Fuck his bitch ass and fuck shorty.

True had always been difficult ever since I met her at the Italian Fiesta on Lake Park a few months ago. She had told me then that she was divorcing her husband. I thought she was going to be one of those chicks that wanted to be wifed since she was used to having a husband. But that was the last thing or her mind. I had never had a woman act like a man before, only wanting sex and nothing more. I was good with that. I wasn't trying to fall in love with anybody. My love was the game. My side chick was money. I had no emotions for anything more. I didn't know how to feel. No one had taught me how. I had no parents and no family. I definitely didn't have any kids. I purposely always strapped up because the last thing I wanted to do was put a kid in the position that I had been raised in. If I couldn't promise a kid a home with two loving parents, I didn't want to have any. I had been raised by group homes and negligent foster parents that never kept me long enough to teach me anything. I didn't love. I didn't care. My only family and friend was my right-hand man, Rakim, who had forced his friendship on me in the streets when we were teenagers. But he was all I had. I didn't allow anyone else to get any closer, especially not a *woman*.

True had a lot of nerve trying to play me when she wasn't even the type of chick I went for. She was too skinny. I liked my women tall and thick to match my frame. I don't mean that fake-body, Instagram model thick. I mean cornbread-fed with thighs that rubbed together type of thick. But True was slim and had the nerve to be constantly losing weight since we had started messing around, and she was short. Lucky for her, she still made my dick hard because she had this striking, natural beauty. Her features made her look Afro-Latino. Her skin was tan and smooth. Her kissable, pouty mouth was under a cute, turned-up nose. Her eyes had undeniable femininity that drew you in. Her short haircut put me in the mind of Meagan Good. Her beauty could make a blind man see.

I definitely wasn't going to let that high yellow, lame, nerdy motherfucka keep me from dicking True down. She would hear from me soon. But now that I knew she had opted to give that pussy to another nigga over me for the night, I was definitely going to make her pay for it.

Back out on the patio, the shorty I had left out there when I peeped True inside was still leaning against the gate. One of the homies off the block, Zell, was still chopping it up with her. Zell wasn't only a homie. He was one of my loyal block boys. Out of all the block boys, he had been working with me the longest. I had taken him under my wing and taught him the game. I saw a prosperous hustling future ahead for him if he kept his mind on the game as he had been.

"Aye, lets ride," I told Trina as I walked up on them.

She looked surprised that I was ready to go so soon since we'd just gotten there. Since True was getting her action tonight, I wasn't trying to let her mess that up by causing any smoke when she saw me with somebody else after I had just cut up. So, it was time to ride out.

Trina, though confused about our sudden departure, didn't argue with me. She grabbed her purse off the table in front of her as I shook up with Zell.

Trina grabbed my hand, ready to leave, and my skin crawled. I didn't like that shit at all. My hand suddenly started itching. But for the sake of ensuring that I didn't piss tonight's pussy off, I allowed her to hold on to my fingertips as we began to walk away.

"Later, Zell," I shot over my shoulder.

"Aye, wait up, Coop." He stopped me, appearing in front of me. "You seen Mac?"

"Last time I saw him, he was on the block. Why? What's up?"

"He ain't been back on the block since this morning. His baby's mama called me lookin' for him."

I shrugged. "I haven't seen him. But make sure you find him. That nigga got my product."

He nodded. "For sure, boss." He moved out of my way to give me and Trina a pathway out of the gate.

I guided Trina by the small of her back towards the exit of the patio. I looked back at Zell with a stern eye. "Find my product." I turned around expecting to see Trina's phat ass, but instead, I was facing eyes just as cold as mine. My guard instantly went up. My hand instantly went to my hip where my piece was. There were at least fifty people on the patio. More people were across the street in the parking lot kicking it. Others were coming and going on the sidewalk. I hated to air this place out, but if I had to, I was prepared.

"State your business," I gritted as I glared into Prince's eyes.

Prince was another hustler from my hood. We rarely bumped heads, only having had beef over turf as younguns when we were just starting out. But the look in his eyes was telling me that he wasn't in my face for a friendly conversation.

Me and Trina locked eyes, and I motioned for her to go to the car. She did so just as Prince spat, "You fuckin' my broad?"

I had to laugh. I *had* to. "You comin' at me over some pussy?"

He stepped closer into my space. We were eye to eye, fire darting between us. I could feel the bouncer's eyes on us a few feet away that were securing the balcony.

Prince then gritted, "I'm coming at you over what's mine."

I couldn't help the slick grin that spread across my beard. What was "his" was a cold piece of work by the name of Issa. She had been fine since grammar school and had only grown better with time. She was a caramel beauty with the measurements that I fantasized about. The only reason I wasn't with her that night was because she was too scared to lie to Prince since he had been hearing about her messing around with me.

I guessed she was right.

"I ain't worried about what's yours," I lied with a shrug. "I got pussy in the car waiting on me, my nigga. You can save this pussy-ass shit."

I was walking away when his soft ass had the nerve to stand in my way. My hand went to my piece. My body tensed until I saw the sincerity and pure pussiness in his eyes.

"Man..." he mumbled. "I'm just asking you man to man to back up."

I laughed at his ass and kept it moving.

I had been dicking Issa down for six months. She was a regular piece of good pussy, phat ass, and great head, so I wasn't giving that up to satisfy that weak-ass nigga.

"Ooooh shiiiiit!" Trina reached back and scratched at my thigh. I could feel her nails digging into my dripping skin, leaking the Hennessy that I had been drinking all day, as I pumped, gracefully in and out of her drenching, wet pussy.

"Don't move," I ordered through grunts.

"I'm cummin'!" she shrieked. Her back hunched tightly.

I leaned forward and pressed her back into the deep arch that I preferred. "Don't move!" Clamping down on her waist, I brought that ass to me, driving all my width and length in deeper.

"Shiiiiiit!"

My eyes fixated on her plump, juicy ass as it slapped against my lap while I murdered that pussy. Trina was exactly how I liked them, thick like cornbread, real woman curves, with that lil' stomach pouch that I could grab on while hitting it from behind.

"Gawd damn," I mumbled. I could see her big titties flying every-where while I infiltrated her soggy opening with no mercy.

"Ahhhhhh! Fuuuuuck!" she shrilled.

"You bet' not move," I grunted.

"Shit, it's so deep!" she shrieked.

"Don't... Arrrrrrgh!" I grabbed the base of the condom, jumped out of her, and leaned against her weak arched ass as I released inside of it. "Fuuuuuck!"

With heavy breaths, I pushed off her. She plopped down onto the bed as I sat on the edge of it, taking off the rubber. I leaned forward and tossed it into the trash can. Then I reached for my phone on the cluttered nightstand.

She needs to clean this motherfucker up.

Trina was one of those chicks that always wanted a man over, but she never cleaned up. Good for her, she had some good pussy.

I had a few text messages. As I unlocked my phone, I checked myself for actually looking for one of them to be from True.

Fuck shorty.

Tonight had been the first time I had caught a chick playing me. I had always figured she was sleeping with somebody else. Hell, I figured that all women had a spare dick in their back pocket. But that was why I did what I did and treated them how I treated them. But seeing it for myself was admittedly messing with my ego. I wanted every woman that I messed with to be at home waiting on this dick until I chose to give it to them.

Right or wrong, every man does.

Three of the text messages were from this chick, Regina, that I had sent off earlier that night. I had told her that we were hanging out that night, but Trina had been more persistent than her and True that night. So, Trina had won.

I ignored Regina's messages and focused on the one from Zell.

Zell: *Still no Mac.*

I locked the phone and tossed it on the bed. As soon as I reached down on the floor for my jeans, I heard Trina sigh.

"Stay the night with me," she whined. I could feel her tugging on my elbow. I snatched back and started throwing on my pants.

"Don't start that shit, man."

But she kept whining, "You always hitting this and leaving."

I shrugged as I grabbed my shirt from the dresser I had tossed it on. "So, you should be used to it."

"You *so* mean," she complained.

"And?" I spat, throwing my shirt on. "Stop being clingy. We ain't together. You know what this is."

"Urrgh!" she groaned, kicking her feet into the air. "Why do I even fuck with you?"

I laughed, taunting her. "Because I got good dick." I turned to walk away before she could argue with me. On my way out of the door, I tripped over a shoe. I grimaced and kicked it across the room. It hit the wall with a loud thud.

"Stop kicking my shit!" she yelped.

"You want a nigga to spend the night, try cleaning this bitch up," I huffed.

"I hate you, Coop!"

I laughed on my way out of her bedroom door. I could hear her still mumbling under her breath. I could imagine what she was saying about me, but she knew better than to let me hear her say it if she still wanted this dick whenever I decided to give it to her again.

I let myself out of her crib and made my way towards my black 2018 BMW. I looked around to make sure no one was around. For a Tuesday night, the neighborhood right off 50th and Cottage Grove was pretty much abandoned.

Once at the back of the car, I popped the trunk open. It looked like the sudden sound had jolted Mac out of his sleep. He was still bound by his ankles and wrists and gagged. Much of the blood on his face had dried up during the hours he had spent in the trunk since that morning. He looked weak, hungry, and dehydrated. I was sure that for a sixty-degree night in April it was hot in that trunk. That was the least he was going to suffer that night, though.

"A'ight. You ready to die for trying to play me?"

Through the gag, he started to breathe heavily, hyperventilating. But every one of the workers on my block knew not to cross me. So, his surprise at his oncoming death was a shock to me. He knew my wrath. He knew I didn't play games when it came to my product or my money. Yet and still, he had been selling dope on my block and coming up short for three weeks, blaming it on other workers and crack heads like I hadn't been selling dope since I was thirteen and knew every trick in the book.

I laughed at the fear in his eyes as I closed the trunk. He may have only stolen a couple thousand from me, compared to the racks I had tucked away, but proving my point was priceless.

As I hopped in the car, I could hear Mac kicking against the trunk and his muffled screams. I laughed as I started the engine, pulled off, and blasted the radio on my way to my destination.

♬ *Fuck a shooter I'm my own shooter*
All this ice I'm my own jeweler
Six lawyers and they all Jewish
I'm the star bitch this is my movie
Pinky ring two-fifty on it
Guess it's safe to say nigga I spent your budget on it
Ran off on the plug twice ♬

This part of my job was draining. I had been doing this for almost fifteen years. I was thirteen when I sold my first bag of heroin. Back then, I was selling dope to feed myself and keep clothes on my back because no one else was there for me. I had been fending for myself ever since. I was the only person who could feed me, take care of me, and put a roof over my head. I never had a mother or father to do so. So, I didn't play when it came to my money. I had killed for less, murdered niggas for testing me and thinking I was game. I was street tested and hood approved. This wasn't no character I was playing. This was me in real life.

But I was tired. I was twenty-eight, which was elderly in drug-game years. I was an "old head." It was time for me to retire and live my life without looking over my shoulder and worrying who was stealing from me or if I was on the indictment list. It was time to invest my money into something legit and become a regular dude. I just had no idea exactly what I wanted to do.

I drove around until the blocks fell asleep. At four in the morning, the block that I sold most of my product from on the southwest side of the city was vacant. The dope boys had disappeared to fall into something tight and wet. The crack heads were tucked away getting high off my supply. Kids and parents were getting their last few hours of sleep before they woke up and started their day.

And me? I was pulling Mac out of the trunk in an alley.

His eyes jolted open from the sudden movement, but they were too weak to stay wide open. They rode low. Buddy was exhausted and famished. I had driven around all day securing my alibi. Now, tucked away in the darkest corner of an alley where I knew no eyes or cameras could see me, I threw Mac down onto his knees.

"Was it worth it?" I asked as I took my blade from my back pocket.

Mac's weary, heavy eyes peered up at me with so much sorrow. But it was too late to be sorry. He should have thought about that shit before he decided to steal from me. I had clothed this punk and fed him. If it wasn't for me, he would be some dirty-ass boy on State Street beating buckets for change. And he'd had the nerve to steal from me?

I snatched a handful of his locs and pulled his head back to expose his neck. I saw his Adam's Apple move up and down slowly, signaling him swallowing hard. He stared into my eyes, and I admired him for at least dying like a man.

In one swift motion, I slit his throat so slowly that it was even more agonizing for him. His muffled screams pierced the night air until the knife slit his vocal cords. Blood splattered against the trash-cluttered pavement where he kneeled. I let his locs go with a jolt that sent him flying to the pavement face first. I heard his teeth crack and facial bones break against the pavement.

Then I left him right there on the block where I'd met him, fed him, and bonded with him, so everyone else could be reminded not to ever fuck with me.

2

REMI

"Why are you being so picky about this?"

I smiled, but Gigi didn't even notice. She was busy roaming through the skirt rack. "It's our anniversary. I gotta be cute for our date."

"You've never been this picky about any other anniversary outfit."

"Because..." I turned around slowly with this big, goofy grin on my face.

My sister, Gigi, short for her horrible name, Gregoria... I know, right? Her father's name was Greg. Our mother's name was Gloria. Ratchet shit... I know. Anyway, Gigi's head cocked to the side dramatically as her eyes bulged with curiosity. She leaned against the nearest clothing rack. Her mink lashes fluttered repeatedly as she watched me with disbelief. "What?"

I sighed deeply and admitted, "I think Banks is going to propose to me."

Gigi instantly rolled her eyes to the ceiling of the Sak's store. My smile vanished as she smacked her lips dismissively. "Girl, bye." She turned away from me and headed for a nearby rack of jeans.

I followed her, insisting, "I'm for real!"

She waved me off. "It's been like ten years, Remi," she reminded me.

Unfortunately, and embarrassingly, she was right. I had been with Banks since I was sixteen years old. We had done everything a couple was supposed to do, except two things: have children and get married. That was because I wanted to do it the right way and in the correct order. I preferred to get married *and then* have children. I had played house for ten years, though. We had been living together. I had taken all his shit. I had supported him through his way up the hustle ladder. I was figuratively his wife, but I refused to have his baby until I was his *legal* wife. I deserved a ring after all these years of putting up with his lies. That was the one thing all these other chicks could never say. They could say they had his dick and that he'd spent money on them. They could even say he had taken them out of town. Other women could even say he had told them he loved them. But none of those hoes could say they were his wife. I needed that. I deserved that. He owed me that.

When Gigi noticed the solemn expression that had replaced the happiness she had snatched from me, she gave me this sympathetic look. "I'm sorry, sissy. I just don't want you to get your hopes up and get your feelings hurt."

I shrugged and tried to look confident as I said, "It's okay. I don't blame you."

I honestly couldn't fault my sister for not having any faith in Banks. For the last five years, I had been anticipating a ring every anniversary, every Christmas, every Valentine's Day, every birthday, and, hell, even every Independence Day. And each time, I was let down. Banks had given me everything—diamonds, cars, clothes, and handbags; everything I did *not* want.

Gigi huffed, slightly rolling her eyes to the back of her head. "Fine. What makes you think he's about to propose."

The simple thought caused my smile to return. "Well, first of all, he made us a reservation at Everest." I waited for Gigi's response to Banks taking me to one of the most expensive restaurants in Chicago. When her eyes slightly bucked and she nodded, I went on. "Right.

And then he told me to make sure I dressed nice and got my nails done. And he's been being secretive as hell! I'm telling you, girl, he is going to propose. *Sooo*, I need a cute outfit."

Finally, Gigi smiled. "A'ight, fine. C'mon. There isn't anything in here. Let's go to the Gucci store."

I felt good having my sister finally in my corner. I had been waiting for this for so long. I honestly didn't care if Banks proposed to me in an expensive restaurant with a half-a-million-dollar ring or if he asked me on the block with a toy ring. No matter what we had been through and no matter how long I had waited, I wanted to marry that man by any means.

I WAS STANDING in the middle of me and Banks' bedroom floor in the thirty-five-hundred-dollar embroidered Gucci dress I had purchased a few hours ago. My curves looked so good in it. I was a thick, curvy girl, standing at 5'7" and two-hundred and eighty pounds. I had curves in places I didn't want them, but with the help of a good waist cincher and Spanx, this dress was hugging every last one of them while giving me an hourglass shape.

I didn't too particularly like all of my curves. I had always been a curvy chick, but over the years, as I fought constant heartache from Banks, I ate my feelings until I was fifty pounds heavier. He never complained about my weight gain to my face. But I knew he didn't like it because he always said that I was so pretty in the face. He loved my pouty mouth, dark skin, high cheekbones, and slanted eyes with heavy, natural lashes. I had a "pretty face" was what he always said, but it was evident that he preferred smaller chicks since every woman that he had cheated on me with was smaller and tighter. I wanted to lose the weight, but I wasn't over the pain caused by Banks' past indiscretions. So, I still ate to mask it.

However, with the help of a good girdle, I looked like a chocolate stallion standing in the Gucci pumps that jolted me up to a regal 5'11" height.

I looked good.

But, to my mother, I guess I looked like a fool.

She lounged in a chaise in my room staring at the price tag in her hand in disbelief. "It's cute, but why did you spend so much on this dress just for your anniversary? Y'all been together forever."

"I think he's going to propose tomorrow." I held my breath, hoping she would be as happy for me as I was.

She slowly looked from the Gucci receipt to me. She blinked slowly and then asked, "You what?"

My heart sank, watching my mother chuckle as she waited for me to answer.

"She thinks he's going to propose tomorrow," Gigi repeated for me from my bed.

My mother snickered and shook her head. "Giiiiirl..."

"Mama!" I whined over Gigi's muffled chuckles. "Wooow," I groaned under my breath.

Shaking my head, I started to take the dress off.

I shouldn't have been surprised. Much like my sister, my mother had very little faith in Banks. I had made the mistake of sharing with my mother and sister every time Banks cheated and every time another woman called my phone. So now, even though I had forgiven him, they hadn't.

"I don't know what you expected me to say to that," Mama said, still chuckling.

At least my sister had stopped laughing, but the sympathetic look she was giving me wasn't helping either.

I kept quiet and started to change back into the clothes I had worn shopping.

My mother didn't keep quiet, however. "It's been ten years. He can't even commit to being a faithful boyfriend. Why the hell would he commit to being in a faithful marriage? I—"

"I get it, Mama," I spat.

Her voice raised a little as she pressed, "Don't get mad at me. I'm just saying."

"Mama, let's go," Gigi thankfully said.

Confusion etched her face. "Now, why are we leaving? Because she can't take the truth?"

Gigi's eyes bucked, and she kept trying to press their exit. "Because I gotta go. I've been gone all day. I gotta go get the kids."

I walked out, tuning my mother out. I walked into the en-suite bathroom, closed the door, and locked it. I sat on the ledge of my jacuzzi. I took deep breaths, trying to fight the urge to cry.

This was my fault. I had done this by telling my sister and mother everything. I should have had friends that I told Banks' dirt to so that when I took him back, my family would still accept him. But I didn't have friends. I had known Banks since I was sixteen. He was my best and only friend. If I wasn't with my sister or mother or both, I was at work, spending my time with him, or cooking or cleaning while waiting for him to come home.

I noticed my cell phone sitting on the sink next to the toilet where I'd left it. I reached for it and unlocked it. I could hear my sister rushing my mother to get her things so they could leave, and I was so grateful. I sat there waiting until they were damn near out of the door before I left out. I started scrolling through my notifications to see if I had missed any calls or text messages from Banks, but he hadn't said anything since we talked in the Gucci store when I was letting him know I was about to make such a big purchase on our credit card.

To pass the time, I scrolled through Instagram and then Facebook. Because my mother and sister had Banks' past infidelities on my mind, I went to his most recent side chicks' page. Her name was Shandra. Though we weren't friends on Facebook, she had always made sure to make every post public since I'd found out about her two years ago. Supposedly, as of a year ago, Banks' had left her alone for good.

My heart started to skip beats when it seemed as if that wasn't the case, however. My breathing got sporadic as I read the last few posts that she had made within the last hour, referring to spending time with an old dip, getting that old thang back, and when the pussy is good that it can take a man away from his main chick. I bit my bottom lip so hard that I could taste blood. I shot up from my seat on the ledge and raced towards the bathroom door. I threw it open and charged out, damn near running Gigi down as she stood close on the other side.

"Oh!" I shrieked as she scared me. "Sorry."

She stared at me strangely, seeing the anxiety all in my face. "You okay?"

I looked around, relieved that my mama was gone out of my bedroom. But I still wasn't about to make the same mistake twice. "I'm good. I'm about to go meet Banks for some drinks."

"Oh okay..." She paused and then slightly pouted. "Sorry about Mama. You know she just wants the best for you."

"I know." I rushed, anxious to get the hell out of the house.

"I do too. And I know Banks is who you want. Marrying him, you would be at your best, so I got your back."

I rushed a smile and mumbled on a shallow breath, "Thanks, sissy."

She reached out and hugged me quickly. "A'ight, let me get your mama outta here."

"That's *yo'* mama," I slurred as I went for my bed where my shoes were.

"Y'all way more alike than you know." She laughed. "See you later. Call me."

"Bye," I shot back in a hurry. My heart eased with relief as she disappeared. "Thank God," I mumbled as I hurriedly slid into my shoes as I heard the alarm system alert that the front door had opened.

I started to race around the house, grabbing my phone, keys, and purse. I then raced towards the door, hoping that Banks hadn't done this, that he hadn't played me yet again, that he would fulfill his promise to do right this time.

I bolted out of the door, hating the familiar feeling of heartbreak that was seeping into my soul. Every time that he had cheated ran through my mind as I jumped into my car and sped off towards Shandra's house. I knew where she stayed because I had followed Banks there so many times last year when I'd found out about her. I had spared none of my dignity, banging on the door, making him come out, asking him to come home, every one of the four times that I had caught him there.

My mother and sister wondered why I stayed through all the hurt. Hell, sometimes I wondered too. We had no kids binding us together. But every time I thought about walking away, I felt like I would be giving another woman the chance to reap the benefits of enjoying the man I had made. I had molded Banks into the successful street hustla that he was. I had experienced the blood, sweat, and tears. So, no way should another woman reap the benefits of him. That was my reward.

Plus, I wondered if it were even possible to find another man at this point. I had gained so much weight. I wasn't sure of myself anymore. I didn't have enough self-esteem to get out there and meet anyone new.

As I approached the block that Shandra lived on, I hoped that I didn't have to do this yet again. I turned the lights off on my Lexus and eased down the street towards the house that I'd found out that Banks had been paying the rent at for the time that he was with her. My heart pounded out of my chest as I squinted as if that would help me see better in the night sky.

"Thank God," I said and exhaled when I didn't see his black, Hummer in her driveway. But Banks wasn't stupid. He knew I would do this. He could have easily gotten dropped off. So, I parked and hopped out. I didn't want her telling social media that I had showed up at her house, so I crept around the back. I peered through the windows, listening, trying to see any and everything. But the house was dark and quiet.

It was only ten at night. Banks wouldn't sleep this late, so it appeared that he wasn't inside. But I wasn't relieved. They could've been anywhere. He'd had her on the block, around his friends in our circle.

I sped off and headed towards the block. He wasn't there either. His Hummer was nowhere. But I still wasn't convinced. I drove everywhere I thought he would be, every club and every hotel that I had caught him with another woman at before.

And he was nowhere.

I didn't even bother calling his phone because he'd talked to me while right next to another woman before.

"Please prove them wrong, baby," I cried into my hands as I sat at a red light. My knee jumped nervously. My stomach was balled up in a nauseating knot.

In a last-ditch effort, I drove by his usual Wednesday-night spot, The Dating Game. Banks had his hand in club promotion as well, and every Wednesday he had a comedy show there. I usually made it my business not to show up in environments like this one with Banks because I was too scared of what I would run up on.

Against my better judgment, I pulled into the lot and hopped out. I was too sporadic to wipe my tears, fix my hair, or adjust my clothes. I ran right past security.

"Aye!!" I heard security behind me as I raced through the glass doors. I sped past the female security guard who would have checked my ID and my purse.

Once inside of the club, I could feel someone pulling on my arm and all eyes on me. That's when I realized how crazy I must have looked. I hurriedly wiped my face as I turned to see who was tugging on me.

It was the female security guard holding a stern expression. "We need to see your ID."

"Aye, she good. This my woman. You know that."

Hearing that, the security guard realized who I was and immediately appeared to be apologetic.

I swung around. My eyes met his beautiful, sandy brown orbs that were encased in narrow, bedroom eyes that had the nerve to twinkle. Even in my anxiety, I appreciated the colorful tattoos that covered his arms and bounced beautifully off his butter-coated skin. Banks was hardcore, but his appearance was that of a pretty boy. His 6'1" frame was athletically cocky. He was draped in diamonds and tats. His full, pink, lips were surrounded by a full, beard, which was as luscious and curly as his bushy eyebrows and tapered fade.

Banks eyed me curiously as he took in my appearance. I started to fix my long, Peruvian, deep-wave, layered weave with my fingers. I then pulled down the T-shirt dress that was riding up a bit from all the chaos.

The security guard walked away as Banks approached me. I looked around for Shandra and thanked God that I didn't see her in the small, intimate crowd of the comedy set.

Thankfully, Banks hugged and kissed me as he always did. He held me for so long that I realized he could not be with another woman. Shandra had just posted those statuses to mess with me.

Finally, relief filled me as the smell of his Tom Ford cologne drowned me.

"What you doin' here, bae? You felt like coming out tonight?" When he let me go and smiled into my eyes, I was reminded why I had forgiven him so much and why I was willing to hold on.

Banks was going to prove them wrong.

God, I hoped so.

TRUE

"Angel?" My mother and I were leaving dinner at Tilly's when we heard someone call her name. She and I slightly jumped at the sound of her name being called by an unfamiliar, deep, male voice. We turned our attention towards the voice to see a handsome, older gentleman smiling down on her.

My mother's skin seemed to sheet white right before my eyes as she stuttered. "Russ...Russell."

My eyes darted towards my mother's sudden girlish nervousness.

"My *God*..." This man, Russell, took a step back to look my mother up and down ever so slowly.

I had never seen my mother blush so red. I suddenly felt like the third wheel.

"I haven't seen you in ages." He looked over at me. "I know this isn't True."

Smiling from ear to ear, she told him, "As a matter of fact, it is, and that is my grandbaby, Joy."

I gave him a half smile that was full of curiosity as to who the hell homeboy was. He nodded hello and then smiled down on Joy. Then his attention was back on what seemed to be a sight for sore eyes to him. "You don't look like a grandmother."

My mother failed at hiding her smile as she nervously ran her hand over the back of her tapered cut.

The tension between the three of us was thick. I was done trying to hide my interest in my mother's jumpiness over this stranger's existence. My mother avoided my eyes as her hand nervously ran over her hair again.

She swallowed hard and snatched Joy's hand into hers. "Well, it was nice seeing you, Russell." She turned away from his need to say more and gave me a stern look. I knew its interpretation without her saying a word. "C'mon, Joy. Let's go."

She walked off before Russell could get another word out. He looked to want to say so much to her, but he was so shocked by her response that he was offended and just walked away. I felt bad for the disappointment in his eyes. I then hurried behind my mother to catch up with her.

"Mama," I called as I caught up with her near the exit. "Who was that?"

"Nobody," she said shortly as she nearly dragged Joy through the door.

On her heels, I teased her, "That didn't look like a nobody. Seems like he knew you."

"Mind your business," she scolded me.

Finally catching up to her, I could see that her face was still wearing that perplexed look. "Unt uh. He was looking at you like you was a snack. Who was that man?"

Her eyes rolled slightly as she marched towards her BMW truck. "He wasn't looking at me like I was no damn snack, girl. Hush."

I was cracking up at how frazzled the sight of that man had made her. "*Yes*, he was."

"He was just somebody from the old hood. Somebody that knew your dad."

"My dad?" I asked shockingly.

She shook her head slightly. "No." She finally gave me her eyes, and they were reluctant. "Sorry, not your biological father. I'm talking about your stepfather."

"Okay, so why did you run away so fast?" I pushed.

She sucked her teeth as she waved my nosiness away. "Mind the business that pays you."

Teasing her more, I smiled hard. "Mmmm hmmm. Well, it seems like he had more to say to you. Gon' head and get those cobwebs knocked out, Mama." She was trying her best to avoid my eyes, but she couldn't help it. Her eyes met my smiling eyes and an uncontrollable smile spread across her face.

We both broke out into uncontrollable giggles. It wasn't even that funny, but we took every opportunity to laugh those days. After dealing with my stepfather's death, it broke my heart that my mother was being put through yet another test of her strength and faith. We both felt a lot of sadness when we were near each other. But, thankfully, tonight there was some joy.

3

COOP

♫Now behold the Lamb
The Precious Lamb of God
Born into sin that I may live again
The Precious Lamb of God

Now behold the Lamb
The Precious Lamb of God
Born into sin that I may live again
The Precious Lamb of God ♫

The choir serenaded the congregation as they filed out of the church behind Mac's casket. I was standing along a wall in the vestibule around the homies and my crew. Looking outside of the open doors of the church, I could see Mac's baby mama hysterically crying and clawing at Mac's casket as they put it in the back of the hearse.

I felt a soft touch on my back that made me tear my eyes away from Mac's baby mama. Issa was standing behind me looking like an angel in the midst of such dreariness. Her cream, quarter-sleeve dress hugged her massive curves. The cotton looked like butter. Her caramel skin was dripping with shea butter. Her juicy lips were glossed with red paint. Long, curls fell thirty inches down her back.

"Hey, you," she said lowly.

All eyes were on us, further proof that the hood-vine had definitely been talking about me and Issa.

"You think you should be speaking to me here?" I whispered.

I could see her forcing back a pout. "You haven't been answering my calls."

I gritted. I didn't like how she called herself checking on me. "I've been taking care of business."

Still pouting, she said, "Prince told me what happened the other night. I'm sorry."

I chuckled. "Don't be."

Her voice was pleading as she said, "Coop..."

Just then, I saw Mac's mother moping towards me. Her face was so tear-soaked that her makeup was causing brown stains on the all-white that she and the rest of Mac's family was wearing.

"I'll call you later," I rushed and told Issa just as Mac's mother reached me. I turned my back on Issa just as Mac's mother was reaching out to embrace me.

"Coop," she cried as I embraced her.

Kissing her cheek, I replied, "Hey, Ms. McCoy."

She started to sob on my three-thousand-dollar suit jacket. "Thank you."

I pulled back, looking into her sorrowful eyes. "What are you thanking me for?"

"For looking out for my son. You helped him feed his sisters and brothers. You took care of him even in death. You paid for his funeral. That was so sweet. I don't know how I could ever repay you."

As I smiled down on her, I felt eyes on me. I looked up and saw

Zell a foot away talking to one of the homies while staring at my exchange with Ms. McCoy.

"You don't have to thank me for that. It was the least I could do."

She smiled up at me, stood on her tiptoes, and kissed the same cheek that I had wiped her son's blood from a few days ago as he lay dying in an alley. "You're so sweet. Please keep in touch."

"You know I will. I got you and his siblings. Don't worry."

"Thank you," she said again, tearfully.

She squeezed my hands before walking away just as Zell walked up.

"Damn, man, this all fucked up," Zell grumbled.

I grimaced inwardly. It was one thing to listen to Mac's mother mourn, but to hear my own homies crying like punks when they knew this motherfucker was dirty was blowing me. Nobody knew who had killed Mac, but they knew that he was stealing from me. They didn't have proof that I had killed him, and no one would ever have the balls to say that shit out loud, but they knew. So, Zell was being a goofy right now.

"He was young. He didn't have to go out like that," Zell went on.

I cracked my neck and focused on Mac's baby mama now passing out in front of the hearse as Zell kept running his mouth. "It's messed up that somebody killed him like that."

My eyes darted towards Zell, who surprisingly had the courage to look me in my eyes. I laughed at his attempt to puff his chest out.

With tears pooling in his eyes, he gritted, "That was my boy. We grew up together. We were like brothers."

Lucky for Zell, I knew his loyalty, so I took into account that he was in his feelings right now. I lightly gripped his shoulder before walking away from him. "Niggas die every day. That's the name of the game."

TRUE

While leaving the doctor's office, my phone started to ring. I looked down at it with weary eyes and cringed when I saw that it was Jameel calling. I wasn't for his attitude today, but I wanted somebody to take my frustrations out on.

"What?" I shot after I answered.

"Hello?" he asked as if he had the wrong number.

"What, Jameel?" I snapped so loudly that a random old lady looked at me strangely as I walked by her on my way to the parking lot.

"I want custody of my daughter, True."

I laughed. I literally threw my head back and started cracking up. I was grateful that he was giving me *something* to smile about that day. "Oh, *now* you wanna be a father? You haven't seen her in the last three months!"

"I figure I need to be a part of her life, so she don't turn out like you, now that I know her mama is out here hoeing."

My eyes bucked as I entered the parking garage. "Excuse me?"

"You heard me," he slurred.

"What are you talking about?"

"Weren't you in Norman's the other day damn near fucking some yellow nigga on the dance floor?"

I laughed. Jameel was delusional. "What business is that of yours, Jameel? We are divorced. You left me, remember?"

This son of a bitch had left me without ever looking back. The bastard didn't even call me to check on his daughter. He only called to nag about the money he was struggling to pay me every month.

"Good thing I did leave your, hoe ass," he mumbled as I arrived at my truck.

"Oh, now I'm a hoe?" I laughed. "Or is the issue that you thought when you left nobody would want me?"

"Don't you have more important things to be worried about than the next dick you're jumping on?"

I laughed again. This was the Jameel that I knew, throwing my reality in my face, trying to demean me, so that I could be some sad woman groveling at his feet.

"Don't you have more important things to be worried about than the woman you left?"

"You got a whole lot of mouth all of a sudden. These niggas got your whack ass feeling froggish."

"Whack?" I repeated. I hated that tears were coming to my eyes. Jameel did not deserve my tears. He did not deserve to continue to hurt me. I couldn't keep giving him that. But even though he had walked out on me a year ago, I was still so shocked that he had turned so cold, so suddenly. He resented me as if I had wasted the last four years of his life. And I couldn't understand how someone who had once loved me so much could now treat me as if I was the worst mistake of his life.

"I want full custody of Joy," Jameel hissed into the phone.

Again, I laughed. "You just don't want to have to pay child support anymore."

"You're motherfuckin' right! Why the fuck am I paying child and spousal support when you aren't even going to be—"

"Fuck you, Jameel!" I hung up, too exhausted to continue this fight. I had enough I was fighting for.

I struggled through the door with a sleeping Joy drooling on my shoulder.

"Hey, True." My mother appeared out of the kitchen no sooner than she heard me coming through the front door. "How did things go at—"

I shot my hand in the air to stop her next words and kept walking past her. "Not right now, Mama." The last thing I needed was to have a long-drawn-out conversation with my mother about some shit we both already knew. I just wanted to lay down and forget this day. I was suddenly regretting allowing my mother to spend so much time here to help once Jameel left.

I cringed as I heard her calling me, "True—"

"Mama, please, just not right now." I went into Joy's bedroom and closed the door. I laid her down on her bed, praying to God that I had done it gently enough to keep her asleep. I didn't feel like putting the fake smile on my face today and mothering.

I needed just to close my eyes and forget.

On my way out of Joy's room, my cell phone rang. I didn't feel like talking to anyone else that day, but to keep the ringing from waking up Joy, I answered without even looking at the Caller ID. "Hello?"

"You still on bullshit?" Coop spat.

As soon as I heard his arrogant, cynical voice, my eyes rolled into the back of my head as I walked up the hall.

Maybe I shouldn't have answered the phone.

That day, I didn't have the strength to battle with his shit talking.

"Hello?" he pressed when I took too long to respond.

"What's up, Coop?" I finally spoke dryly.

"What's wrong with you?" he shot.

I couldn't even believe he cared enough to ask. "Nothing. What's up?"

"Tryin' to see you."

Urgh! His cockiness was repulsive, but I was surprised that after Tuesday night he wanted to see me.

He doesn't care who else I'm sleeping with as long as he gets some, I guess.

This just proved that Coop couldn't care less about me outside of the sex, but lucky for him, the feeling was mutual. And that day, I desperately needed to take my mind off things.

I sighed deeply, full of frustration. "I'm on my way."

ANGEL

"Mama, I'll be back," True announced.

I couldn't even look at her. I knew she was dealing with so much. She had more on her shoulders than most twenty-five-year-old women. I felt for my daughter every day. I wanted nothing more than to take it all off her shoulders and put it on mine. She was my baby —*mine*. I wanted to protect her and shield her from all sadness and pain. She had to know the desperation of that need because she had her own daughter that she wanted the same for. Still, she was so busy dealing with her own shit that she'd forgotten I was right here, *right here*, dealing with it with her.

I could only stare at the television that was playing re-runs of *Girlfriends*. I couldn't bear to give True the scrutiny that I felt was in my eyes. Even though her shortness had hurt my feelings, I knew the place where it was coming from. I loved her too much to chastise her for it. But still, it hurt.

I heard her sigh heavily. Then I could feel her walking towards me as I sat on the couch with my arms folded. I could feel the tears stinging my eyes as I felt her sit next to me.

I cried a lot.

Mostly for her.

"I'm sorry, Ma. I—"

I quickly put my hand up to stop her words because I always tried to be strong for her. Had she said one sweet, loving word, I would have broken down in uncontrollable tears. There would be a time that I would be allowed to cry freely but now wasn't that time. Because she was carrying this load with astonishing strength, I had to be strong for her.

I swallowed hard to digest the huge ball of sadness that always appeared there when she was near me. After taking a deep breath, I tapped her knee to let her know it was okay. Anything she did was okay. She could spit in my face, and it would still be okay.

"Where are you going?" I asked her.

"To see a friend. I need it. Watch Joy for me?"

"Of course."

I still couldn't look at her, but I felt her lean over and kiss my cheek. "See you later, Ma. I won't be long."

I just nodded as she hopped off the couch and headed towards the front door. As she left out of it, my cell phone rang. I picked it up from the cushion next to me. My eyes instantly rolled to the ceiling as I saw Tyrone's name flashing on the display screen.

"What?" I answered.

Tyrone was a guy I had allowed to take me to dinner when I needed someone to take my mind off things. I hadn't seriously dated since my husband died, so I hadn't been in a relationship since. However, I had entertained a few here and there, and all those men had failed miserably.

Just like this fool.

"That's how you feel?"

"Yes, that's how I feel. I don't have time for your games, Tyrone. I'm dealing with enough as is. You know what's going on with my daughter. Why would you add to my misery?"

After countless conversations over steak and potatoes, Tyrone knew my life. He knew every agonizing part of it. And, yet, last week, he still allowed some tramp to call me, after she'd gone through his phone, to tell me that I wouldn't be going on any more dinners with her man.

Yes, even at the age of forty, I was still dealing with messy men and the women who loved them. That's why I stayed away from them.

Russell, who'd found me on Facebook a few days ago, had been sending me inbox messages. He'd given me his number and asked me to dinner, but I just couldn't. Russell was way too close to home.

"Baby, it was a mistake," Tyrone annoyingly attempting to persuade me.

Again, my eyes were rolling. "A mistake that is going to cost you me."

"What you expect me to do, baby? You're not giving me any."

I chuckled. Men always used that against me. But they constantly showed me why my celibacy was necessary. I hadn't had sex with anyone since my late husband because of this very reason.

Chuckling cynically with a shake of my head, I replied, "I'm glad I didn't. Lose my number."

TRUE

As I walked into Coop's house on 97th and California, I could smell the weed in the air. He had left the door open for me, so I looked around for him in the large living room. Coop was so rough around the edges, and his attitude was ugly, but his three-hundred-thousand-dollar house in Evergreen Park was beautiful. I kicked my shoes off at the front door, looking around for him. Through the open concept of the home, I peeped him on the patio through the glass doors in the kitchen. I glided over the maple flooring towards the patio, leaving my purse on the kitchen island as I walked by.

"Hey..." His appearance stopped me dead in my tracks and took my words away.

He was lounging on an outdoor couch; his large, thick frame draped in a high-end suit. I appreciated the way it custom fit his frame. His strong arms seemed to be ripping at the seams of the jacket. His thick thighs threatened the seams of his pants as he sat riding back on the patio furniture. His beard was glistening in the setting, April sun. I had never seen his ignorance look so exquisite.

I cleared my throat and forced out, "H-hey, you."

I didn't feel like beating him to being an asshole. Not today. I didn't feel like the beef. As he looked up at me, it was as if he could see it in my face. So, he was actually calm and humane as he replied, "What's up?"

"Nothing," I lied. "Why are you so dressed up?"

"I had to go to a funeral today."

I shivered at the word. I hated to even think of funerals. "Somebody close?" I forced myself to ask. But this was the last conversation I wanted to have.

"Yeah."

My heart went out to him. "Sorry to hear that."

"Don't be. That's how the game goes sometimes."

He moved his feet off of the space on the couch next to him, and I sat beside him. He looked at me strangely as I eyed the weed pen in his hand that he was smoking from.

When he smiled slowly, I wished I could stay in this moment with him. Sitting there with that caring smile on his face, he seemed so sweet and beautiful.

Even though he and I had only been having sex for the last three months, we had managed to have decent conversations when he was like this. So, I knew that under his hardcore exterior was a much milder man that I would only see now and then.

I guessed that now was one of those rare times.

"You want to hit it, don't you?" he asked with a teasing smile that made me forget my worries. It was amazing how beautiful this flawed man was. His smile was so gorgeous, with lips that normally spilled such ugliness.

I playfully nudged him in the side. "You know I do. Stop playing."

As he handed the weed to me, he said, "When I met you, I would have never thought you smoked weed so much."

My eyebrow rose as our eyes met. "Why not?"

I could see the same fire in his eyes that was burning in them that night at Norman's Bistro. So, I knew that he hadn't gotten over it.

He shrugged. "You didn't seem like the type."

I kept staring in those harsh yet stunning eyes. I drowned into the intensity. I wanted it. I needed it. "What's the type?"

"Down to earth."

Surprised, my mouth dropped. "So, I'm bougie?"

He shook his head, his gorgeous smile spreading deeper into his beard. "Nah, you just looked that way."

"So, bougie girls don't smoke weed?" I pressed.

Coop shook his head. "Not the ones I've met."

I slightly shrugged. "You just have this stereotypical view that only hood chicks do drugs because you're from the hood. That's all you've seen."

He nodded. "You're probably right."

Shocked, my eyes bucked. I slightly sat back and stared at him. "Whaaaaaaat? You're agreeing with me?"

Finally, his intense eyes shied away from mine. Watching him blush was adorable to see. "Shut up."

He must be high.

Blushing wasn't like him at all.

"For real, though. Why do you smoke so much?" he asked as he rested his arm behind me on the couch.

I sat back and got comfortable. "Stop asking so many questions."

"I was just wondering. It's not a good look for a pretty girl like you."

My mouth flew open. I forced it to close so that I could hit the pen.

"What?" he asked curiously.

"You called me pretty," I acknowledged with a smile as I exhaled the weed smoke.

Again, he blushed, and I thought it was so damn cute. "You know I think you're pretty."

I shrugged. "You never say it."

He gave me his penetrating, flirtatious stare, and I could feel the seat of my panties flood with moisture. He licked his lips and told me, "I never knew you wanted to hear it."

"I mean it wouldn't hurt to hear it."

"Well, you're pretty.... And you're skinny as hell," he joked as he pinched my side.

"Whatever!" I fussed as I leaned into him. I was slowly starting to feel the effects of the weed. I enjoyed the feeling of that day's stress floating away.

"Yes, you are," he stressed. "You can dodge a raindrop, can't you?" he joked.

I started cracking up, and, damn, it felt good to laugh.

He nudged me, chuckling. "You know it's true. You wash your ass with floss?"

My mouth dropped as I continued to cackle. "Whatever! I am *not* that damn little!"

Usually, I was self-conscious about my weight. I was already slim, but when I started to drastically lose weight, losing the little curves that I had, I felt like a boy. But Coop had a way of making me laugh at his jokes, even though they were aimed towards me and lined with honesty.

Our eyes met again as our giggles faded and that intensity between us returned. I squeezed my thighs together, fighting the throbbing feeling between them. I swallowed hard and handed him back the pen. I watched curiously as he sat it down on the small table in front of him. Before I knew it, he reached over and pulled me onto his lap. Before I could say anything, he started kissing me, while taking off his suit jacket. Then he pulled up my dress. I could feel as his hand left my ass and went into his slacks. He pulled out that beautiful piece of long, thick art and used it to push my panties to the side.

He forced himself inside of me with such a thrust that I gasped. My eyes flew open, and I stared into his, wondering what these death strokes were for. He grabbed the back of my neck, and while biting his lip, said, "I told you that I was gon' make you pay for lying to me."

He grabbed my waist and controlled the strokes, even though I was sitting on his lap. He rocked me back and forth, up and down, tossing me all over the dick.

"You 'bout to get it," he groaned.

"Oooooh shiiiiit."

REMI

My hands were shaking as I walked up to my house. Tonight was me and Banks' anniversary dinner. We hadn't even gotten there, and I was already so nervous. I kept telling myself not to get my hopes up just in case he didn't propose. But I could feel that this was it.

This *had* to be it.

I had just gotten my makeup done, and I had already struggled into my Gucci dress afterward. I was now rushing into the house so Banks and I could leave for our eight o'clock reservation.

"Baaaabe..." I stopped in my tracks as my eyes fell on Banks and his right hand, Bennie, sitting at the dining room table. I heard sounds behind me. I spun around, and my heart sank when I saw his other two guys, JD and Jason, and their girlfriends, Niyah and Iyana, sitting on my couch watching TV. Music was playing. Blunts were in rotation.

"What's going on?" I asked as I looked around slowly. I walked towards Banks, asking, "Are they coming with us?"

"Nah, babe," Banks said. He sat his cup down on the table and stood up to greet me. As he hugged me, he said, "We aren't going to dinner anymore." He kissed my cheek quickly and then looked me over. "You look nice."

Shocked, I stuttered, "W-why aren't we going?"

"We're gonna kick it here for a while and then go to the strip club. One of the guys is having a birthday party at Red Diamonds tonight."

"What about our anniversary?"

He smiled, assuring me, "It's still a celebration, baby. Our people just wanted to celebrate with us."

"Yeah, Remi, we tryin' to kick it and see some hoes tonight," Bennie cut in. When I cut my eyes at him, he laughed. "Happy Anniversary."

Arrrrrrrrgh! I screamed on the inside.

When I looked back at Banks, he was giving my dress a once over. "You might wanna change outta that. That's too fancy for Red Diamonds."

I wasn't even trying to hide how floored I was, but Banks didn't see my shock anyway. He quickly smacked me on my ass and went back to sit at the table where he was rolling a blunt.

I forced back my disappointed tears and disappeared into my bedroom. My heart was so heavy as I removed the Gucci dress and girdle that was holding in all my imperfections. Standing in front of the mirror on our dresser, I looked at my stretch marks, rolls, thighs decorated with cellulite and voluptuousness and wondered was that why I hadn't gotten my ring today.

I didn't even blame Banks. I blamed myself for even getting my hopes up. Apparently, I was still that naïve woman he had been with for ten years, living a fairy tale instead of my reality. However, part of my reality was that I had my man. If he wasn't going to marry me today, then he would ask me eventually. No matter the women he had cheated with, he always stayed with me. So, I swallowed my disappointment and changed into a pair of Fashion Nova high-waist jeans that held in my imperfections while accentuating my ass. I threw on a Balmain, lightweight bomber jacket since the weather still dropped at night in Chicago in April.

I opted to wait to put my matching heels on until Banks was ready to go. I took another deep breath to get my emotions under control before going back into the living room. I immediately spotted Niyah and Iyana, resentful of their perfect shapes that were hardly covered by thin, short, form-fitted dresses. All the dope boys' girlfriends had perfect breasts, phat asses, and invisible waists that their men had purchased in Miami or the Dominican for half the price. Banks always suggested that I get my body done too, which further let me know what his preference was. But the doctor had told me long ago that I needed to lose weight and get my health together before I underwent such aggressive surgeries.

"Aye, baby, before you sit down, can you go get my Rolex out the drawer?" Banks asked, still seated at the table, weed smoke encasing him. "We ready to bounce."

I made an about face and went back into the bedroom, thinking, *It's going to be okay, Remi. Just be patient. Be patient, girl.*

But how patient did I have to be?! How long did I have to wait? How much more loving did I have to be? What else did I have to do to show him that I was wifey material?

I grimaced as I tore the drawer open of our nightstand where Banks usually kept his valuable jewelry. His two-carat cross pendant chain was there. I saw his Versace watch, Cartier bracelet, and multi-carat diamond earrings. But no Rolex.

"Bae, it's not in here!" I shouted.

"Look in the top drawer on the left!"

I frowned, mocking him silently and making faces as I started to close the drawer, but I stopped when I saw a watch box in the back of the drawer that I was already in. I figured that was his watch, so I reached back there and grabbed it. I shut the drawer as I opened the box to get the watch out.

"I found..." I stopped in my tracks when I saw the smaller velvet box tucked away inside of the watch box. My heart pounded out of my chest. I started to feel weak, and the room started to spin as I started to scream at the top of my lungs jumping up and down. "Aaaaaaaaaaaaaaaaaahhhhh!"

I tossed the watch box and tore open the velvet box. My eyes laid on a three-carat, tri-stone engagement ring set in platinum and lost my mind. "Oh my Goooooooooooooooood!"

Tears flooded my eyes as I took off running, but I was stopped suddenly when Banks came racing inside the room.

"What's wrong?" he asked as I ran up on him.

"Baby!" I squealed. "Oh my God! Baby! You tricked me!"

I threw my arms around him. Everyone else raced inside our bedroom to see what the hell was going on.

I waved the ring at Niyah and Iyana, chanting, "He got my ring! He got my ring!"

"Aaaaaaaaawww!" they both chanted and immediately got out their phones to capture the moment.

I finally let Banks go and handed them the ring. But I was so excited that I wouldn't let him get a word in. I grabbed both sides of his face and started to kiss him over and over again. My tears sank into his beard as I wrapped my arms around him so tightly that I was suffocating him.

Finally, I let him go again and stuck my hand out. "Yes! Yes! Yes! Yes!"

Everyone behind us laughed at my eagerness.

"Girl, you didn't even give him a chance to ask," Niyah said.

Banks and I laughed as he grabbed my hand and slid the ring on my finger. He stopped short when it wouldn't fit.

"Damn, it's too small," he told me.

"That's okay," I quickly insisted. "We'll just go get it sized tomorrow."

"Cool," Banks said putting it back in the box smiling into my face.

Grabbing his beard, I slightly pulled his face to mine. "I love you."

And for the first time in years, my heart relaxed. Now, I had no worries of who could take him from me because he had chosen me, and he had finally proven them all wrong.

4

TRUE

A MONTH LATER –

I had never known that a man knowing that you are sleeping with someone else would draw him to you so much. A month after bumping into Coop at Norman's Bistro, we were a lot closer than we had ever been before. We saw each other more often; every week now, versus once every couple of weeks. He started to take me on real dates, talk to me about my day, and he was a lot less of an asshole. It was like we were... *dating.*

Don't get me wrong. I wasn't falling for him, and he was still against all things resembling a relationship. Our time together was just oddly becoming more consistent.

"Are you going out with Coop again?"

I cringed as I walked towards the front door. I swallowed hard and turned towards my mother's judgmental eyes.

Knowing where this was going, I answered, "Yes."

Her perfectly arched eyebrow rose. "Do you like him?"

Admittedly, I did. As I said, I wasn't falling in love. I couldn't fall in love. There was no time for that. That wasn't an option for a person in my position. But over the last month, Coop had shed his hard shell and shown me who he *could* be. By now, I had grown comfortable with Coop. We had been spending so much time together that he was slowly getting rid of the other players on my team. Clearly, I hadn't learned from my mistakes with Jameel because I was falling for another asshole. But there was something so authentic about Coop when he took off that hardcore mask.

I would never tell him that, though. There was no use.

"Yeah, I guess I do," I admitted.

My mother's arms folded across her chest as she stared at me with those motherly eyes. "Are you falling for him?"

My eyes rolled to the ceiling. "No, Ma, I know better. He's just fun to be around."

That's truly all that it was. I guess in addition to the sex, Coop and I were becoming *friends*.

"What's the use in dating somebody right now?" my mother probed.

"Well, you said you wanted another grandbaby," I joked. Then I smiled, hoping it would get her to smile too.

"I do. But..." Her voice trailed off with sadness.

I sighed, feeling defeated that I hadn't gotten her to smile. "I was just playing. I am just having fun with Coop, Ma."

Her lips pressed together. "It's fun until one or both of you get feelings."

Not wanting to argue with her, hoping that it would ensure a sooner exit for me, I didn't say anything.

Yet, she pressed, "Did you tell him?"

"No," I answered shamefully.

"Well, don't you think you should?"

I allowed the frustration that her question had caused to flood my face. "Why?"

Shocked, my mother repeated, "Why?" She slightly sat up. Her elbows rested on her knees as she stared at me. She was in full Mama mode now. "Don't you think he needs to know?"

"No, he doesn't," I argued.

"Just because Jameel left you, it doesn't mean everybody—"

"Mama!" She jumped a bit, and I felt bad. I took a deep breath, calming myself down. "I'm sorry. I just... I just don't want to talk about it. When I'm out there dating and having fun, I don't think about it. It's like it doesn't exist. It's my escape. It's all that I have, besides you and Joy. And I enjoy it. I don't want to ruin it by talking about it."

My mother nodded, but I could see the regret all over her face. I went towards her on the couch, bent down, and kissed her cheek. "I'll be back. Thanks for watching Joy."

"You don't have to thank me for watching my baby. I wish you had some more of 'em for me to watch." There was a bit of sadness in her eyes that I sympathized.

However, I only said, "See you later." I wanted to keep this conversation from going to the dark place that I was running away from.

COOP

"Aye, shorty, come here."

I laughed at my right hand, Rakim, as he hung out of the passenger's window of my Beamer, hollering at this dirty-foot shorty while I pumped the gas. She was switching her lopsided booty hard as hell in some dingy-ass leggings that were see-thru, so they showed her polka dot panties underneath.

Her bum ass had the nerve to turn around, eyeball Rakim, ball her face up, and spit, "Ewwwwe. *No.*"

My eyes bucked. Shorty had a lot of nerve. Her PINK hoodie needed to be washed. Her gym shoes were dingy and probably from Walmart.

"Ewe?" I shot back. "You gon' let her get on you like that?" I asked Rakim.

"Man, fuck her!"

"Fuck *you!*" she spat at him.

I laughed at her. "Aye, shawty, stand down. Dirty ass looking like you got more claps than an auditorium."

Her face dropped. She was embarrassed, so she had lost all of that mouth quick. She tucked her dirty tail and scampered into the store.

Rakim hung out of the passenger's window, laughing. "Wow, dawg, for real?"

"She was trying to play you. I don't know why you was trying to holla at her anyway. Dirty ass probably only shower after three periods like a fucking hockey player or some shit."

Rakim started laughing even harder as he sat back in the car. I finished pumping the gas and hopped in the driver's side just as my phone started to ring.

I cringed when I saw it was Issa. Between hustling and True, I hadn't been able to get up with shorty. I had stood her up a few times, hadn't responded to a few text messages, and hadn't returned a shit-load of her calls.

Unconsciously, I had given Prince what he wanted after all.

"What up?" I answered reluctantly.

"Really?!" she popped. "That's what you on? You let another nigga tell you to stop fucking with your broad?"

I laughed at her ass. "You ain't *my* broad."

She instantly lost all that attitude. "This pussy was yours, though, baby," she whined. "Please don't let Prince come between us."

I looked at the phone as if that would make her make sense. "Ain't you still with that nigga?"

She sucked her teeth. "Are you going to wife me and pay my bills?"

"Fuck no."

"Then that's why I'm still with him, but I want *you*, though. I miss you and *it*. Don't you miss this pussy?"

Then this motherfucker, Rakim, sends it up by saying out loud, "He's fucking somebody else, Issa!"

I laughed softly while Issa gasped. "Are you fucking serious, Coop?!"

Still chuckling, I told her, "Aye, I gotta go."

"Coop!" she shouted.

I hung up on her while Rakim laughed his ass off. "Ahhhh! Hell nah!"

"Thanks a lot, motherfucka." I threw the car in drive, shaking my head, and pulled out of the gas station.

"I saw your girl, Trina, last night at V75," Rakim told me. "She was asking about you. You ain't been fucking with her either?"

"Nah, she's a dirty motherfucker too. I worry about getting robbed by hood niggas in the streets every day, and then I gotta go over there and worry about getting robbed by the rats? Nah, fuck that. I don't know whether it's her or a roach sucking my dick."

Rakim bent over laughing. "You know that girl wasn't that dirty. You wouldn't even lay your head in a place like that."

I nodded. "You're right. She was just junky than a motherfucker and clingy as shit. So, I haven't seen her in a few weeks."

I felt him looking at me. So, I quickly turned towards him before putting my eyes back on the road. "What?"

With a smirk, he told me, "Stop lying."

"What I'm lying about?"

"Trina being junky and clingy don't have shit to do with why you aren't fucking her no more."

"What it got to do with?" I challenged him.

"*True.*"

I had to force back my grin at the mention of her name. Since he was my right hand, Rakim was the only person who knew how I had been spending more and more time with True. I was too embarrassed to let anybody know how I had started liking a woman after I caught her up playing me. But I had never had a woman boss up on me like that. Her pulling that move had definitely made me pay more attention to her. It was like they say, everybody wants what they can't have, and since True acted like I couldn't have her, I wanted to captivate her. She was a challenge to me, and that made her different than any other woman who was begging and waiting patiently to suck my dick. So, she had my attention.

However, I would never tell her that. True was the first woman that I'd fucked that never asked me about other women, who else I was fucking, and if I wanted to be with her. She still wasn't trying to be tied down, and neither was I.

Ignoring that bitch-like feeling in my stomach that came every time I thought about her, I shrugged. "She's cool."

Rakim smirked. "She's more than cool."

"No, she's not," I shot back. "She's just cool to be around. She's less of a headache than most females."

Rakim folded his arms and stared at me. "If not, then why are you taking me home, instead of taking us to see them hoes waiting on us?"

"Because I would rather see True," I said with confidence.

Rakim laughed so hard that his head fell back on the headrest.

"Fuck you," I cursed.

"It's cool if you're falling for a chick."

I spat, "I ain't falling nowhere. She's just cool to be around. She's different."

Rakim nodded.

"Now, stop talking about it before I knock yo' ugly ass out."

"Whatever, pretty boy motherfucker." Changing the subject, he said, "Anyway, I gotta holla at you about something I heard Zell is pillow talking with his baby mama. He thinks you're being reckless and killed Mac."

My eyebrows rose. "He said that to his baby mama?"

"Yeah."

"How you know?" I quickly looked over at Rakim who was wearing a slick, devilish grin. I put my eyes back on the road and asked, "You fucking Candi?"

Candi was Zell's baby mama.

Rakim nodded once. "Here and there."

Frowning, I reminded him, "She like eighteen, dawg."

His devious grin told me that he was well aware of her age. "I know. That pussy *tiiiiight* too."

I shook my head. "You foul, dawg."

He shrugged with a careless smirk. "Anyway, you gotta take care of that lil' nigga. I know he like a lil' brother to you, but he can't keep running his mouth like a bitch. He say that shit to the wrong mother-fucker and all of this is done. Game over. He needs to be dealt with."

I nodded. "Say less."

"Whaaaat?!" True shrieked. She held a smile as she looked into the bag I'd handed her when she walked into my spot.

I chuckled. "Shut up."

"Oooooh!" She continued fucking with me, teasing me as she scurried over to the couch. "You brought me my favorite? Ahhhhhh!"

"Didn't I say shut yo' ass up?" I snapped with a blush.

She looked up at me, grinning from ear to ear. "I'm geeked. You brought me one... two... three... four... *five* weed pens. And they are lemon haze." She paused and looked up at me with starry eyes. "You like me. You really *liiiike* me."

I brushed her off. "Shut the fuck up before I take them from you. I was just tired of yo' ass smoking all of my shit. Now, you have your own."

The smile on her face was unbelievable as she sat on my couch Indian style and turned one of the pens. I sat across from her on the chaise attached to it and watched her with a smile on my face, as if I was a daddy watching my baby opening her presents on Christmas.

Out of all the pens I had let her hit, she particularly liked the lemon haze oil because of the smell of zest, citrus, and a lingering sweetness that it left in the air. She particularly liked how it left her feeling energetic and lively since it particularly helped smokers that suffered from depression and fatigue. Usually, when she and I would meet up, no matter the smile on her face, I could see the exhaustion in her eyes. But after hitting the pen a few times, she was full of life like her worries had vanished. And she could have sex for hours.

She took the first hit slowly, blowing it out even slower, and then meeting my eyes with a happy twinkle in hers. "You are so nice, once a person gets to know you. I never knew you would be so cool to be around."

I rolled my eyes. "Is it a point to that?"

"Why are you such an asshole then?" she pressed. "Why not just be this cool person all the time?"

I simply shrugged. "People don't respect nice."

"So, you're an asshole just to get respect from people? It's a facade?"

I confidently shook my head. "Ain't shit fake about me, shorty."

"Then what is it?" she asked as she kicked off her sandals and started to run her toes over the carpet. As she did, I admired her fresh, French manicured toes.

"I've had to be this way for so long that I guess its second nature. It's how I survived. I had nobody else to take care of me. I had to fend for myself. It was just me out there."

"Where were your parents?"

Again, I shrugged. "I don't know."

True raised an eyebrow and hit the pen again. She then asked with a throat full of smoke, "You don't know?"

"No. From as long as I can remember, I was bounced from foster home to foster home to group home." Her eyes bucked slightly as she listened intently. "Everybody had a different story on where my parents were. I figured they were all lies and, eventually, I forgot about my parents. If I wasn't fighting off the kids in the group home, I was fighting off the motherfuckers who just wanted the check when they took me in but didn't want the responsibility of actually caring for me. So, there was never a chance to be nice. I had to be a motherfucker to keep people off me. Most of my foster parents didn't give a fuck about me. Most of 'em mistreated me. Some of 'em even abused me. The last ones were so abusive that I ran and never went back. I was twelve then. Ever since then, I've been out here fending for myself."

I looked away from the sympathy in her eyes. I didn't want sympathy from anybody. *It is what it is.*

That part of my life was over. I hadn't folded back then, and I would never fold for a motherfucker now. I had to beat people to being the beast before they beasted up on me. That's how you survived in this world.

"You get it now?" I asked her.

"Yeah," she answered softly as she blew out a cloud of smoke slowly. "But is that what you want to be remembered for?"

I was happy that she hadn't pried with more questions about what I had gone through as a child. That's why I fucked with her, despite wanting my distance from people. She didn't try to get too close, and neither did I, still while enjoying each other's company.

"What you mean?" I asked.

"I mean when you die, do you want that to be what people remember you for? Do you want everyone at your funeral saying you were some asshole they all feared?"

I thought for a few seconds before replying, "I never thought about it like that."

"You should because life is short. Very, unexpectedly short..." She looked like she had phased out for a split second and then came back to reality. "But how we are remembered lasts forever."

I let that sink in for a minute. We both sat in silence as she puffed on her pen. I puffed on what she said, realizing that all I had in my legacy was murder and mayhem. Everybody feared me, but who loved me? Who truly loved me?

"You done being Iyanla Vanzant?" I joked, avoiding the question.

Fuck that deep, thought-provoking shit True was on.

Her head fell back as she laughed. "Whatever. I was just trying to put something on your mind."

"Well, I'm trying to put something on your mind too," I said as I grabbed the bulge forcing its way out of my basketball shorts.

As I stood up from the couch and started walking towards her, she smiled slowly as she sat back on the couch, opening her legs, and inviting me in.

"Like what?" she beamed.

As I kneeled in front of her, she licked her lips slowly and seductively continued to hit the pen. I pushed up her short-sleeve T-shirt dress and exposed her shaved chocolate pussy. I spread her legs as I brought my face closer to her leaking opening, her eyes bucked. I had never given her head before—*ever*. That was just something I didn't do often. I could count on one hand how many times I had done it in my life, but True made me so comfortable that I just wanted to taste her. So, I did.

5

REMI

"Oh gawd," I panted as I felt Banks' strokes getting deeper and faster.

As he lay on top of me, drilling my soppy, wet pussy, I could feel his heavy breath against my neck. It got heavier as his strokes got even more punishable.

"Ah! Fuck!" I gritted, forcing myself to take the pain because the pleasure that came with it was so worth it. I turned my head, and our lips met. As we tongue kissed, our heavy breaths intertwined with one another's. I could feel his dick forming into concrete as he reached down, grabbed one of my heavy, thick thighs, and brought my knee to my breast, causing him to fall into my ocean even deeper.

"Ooooooh," I cried. Literally, tears slid down my face and onto the satin pillow that I always slept on to protect my hair.

Banks continued to kiss me, tasting the saltiness of the tears that slid down my cheeks and into my mouth. He leaned to his side and, while holding my leg tightly, he started to beat this pussy into a flood of juices that spilled all over his dick.

"Aaaaaaaaaaahhh," I screamed as I creamed. "Oh my—" He stopped my praises by lightly biting my bottom lip and grunting as he also started to cum.

Then, with a jolt, he jumped out of me, and my heart sank. For years, I had made him pull out because I refused to get pregnant if he wasn't willing to marry me. But it had been a month and a half since he'd proposed, and he was still pulling out.

"Arrrrgh!" he grunted as he released on my stomach. I lay there, breathing heavily as he caught his breath and jacked himself until all his seed had been released. Then he reached over to the nightstand, grabbed a towel, and wiped my stomach clean.

When Banks was done, he lay beside me on his side and cuddled with me, laying his hand on my stomach.

I lightly pushed his hand away. "Stop."

Banks giggled and squeezed the pouch sitting on top of my pelvis.

"Stop playiiiiing!" I cringed. I smacked his hand away and attempted to roll away from him.

He overpowered me, pulling me back towards him. "Don't run away from me."

I pouted. "Then stop. You know I hate that."

"Then why don't you fix it if you hate it?"

"What you mean?" I asked, looking up at him.

"Get your body snatched like all the rest of these chicks. I got the money. You can go to the Dominican Republic and come back with one of those bad-ass bodies."

That left a lump in my throat. So, clearly, he didn't think I had a "bad-ass body" now. He always complimented me on my ass, but that was it. I knew he didn't appreciate the weight gain, but he clearly appreciated those chicks with "bad-ass bodies."

"I need to lose weight first," I forced myself to say past my embarrassment.

"Yeah, you do."

Ouch!

I cut my eyes at him. "Damn, you didn't have to agree so fast."

"I mean I heard about that shit. I know you gotta lose weight before that type of surgery. Otherwise, you gon' look big with a small stomach."

I flinched. "Ouch!"

"What?"

I couldn't look at him as I asked, "So, you think I'm *big*?" I just looked at the ceiling.

I could feel Banks staring at me, however, as he replied, "Babe, be real. You *have* gained weight since we got together."

Chewing the inside of my mouth, I admitted, "You're right. I just didn't think you thought I was big."

"I didn't say big. You just gained weight."

Now, I was embarrassingly biting on my bottom lip. "I know. I need to lose weight."

"Then what are you waiting on?"

I cringed and decided to change the subject. "I'm waiting on *my ring*." He chuckled as I went on. "What is taking them so long to size it?"

"I decided to add a few more diamonds to it. It's coming." He kissed my forehead.

Hearing that washed the sadness away, and it was replaced with so much joy. Then I instantly felt regret again. Banks had been so thoughtful of me. I needed to be thoughtful of him and be the woman he wanted to see every time he looked at me.

A FEW HOURS LATER, I was on my way to work. Along the way, I was consumed by reprimanding thoughts of how I had let myself get so big. I told myself this was *it*. Starting the next day, I was going on a diet. I had finally gotten my ring from Banks, and it was clear that he wanted me to lose the weight and look better. So, if he could give me what I wanted, then I was going to give him what he wanted. I was going to lose fifty pounds and then hop a flight to the Dominican and get my stomach and waist snatched. Hell, maybe I would even have my breasts done too.

As I arrived at my patient's house, I was so determined. I should have been doing it for me, but however it was going to get done, so be it.

I got out of the car, planning my lunch for the day. If this was going to be my last day being a fat girl, I was going to *max*. As I approached my patient's house and rang the bell, I started to scroll the UberEATS app for lunch options.

I decided on Five Guys just as the door started to open. On the other side of it appeared a very solemn-faced Olivia, the younger sister of Lucille, my patient. Although she was her younger sister, Olivia was in her mid-fifties, and Lucille was in her late sixties.

Olivia's sadness was more visible than usual. Her head seemed heavy as if she could barely hold it up. Her eyes were glassed over and red.

I sighed, realizing what must have happened, and my shoulders sank. "She passed?"

As she nodded, the tears pooling in her eyes spilled out. She covered her face and began to wail. I threw my arms around her and repeated the phrase that I had said so many times in my career. "I'm so sorry for your loss."

This was customary in my career. I was a Hospice nurse, so I knew when I met patients that they soon would die. But for the ones that I grew close to, the ones whose families cooked for me, and got to know me, it never got easier.

COOP

"What are you thinking about?"

I looked over at True. She was staring at me as I stared up at the ceiling. I hadn't even realized that she was awake.

"Retiring," I answered.

I couldn't believe it myself, but True had me thinking about settling down. For the last few weeks, we had been pretty tight. The man in me didn't want her giving that pussy to someone else, so I was selfishly taking up all of her time. And for the first time in my life, I was around a woman who didn't irk me, didn't try to change me, and was cool as shit. Being around True made me think about my life, doing better, and being better.

She looked obviously surprised. "Retiring? From what? You ain't got no damn job."

I chuckled. "Fuck you. Yes, I do."

"Mmm humph..." She giggled.

"I meant retiring from hustling."

Her eyebrows rose. "Oh, really?"

I nodded and said simply, "Yeah."

She rolled over onto her stomach and rested her chin in the palm of her hand, staring at me. "Retire and do what? Play golf or something?"

I bit my lip with this threatening smile on my face. "You woke up on asshole mode this morning, huh?"

"I learned from the best," she teased.

"Nah, *asshole*, I ain't gon' play golf. I actually wanna invest my money into something. I just don't know what."

"What do you like to do besides hustle? What are you good at?" she pressed.

"Telling people what to do."

"I think you would be good at opening a club."

I shook my head as I put my hands behind my head. When I did, she cuddled up under my arm. "Nah, I wanna do something more meaningful."

She looked up at me shockingly. "Meaningful?"

"Yes, meaningful."

"Like what?"

"Like an after-school center... Probably just for boys. Like a safe haven in the hood."

I could feel True staring at me, so I looked down and saw her looking up at me with admiration. There was a softness in her eyes as if she was proud of me.

I had never had anybody look at me like that.

"Mommyyyy!" Suddenly, her daughter's voice shot through the air.

"Oh shit!" True whispered in a panic as she hopped out of bed. She started to run frantically around her room looking for something to throw on.

When Joy started to wiggle the doorknob, shorty damn near pissed herself.

"No! No! No, baby!" she chanted as she ran towards the door and leaned against it. "Wait, don't come in!"

"I'm hungryyyyy!"

"Okay," she rushed to say. "I just woke up. Here I come."

I chuckled as I watched True throw her robe on with panic in her eyes. She looked like she felt so guilty. It was the same look on her face that she always had whenever she let me spend the night. And I had been spending the night at her crib a lot.

Shorty was slowly changing me without even trying. It was like the more she showed me that she wasn't like the other chicks, the more I wanted to be around her. As she left the room, squeezing through the small opening in the door she'd created so her daughter couldn't see inside, I caught myself watching her with an admiring smile.

I was actually admiring somebody.

Shit felt weird.

And True caught me. With a quick glance before closing the door, she caught me staring and blushed. I like that blush. I liked that smile. And after a month a half, I liked that girl.

Against my own will, her simply being herself had slowly caused me to only pay attention to her, want to be around her, and only want to fuck her.

I didn't like that feeling. This wasn't me. I wasn't trying to play these games.

"You okay?"

I had been staring up at the ceiling for so long that I didn't even notice that True had come back into the room. I glanced at the door and saw that it was closed shut tight again.

True smiled bashfully and sat on the bed beside me, her robe wrapped tightly around the body I had been wreaking havoc on all night. "She's eating cereal," she told me. "What's wrong?"

"Are we fucking other people or what?"

The question had caught her off guard. Her eyes bucked slightly as regret came over her face. It was as if she was sad to see the caring dude that she had made emerge, wash away. Now the ignorant nigga she'd met had reappear.

"Huh?" she asked, though she had heard me loud and clear.

I cut my eyes at her. "You heard me. Are we still fucking other people or is it just you and me?"

She smiled at the question. Her shoulders sank. She was touched, but fuck all that, I was embarrassed that I had even asked. I stared up at the ceiling, hating that I cared to know. Besides, it was obvious. She still hadn't let her daughter lay eyes on me, which made me think there was somebody else in her life. Any other chick would have been low key trying to make me be a father figure by now.

"Who said that I was fucking other people?" she asked, trying to front.

I cut my eyes at her again. "Bitch, please."

Her mouth dropped as she punched me in the stomach. "Really?!"

"You know you was out there like a race car driver, burning fifty rubbers a day."

"Asshole!" she shrieked quietly with laughter as she pinched my side.

I laughed and shrugged before I swatted her hand away. "Aye, I just wanna know if I should go fuck this other chick later on tonight." I was trying to appear cool by fronting like I didn't care. But I swallowed the tension that had formed in my throat out of fear that she was about to let me down.

"You play all day," she replied as she continued to shake her head at my jokes.

"Who said I was playing?"

She stared at me, shaking her head. "The problem is I don't know if you're playing or not."

I just watched her, waiting for her to finally answer the fucking question as I secretly wished she would say the right thing.

I wanted to shoot myself for actually wishing it.

She continued to stare at me too.

The seconds ticked by.

It felt like forever before True finally sighed. She looked down, avoiding my eyes, toying with the tie on her robe. "I told you that I'm not trying to commit to anybody right now."

I didn't want to react like this, but I couldn't help it. I sat up, threw the covers off me, and got out of the bed. Embarrassment was causing me to run up out of there.

I could feel her eyes on me as I searched for my clothes. "Coop—"

"It's cool," I said, avoiding her eyes.

"Then why are you leaving?"

"I got moves to make."

I could feel her still staring at me as I threw my clothes on. This was shorty's second time embarrassing me. The first time was when she had the audacity to shit on me just to sit on another man's dick. Now, she was telling me that she didn't want to be in a relationship like *I* was the bitch.

I had once again let this woman embarrass me, but there wouldn't be a next time. I had stupidly let my guard down because she was a challenge. I would laugh at my homies for doing that, and here I was being the joke.

Without looking at her, I spit, "You gon' get your daughter out the way so she don't see last night's dick leaving out of her mommy's room?"

I heard her huff and then, out of my peripheral, I saw her marching towards the door, holding her robe closed. She left out and slammed the door. I was pacing the floor. I didn't like this; this soft shit. I needed to get out of there.

As soon as I heard her tell Joy that she could go to the back to watch TV in her room while she showered, I opened the bedroom door quietly. I peeked my head out and saw her and Joy walking down the hall. As soon as she ushered Joy into her bedroom, I crept out and left, knowing I was never going to speak to shorty again. She had this fucked up. Women begged to even be in my presence, let alone have me choose them.

Shorty was gon' learn.

TRUE

I didn't have time for Coop's temper tantrums. I had bigger things to deal with.

A few hours after he stormed out of my house, my heart was beating frantically as I waited for the nurse to return to the examination room. I hadn't gone to my usual doctor. That day, I had gone to the nearest Planned Parenthood.

"Miss Jenkins?" My heart jumped as I heard the voice along with the knock on the door.

"You can come in."

As the doorknob turned and the nurse stepped in, I felt the flutters in my stomach turn into a whirlwind, making me nauseous.

She walked in, avoiding my eyes. She sat down at the desk inside the room and finally looked at me.

I grimaced. "Just tell me."

She lashed a half-ass smile as she replied, "You were right."

I cringed with disappointment. "Damn."

"You *are* pregnant."

I knew it. I'd felt it in my soul. This was only the second time I'd been pregnant, but I knew my body.

"Considering your circumstances, you do have options, however…"

I didn't hear anything else. She was talking. Her mouth was moving. But I didn't hear anything. Not one word. The overflow of thoughts in my mind was drowning out anything that lady was saying. I was pregnant by Coop, and, considering how he had snuck out of my house without saying anything else to me earlier that morning, I knew his mean, spiteful ass had no plans on ever speaking to me again.

An hour later, I was at my mother's house to pick up Joy. As soon as I told her the news, she was mortified.

"No!" she spoke firmly, seemingly more mortified than I was.

"Mama," I pleaded for her to agree with this.

She sat at her dining room table, looking at me in pure disbelief. "You can't."

I had already been shunning her to her own house because I was spending so much time at mine with Coop. Now, this? My mother was horrified for me.

"Why not?" I asked her, because as a matter of fact, I was not mortified at all. After sitting with knowing that I was pregnant, for an hour in my spot in the parking lot at Planned Parenthood and realizing that finally, my body had life in it, I felt like I had no choice, despite my circumstances, to have this baby.

"Don't you think you're going through enough?" my mother asked.

It was bad timing, super bad timing. But after learning I was pregnant, I realized I was happy. For once in a very long time, I had some *good* news, something to look forward to.

"I want to give this to you," I told her as I sat down at the table next to her. "You've been saying you wanted another grandbaby for so long."

"True…" She didn't have any more words. She just looked at me and shook her head in disbelief.

"I *need* to do this, Mama," I pleaded with her.

She bit her lip in frustration. Then her nails clawed at the table as if she was reaching for some stability. "It might make matters worse."

"I talked to the doctor about that. It won't." My mother still wasn't convinced. With her lips pressed together, she shook her head slowly as I begged for her support. "Let me do this for you."

"For *me*?" she asked. "You don't have to worry about me."

"But I do. That's all I do. This will bring you some joy, *us* some joy. So, I am going to do this, Mama."

She stared at me long and hard. I smiled and reached for her hand and lovingly laid my hand over it.

"Fine," she snapped, giving in. "But if you are going to have this baby, then you need to move in with me."

"Mamaaa!" I whined.

"You need to anyway."

"Mama, I already told you. After all of this, I need to at least have my freedom and my own space. I can't have nothing else, so I at least want this all to play out in my own space."

"Fine." She silenced with a sigh as she held my hand that lay on top of hers.

It pained me to frustrate her, but she would soon see that this was for the best. "I'm doing this for you, Mama."

"Thank you, baby. I'm still praying that God will give us a miracle, though." Finally, a smile slowly spread across her face. My heart melted. I didn't know how many more chances I would have to put a smile on my mama's face, so I treasured the opportunity to do it while I still had time.

6

REMI

"Hey, Remi. What you doin' here so early?"

I smiled as I walked towards Mark, one of the bouncers at The Dating Game. "I came to bring my man something to eat before the comedy show starts. Where is he?"

He gave me a quick hug as he answered, "He's in the back talking to the owner."

"I'll wait at the bar then." I sashayed over to the bar and took a seat, placing the bag of pasta from Pizza Capri in front of me. I took a big whiff of it and closed my eyes as I savored the smell of the salmon pasta simmered in tomato cream sauce. I wanted some so fucking bad. It was my favorite and Banks' too, but my get-snatched diet had officially begun. I had been on my diet for two days, and the struggle was *so* real. I had a goal to be fifty pounds lighter by Christmas, so I had six months. After the New Year, I planned on being on my way to the Dominican to get snatched. I wanted a tummy tuck, breast lift, and hella lipo. And by next summer, I would be in a thirty-thousand-dollar Pnani Tornai wedding dress looking like a snack instead of a fucking buffet full of rolls and cakes.

Every time I had to eat a salad instead of some Harold's Chicken, I was mad as fuck at myself for letting myself go so much. But I blamed

Banks. Not only was he the cause of the emotions that had driven me to eat my sadness, but he had also continued to dick me down while I gained every pound. He kept fucking me while I gorged and then fucked the shapely, healthy, skinny chicks behind my back. He had me thinking I was sexy out here in these streets and then waited until I was fifty pounds heavier to tell me that he had noticed that I'd gained weight.

But that was all I had needed to hear to get my shit together.

"Can I get you something to drink?"

I looked up from my thoughts and noticed one of the bartenders waiting to take my order.

This heffa. My insides sneered at the perfectly-built bartender. She was the exact reason why I didn't need any more calories. "I'll take a glass of wine."

"What kind?"

"Merlot is fine."

She nodded, and I watched her with envy as she poured my wine. Her body was perfect. Every single part of it was small and toned. The only thing big on her was the big ass and wide hips that made her leggings see-thru. She had on a cropped top that revealed a nearly invisible waist. These were the types of women that my man was around all the time, and here I was letting myself go.

"Here you go." As she handed me the flute, I noticed her finger-nails. They were beautiful, designed in fluorescent colors and an immense amount of rhinestones.

"Your nails are so pretty," I told her. "Can I see?"

She smiled. "Sure," she said as she stuck her left hand out proudly.

I leaned over, taking a sip as I admired her hand. And then I nearly choked on the Merlot as it slid now my throat.

"You okay?" she asked as I started coughing.

She snatched back her hand, watching me oddly as I coughed a few times. I was gasping trying to catch my breath as I forced out, "That's my ring."

On her finger was *my* three-carat, three-stone engagement ring. It was on her dainty little hand. I knew it. I had stared at it long enough to know every diamond, curve, and detail of it.

Finally catching my breath, I snapped, "That's my ring!"

"Huh?" she was utterly confused as anger poured over my eyes.

Next thing I knew, I snapped again. I snatched that lil' bitch up and pulled her over the bar. I could hear people yelling and scampering around me, but I could also hear my fists connecting with her face as I stood over her cowering body.

She tried to fight back. She tried to kick and punch, but I grabbed her left hand and bent it back.

"Ooooowww!" she howled.

"Give me my fucking ring, bitch!" I screamed as I took the ring off her finger.

Just then, I was snatched up by someone much bigger than me because I was unable to get out of their grasp.

"Let me go!" I yelped.

"Don't do this, Remi." I recognized the voice as Mark's.

He was carrying me towards the front door until I saw Banks rushing out of the back. He looked at me and then down at the bartender and raced towards *her* to help *her*.

That's when strength I didn't even know I had, surfaced. I fought my way out of Mark's grasp and ran towards them, screaming, "Why the fuck did she have my ring on, Banks?!"

I was crying, watching him help her to her feet. He immediately stood in front of her, to protect her from me snatching her up again. He met me and held me in a bear hug. Feeling his arms around me, I was too weak to fight. My bite was gone replaced with heartbreak.

"Why does she have my ring on, Banks?" I asked as I began to sob.

I stopped fighting finally. I stood still, and he let me go. We looked into each other's eyes, and I saw that he stared back at me completely unapologetic.

He finally shrugged and simply replied, "You went in the wrong drawer."

My eyes squinted in confusion. "What?"

He stuck his hands into his pockets and stood confidently. "You went in the wrong

drawer that night," he announced so easily with relief as if he had been waiting so long to finally admit it. "When I asked you to get my watch, you went in the wrong drawer."

My soul left my body. I was still alive, but I was now dead inside.

I stuttered, trying to wrap my head around this level of utter betrayal. "So... So..."

"*I'm* his fiancée, bitch!" The bartender appeared next to Banks, blood spewing from her nose, but proudly holding on to his arm.

I slowly looked towards her and then back at him. He stood there just as proudly as she did. I wanted to bash their faces together, but I couldn't do this anymore. Fighting women over him, fighting *for* him had come to an end. Not if I wanted to survive. Not if I didn't want to lose it.

With a weak arm, I threw the ring at their feet. I then turned on heavy-burdened heels and walked towards the entrance. The patrons and bouncers watched me with so much pity that I was even more embarrassed. But I didn't cringe. They were right to look at me that way. I had let Banks do it again. I had let him fool me again, trick me again, and manipulate me again. But only this time, as I walked out of that club, I knew I would never be the same.

COOP

"Why are we in here?" Rakim asked as he looked around the jewelry store with a frown like it stunk.

"I'm looking for something."

"Looking for what?" he pressed as he followed closely behind me.

"I don't know. Something to make True talk to me."

"Wait. What?"

I avoided his eyes as I stopped at a counter with some dope necklaces inside. "I walked out on her two days ago, and now she won't answer the phone."

"*Sooo*, you want to buy her jewelry?" The confusion in his voice was annoying.

I cut my eyes at him. This nigga was getting on my nerves with the 21 Questions.

"Ain't that what men do when they fuck up with their girl?"

Rakim shrugged. "Yeah, some men do that, but not *you*."

I sucked my teeth before saying, "Man, fuck you." I went back to looking over the necklaces.

"Yo', you seriously tryin' to buy her something?" Rakim pressed.

"We in here, ain't we?"

"But when she become your girl?"

"She's not." And I honestly felt regret when I said that. I hated this, caring, giving a fuck, wanting her. That's why I should have never given her more than some dick.

But I hadn't. I had fucked up and started to like her for more than that wet pussy. I had given her more than a few nuts. I had laid up with her, gotten to know her, and I liked her.

I could feel Rakim staring at me as I peered into the case of necklaces. Then I heard him gasp. "Yoooo', you *want* her to be your girl."

Embarrassment made the hairs on my neck stand up. I already felt like a bitch doing this, and he was making it worse. But I needed his help, so I had to bring him. I had never bought a woman a gift. I hadn't had a mother or father figure in my life, but I knew from watching TV that when a man wanted to get back in a woman's good graces, he had to buy her something nice.

After walking out on True, I was good until that night. I was so used to hearing her voice before I shut it down for the night or being next to her as I went to sleep that it didn't feel right that we were beefing. So, I called her, and she didn't answer. Since, I had been blowing her phone up with no answer. I thought if maybe I sent her a pic of this nice gift, she would accept my apology. I was salty that she didn't want to be my girl, but after all this time, shorty was a pretty good friend to me. Growing up the way I had, being shipped from one foster home to the next, living in group homes, raising myself on the streets, I barely had any real friends, and I had no family. Very few people genuinely gave a fuck about me. Shit, Rakim had been my only friend and family. Since outside of the sex, True had become my friend also, I missed her.

"She ain't gon' ever be my girl. She don't want that and neither do I," I lied. "But I pissed her off and—"

"And you care?" he asked, shockingly.

"*Yes*, motherfucker. Gawd damn!" I snapped loud enough that the store clerks looked at me.

"Aye, I'm just shocked," Rakim explained. "You *actually* give a fuck about somebody."

I frowned at his statement. "I give a fuck about you, don't I?"

"Yeah, we been fam for years, though. And I made you rock with me so we could get this money. You started rocking with me because you finally started trusting me once you weren't homeless no more after we started making money together. I had to prove my loyalty to you. I ain't never seen you care about nobody else."

I just looked at him. I didn't have a quick, witty comeback for that.

Then this goofy started to look at me with this weird smile pressing through his beard.

"What you staring at?" I asked.

"Enjoying the view."

I pushed him in the chest. As he stumbled back a few steps, laughing at me, I told him, "You soft-ass nigga... Fuck you, and help me pick something out."

He finally stopped talking shit and started looking over the necklaces with me.

As we did, he told me, "Zell's baby mama said that he's still running his mouth."

"Shit," I groaned.

"He young. He don't know no better. You gotta shut him up, though. I know you don't want to. I know he been on our team for a minute, but he's a threat. He gotta go."

"Say less."

TRUE

I took a deep breath as I rang Coop's doorbell. After two days of him blowing up my phone, I had finally decided to answer. I had missed him over those two days, but I needed the space to think this through thoroughly.

I knew that once I told him everything, he would be so pissed that the old Coop would reappear, and he would never speak to me again. Behind that asshole was a caring man that had slowly been revealing himself to me. I hated to shift his world like this, but I couldn't have his baby without him knowing everything. So, I had to tell him.

When the door slowly opened, I took in his presence like a breath of fresh air. He was like a tall, burly statue of masculinity. It amazed me how such a beast of an angry man could have sparkling eyes, but his did just that in the setting sun rays that snuck through the door as I walked inside. My knees knocked along the way. My heart skipped beats as I removed my shoes and inched toward the couch. I sat down, laying my eyes on a beautifully-wrapped, small rectangular box sitting on the coffee table in front of me.

"That's yours."

I looked from the gift to Coop. As he stood in front of me, I had never seen him look so humble.

"You got me a present?" I couldn't believe it. The vicious, heartless man that I had met had completely changed for me, and I had to break his heart.

"Yeah. Open it."

"Sit down, Coop."

He looked oddly at my seriousness. His eyes wondered why I wouldn't open the beautifully-wrapped gift. He came towards me and sat beside me. He picked up the gift and handed it to me. I sat it down in my lap and swallowed my fear.

He started to be more compassionate than I had ever seen him. "I know you're mad at me. I was wrong for walking out on you."

My heart went out to this gentle giant. Tears welled up in my eyes. He had let his guard down... just for me to let him down. "Coop—"

"Just listen," he interrupted me. "I know you're not ready for a relationship, and that's cool. I just don't want to lose you as a friend. I only got one, and I never knew I would have another one. I—"

"Coop—"

"Let me fin—"

"I have cancer, Coop." The words tumbled from my mouth like boulders that crushed his spirit.

Finally, I had his attention. He stared at me with wide eyes and asked breathlessly, "What?"

I took a deep breath and just forced it all to come out at once. "I have an inoperable brain tumor. That means they can't take it out. There is nothing they can do for me."

His confusion made him stumble over his words. "S-so what that mean?"

"I only have another year at most to live. All of 2017, I went through chemo and radiation. The tumor shrank, but then right before Jameel left, it started to grow again. I decided to stop the treatment when Jameel left me. I was tired of being so sick, just to end up dying anyway. I chose to live the rest of my days having fun without feeling the effects of chemo. The doctor... well, the *doctors,* because I have gone to so many for second opinions, say I only have about another year to live. A few months ago, I had found out that I am now

Stage 3. I'm dying, Coop. There is no way around it, no treatments that will stop it, no miracles to wait for. I am dying. That's why I *can't* want to be in a relationship with you."

"So, *that's* why you smoke so much weed."

I nodded. "Yes. It helps with the headache pain."

Confusion and disbelief had silenced him. I didn't force him to say anything either. I had had that same reaction when the doctors told me my prognosis two years ago. I had tried to fight back then, when it was only stage 2. I had gone through radiation and chemo. That's why I was too sick to please Jameel. That's why I had been too weak to be a good wife to him. That's why he had left me. But once he walked out on me and the doctors told me the tumor had grown, after all the throwing up, dizziness, weight loss, hair loss, fatigue, and losing my husband, I was done. Since I was dying, I was going to do it feeling the best I could.

Coop was so messed up that he was stuttering over his words. "Are...are you...you sure? Have you gone to a specialist?"

I sadly nodded my head, feeling sorry for the little hope in his eyes. "I have. There is nothing that can be done."

As Coop moaned, "Yoooo'," I could hear the hurt in his voice as he stood up slowly and started to pace. "Why didn't you tell me this before?"

I winced because it was hard to admit it in his face. "Because you were just supposed to be fun."

His nose flared. Even though when he met me, I was just the same to him, he didn't like hearing it. "But when it started to be more than fun, why not tell me?"

"I-I couldn't. When I'm with you, I'm not dying."

That was true. When I was out having my fun, I was living, the total opposite of what I knew was happening to me. Everyone is destined to die eventually, but I knew when and I knew how. And that was scarier than not knowing. I knew that my daughter would go to prom, have babies, and get married, all without me. I knew that my mother would have to bury me. So, I snuck in every delusional moment of happiness I could.

Watching Coop, I knew that I had hurt someone along the way.

"But you are dying. So, when you saw me getting close to you, why not tell me?! You knew I had a hard time getting close to people."

"I know!" I said, jumping to my feet. "I'm sorry." I went towards him, but he backed away with such fury in his eyes that I knew better than to continue to approach him.

"Fuck that!" he snapped with the savagery of a beast. "Why let me fall for you when you knew you were dying?!"

"Because I was falling for you too and I didn't want to hurt you!" I insisted.

"So, why are you telling me now?!" he yelled.

We stood there, yelling at one another with so much intense fire between us. We were two people who truly cared for each other, but we were also two people who had also truly hurt one another.

"Because I'm pregnant!" I admitted in a way that I didn't want to. I didn't want to yell or fight. I didn't want to die with hate for me in anyone's heart. I had already lost that fight with Jameel. I couldn't add anyone else to the list.

Staring at me in disbelief, he asked, "You're what?"

Sitting down on the arm of his couch, I explained, "I found out two days ago...and I'm keeping it."

He frowned, bewildered. "Why? You're dying."

Leaning forward, I tried to grab his hand, but he snatched it away so hard that I heard the air in the room whip around it.

I grimaced and tried to make him understand. "But this baby will live, and since I am dying, since I am begging God to give me just a *few* more months, hell, a few more *days*, who am I to take a life?" Disapproval was all over his face, but I didn't care. I wasn't doing this for him. I wasn't doing this for me. I was doing this for my mother and for the opportunity to do something good before I left this earth. "When my mother lost my stepfather, it was devastating for her. She never got over it. And now..." I got choked up. This was the hardest part of dying, knowing that I was the one responsible for putting my mother through this pain again. "Now, she has to go through the pain of losing me. I feel so guilty. So, I want to gift her with life, a life that will be a part of me. It's not about you."

My words didn't make any of Coop's discomfort or anger go away. His cold eyes held no sympathy for me. With his hands in his pockets, he stood firm in his anger, staring at me with cold eyes. "You know how I was raised. You know I don't have any parents. Why do you think I haven't had kids already? You think I want to have a baby by someone who is not going to be here for my child? You think I wanna do that to someone else?!"

I silenced in shame. I hadn't thought about that. I had been selfish when deciding to have this baby. I had only thought of myself, my situation, and my mama. But I had the right to be selfish. I was the one dying, not him.

"Get out," Coop hissed so menacingly that I was surprised that he could be *this* angry towards me. I knew he would be angry once he knew everything that I had been keeping from him, but this was so much more than anger.

This was a hate-filled rage.

My heart ached as I asked, "What?"

"Get the fuck out."

I jumped to my feet and began to beg, "Coop..."

He bit his bottom lip as he walked further away from me. "Fuck that! You put me in this position knowing that you were dying. That's fucked up! I'm done with you. You played me more times than I let the next motherfucker get away with. You gotta go. Have the baby, do whatever you wanna do, but do it without me. I'm done letting you fuck with my head. Get the fuck out."

"Coop—"

My words were cut off with a gasp as he hurled something across the room. I ran towards the door as I saw it hurling towards me. Whatever it was shattered into the wall, instead of me.

"*Get the fuck out!*" he bellowed, and this time I didn't argue. I rushed into my shoes and then hurried out of his front door, away from my fake existence, and ran back to my reality, back to my dark space.

7

COOP

Too angry to even allow what all True had told me to marinate, I bolted out of the house right after her. I didn't go after her, though. Fuck her. I was that nigga. I was rich. I was good before I met her, and I would be even better now that she was out of my life. This was how I dealt with losing loved ones, even the families that didn't treat me right. When I got bounced from house to house as a shorty, I just turned the other cheek, as if the hurt had never happened. True had gotten close to me, knowing she wouldn't be here long, so that's how I was going to handle True; like it never fucking happened.

True had me fucked up. I couldn't even feel bad for shorty's illness when she was willing to put my child through the same bullshit. Her mother, her family, would *have* to lose her. They were forced to deal with the loss of her. But me and my child hadn't been. She was forcing us to take part in this grief that would affect us long after she was gone. She was bringing a child into the world to purposely feel the hurt and disappointment like I had when I had to spend Mother's Day, Father's Day, and every other fucking holiday feeling like shit because I had no parents.

I didn't have time for this dramatic shit. True clearly was good for playing mind games. She had been since the beginning of us. I wasn't about to do these dramatics with her. I was rich. I was good before I'd met her and I would be good now that I was no longer fucking with her.

As I sped through the city, I hoped my absence would make her realize the insanity of what she was doing so she wouldn't have that baby. I had purposely made sure I never got a chick knocked up. I wasn't trying to bring a child into this world to be raised in fucked up circumstances. And I considered any kid being raised with one or no parent to be a fucked up circumstance. It wasn't meant to be like that. Kids weren't supposed to be out here raising themselves because they had no parents or because their parents were on drugs or locked up. A daughter shouldn't be missing the influence of her mother or the protection of her father. A son shouldn't have to go without knowing how to love a woman or what love from a real woman was because he had no mother or father. God didn't mean for it to be that way. I was a terrible example of the outcome of those situations. I wasn't trying to have my son or daughter out here like that. I wanted no parts of it, nor could I stomach witnessing it. So, if this was what True was going to do, she was going to do it without me.

"Coop, I hope you ready for war, motherfucka! Prince is gonna murk your ass, and I am going to dance on your grave, you bitch-made nig—"

I hung up, groaning and shaking my head.

"What was that?" Rakim asked from the passenger's seat. I had picked him up after getting a 9-1-1 text from him.

I gritted. "Issa's talking crazy on my voicemail."

I hadn't told Rakim what True had told me, not any of it. I was in such disbelief that I couldn't even repeat it. I couldn't stomach saying it out loud.

Rakim smirked with a shake of his head. "Yo', she still stalkin'?"

Nodding, I pulled away from Rakim's apartment in Hyde Park. "Hell yeah."

"I'm hearing Prince wants smoke."

My eyebrow rose. "Word?"

"Word. His bitch ass went through Issa's phone and saw all the times she's been calling you. He hot."

"How you know all this? You fucking his baby mama too, nigga?" I grilled.

Rakim chuckled. "Nah. I'm fucking one of Issa's home girls."

I raised an eyebrow. "So, he hot at me? Not her hoe ass?"

Rakim nodded, raking his beard with his fingers. "Exactly. He's a bitch. But you know he trigga happy and talkin' 'bout he at you... And it's one more thing."

I sucked my teeth with a frown. "Fuck, nigga, do you ever have good news?"

Rakim shrugged nonchalantly. "I'm your eyes and ears on the street. This my job."

"Go ahead, man."

"We gotta take care of Zell."

I cringed. "Candi say he still talking shit?"

"Yeah. I know he's been under you since he was a shorty, but he's too weak. He's an indictment waiting to happen. One interrogation and that motherfucker's lips are gonna start flapping. We gotta get rid of his ass."

In this game, I was used to dealing with some foul shit. A lot of hustlers I knew had been taken out by this game. Hell, my life had started by losing two of the most important people to a person—my parents.

However, today, I had never felt this type of pain; losing two people that I cared about. I had been trying to ignore it since she'd told me the words, but in that moment, I couldn't ignore it anymore. Faced with having to take the life of one of my closest people, I thought about life and how True, such a seemingly loyal and caring person, was losing hers out of her control. I couldn't take being around that type of hurt. My earlier life had been filled with pain, and I had been dodging it ever since for a reason. I had allowed her to make me loosen my grip on my control over my life. But no more. I had temporarily made the mistake of leading with my feelings. But no more and never again.

"Text him and tell him we're on our way to pick him up."

Rakim grabbed his phone with a nod and started typing. "Say less."

FIFTEEN MINUTES LATER, we pulled up in front of Zell's apartment building in my hood. Rakim hopped out to hit the corners and trap houses to ensure they were bussin'. While I waited for Zell to come out of the building, I grabbed my piece from the glove compartment and placed it in the compartment in my driver's side door.

Then I snatched my phone from the cup holder and sent him a text message telling him that I was in front and to bring his ass outside.

Rage was boiling over. I glowered as I bit my lip, telling myself not to take my anger toward True out on Zell. I tried to remind myself that Zell was one of the most loyal hustlers on my team. I didn't have blood relatives, but I had a few niggas that I knew were loyal to me. Rakim was the main one. I *thought* Zell was the other.

But the angry, hurt little boy who'd had to raise himself was present in the car. The guy whose heart had softened because of True had faded away. He had run away because of how hurt he was. The savage was back.

Zell soon appeared from the building. Concern was etched all over his face, wondering what this sudden, urgent meeting was all about.

Zell hopped in the car, filling the inside with the aroma of loud. I reached for my own blunt that was already rolled and perched in the ashtray.

After sliding it between my lips, I threw my ride in drive. "What up, bro?" I greeted Zell as I pulled off.

As I fired the blunt up, he gave me a dry, "What up?"

"You tell me."

"What you talkin' about?" His voice was shaky. I looked over at him quickly and peeped the nervousness in his expression and sweat beads on his brow, despite my good-ass air blowing in this bitch. Then I focused back on the road.

"Do I need to worry about you?" I asked him point blank.

"N-n-nah," he stuttered. "You ain't gotta worry about me. Why you ask me that?"

For the first time in my years in the game, I was stuck. I knew what I had to do, knew what I needed to do, and what was necessary to protect me, my business, and the people who depended on me to eat. But looking at him, my cold heart went out to him. To take out one of the few people who had always rocked with me was giving me a sympathetic feeling that was new to me since falling for True. Her words were ringing in my ears. Now that I knew she was expecting death soon, her words made so much more sense when she had asked me how I wanted to be remembered. Her words now had so much more meaning. Even more so, the thoughtfulness behind those words were so much deeper. She cared enough about me to take care of me when she was the one who needed to be taken care of.

I suddenly pulled over with a jolt that sent Zell's face flying into the passenger's window.

I threw the car in park while reaching for my piece with my other hand. Before Zell knew what was happening, I placed the gun to his head and cocked it.

He threw his hands up in surrender and started to stutter uncontrollably. "Y-y-y-y-o, man. What the fuck?!"

"You running your mouth, lil' nigga?" I barked as I pressed the gun into his head, forcing his head to bang against the window. "You got a problem with how I run my motherfucking organization, nigga?"

"N-n-n-nah, man! I swear!" he tried to ensure me.

I gritted, "I'm hearing different."

"Whoever said that shit is lying!" he insisted with tears coming to his eyes.

"You want your life?"

He nodded vigorously. "Yes."

My jaws clenched as I asked, "You sure, bitch?"

His eyes filled with tears. "I promise! Man, please?!"

Leaning forward caused the gun to press deeper into his temple. He winced as he looked up at the roof of the car, seemingly praying silently.

"Then this is what you gon' do," I told him. "You gon' pack your shit and get the fuck outta town. You ain't trusted in this crew no more. Since you've been running your mouth like a bitch, run your ass out of town *tonight*. You understand?"

Again, he nodded strongly. "Y-yeah."

"You hear me?!" I barked.

"Yes!" he promised. "I swear. I swear! I'm gone. I promise."

Gnawing on my bottom lip, I reluctantly removed the gun from his head and sped away from the curb, back towards his apartment building. I hated that this True situation had changed me. It had changed me to the point that I was actually seeing my love for this weak-ass motherfucka. But, as he sat there with tears streaming down his face, I knew his years of loyalty deserved more from me than a bullet in the head. And now, knowing that True would soon lose her life so young, I was looking at my own life differently and with more appreciation. I suddenly cared about family, relationships, and connections.

I hated her for that shit.

"Get the fuck out!" I barked. The bite in my bark had more to do with True than with Zell, but it was vicious enough to make Zell hop out, just as the back door opened. I whipped my head around to see Rakim hopping into the back.

I shook my head, reluctantly, seeing the questions in his face as I sped off.

"Yo', why the fuck that nigga still alive?" Rakim asked.

"He's leaving town," I announced.

Rakim's voice was full of surprise. "That's good enough for you?"

Grimacing, I told him, "I said it, didn't I, motherfucka?"

"I'm just sayin', bro," Rakim pushed. "What if he talks?"

Taking my eyes off the road for a second, I looked over at the pool of piss in the passenger's seat. "He won't."

Just then, a truck driving sporadically behind me caught my attention in the rearview mirror.

"What the fuck?" I muttered as I glared through the mirror.

Just as Rakim asked me, "What's going on?" shots started blasting off from the truck and pierced through the back window. I could hear the bullets passing my head, firing over and over again like fireworks. Glass shattered all around us. Bullets pierced the windshield as I attempted to keep control of my ride.

"*Fuck!*" I barked as my foot pressed the gas. Now, going over a hundred miles an hour towards the onramp on 90/94, I swerved, attempting to dodge the bullets flying through my ride.

"Aaaaaaaargh!" I heard Rakim yelp from the back seat. "Fuck, fam! I been hit. They shot me, bro!"

Just as I turned around to check on him, more bullets flew through the back window, causing me to duck and steer blindly. Horns blasted around us. Glass continued to fly.

"I need to go to the hospital, bro!" Rakim pleaded.

Pressing the gas to go one-twenty, I ensured him, "I'm trying, fam. I'm trying."

Finally, the gunfire stopped just as I heard tires screeching. But I couldn't tell whether the tires screeching were from the shooter, my ride, or others around me that I was swerving into.

I glanced into the rearview mirror and was relieved when I saw the truck exiting on the passing onramp.

"Arrrgh," Rakim growled. "I'm dying, bro. I'm dying."

Frantically, I pulled over on the shoulder of the expressway. I jumped out of the car. I noticed that many vehicles had pulled over on the shoulder during the mayhem. I rushed to the rear passenger's side door. I threw it open and jumped inside. I crawled over Rakim as he leaned against the opposite door, holding his neck, which was spewing blood.

He struggled to speak through gritted teeth. He was holding on to life with every ounce of his strength as blood splattered from his mouth with every word. "It... It was... That...that nigga, Prince."

I tore my shirt off and pressed it against his neck tightly. I could hear multiple sirens in the distance, which meant someone had called the police.

"It was him," Rakim swore.

"Don't talk," I urged.

"Get that, nigga." I pressed my shirt into his wound harder, but Rakim pushed my hand away as if there was no use. "Make sure you get that, nig…" His words disappeared into the sounds of him choking and coughing. As he did so, blood spewed all over the upholstery and my face. I cringed at the sight of seeing my only family, my only friend left, die in front of me. It caused an unfamiliar sharp pain to pierce through my heart and trickle down to my gut.

I was watching the only person I loved in this world leave me. It was nauseatingly heartbreaking. I had never cared this much or hurt this much until that day.

I pressed the shirt against his neck despite his rejection. "Hold on, bro. *Hold on.*"

8

REMI

"Here, girl."

My head was so heavy as I lifted to see what Niyah was handing me. It was another red cup full of the 1738 that we had been drinking all night. I had been drowning my broken heart in it, hoping that it would stop hurting. Niyah was drinking with me just because. I had run here the night I found out about Banks' utter betrayal and had yet to leave. I didn't have the heart to talk to my sister. It was too embarrassing to tell her that she was right. I for damn sure couldn't tell my mother. And since I didn't have any friends, I called Niyah. She and Iyana were the closest two female associates I had to listen to me ask myself the same questions over and over again. How did I not know? Who was she? Why had he chosen her over me?

It had just been shy of twenty-four hours since Banks had humiliated me while ruining me for the rest of my life, and I hadn't heard from him. I had sent him pages and pages of irate text messages without receiving one response from him. I sat on Niyah's couch, wondering how I was going to live on. All I knew was Banks. And even though he had hurt me over and over again, I would give anything to trade *this* betrayal for one of those bitches he had only fucked while we were together. Because this betrayal was different. He hadn't gotten caught but professed his love for me, despite his infidelities. He had been quiet, telling me he had indeed given that ring to the right woman.

My attention was briefly pulled away from my thoughts when Iyana came barreling into the house. Being best friends, she and Niyah shared an apartment on the southeast side of Chicago.

"Biiiiiitch," Iyana sang as she plopped down on the couch. The sound of that and the look on her face told me she had some tea.

"What?" Niyah pried.

I was reluctant to ask.

Iyana's eyes seemed to water as she told us, "I got the tea on that bartender bitch."

Niyah gasped, and I held my breath.

"From who?" Niyah asked.

"One of the other bartenders that work at the club was at the beauty shop today running her mouth about what went down last night, and my sister happened to be there."

"Great," I moaned, shaking my head. "The whole city knows what happened."

"What she say?" Niyah asked, and I regretted it. I wasn't ready to hear this. I couldn't take it.

Iyana paused and gave me a sympathetic look.

I sighed and told her, "Just tell me." I knew it would hurt me, possibly even kill me by ripping the rest of my heart out of my chest. But I needed to know.

Reluctantly, Iyana continued to put the dirt on top of my grave. "Her name is Brandi. They've been fucking around for like six months and—"

Niyah gasped again before I could even verbally respond, but quietly, I was unraveling on the inside even more.

"And they're engaged already?!" Niyah snapped.

Iyana's eyes once again reluctantly caught mine. "Yeah. Banks proposed to her the day after he gave you the ring, Remi." My head fell into my hands as her words continued to bury me alive. "He met her at The Dating Game when she started bartending there. And... And... She's pregnant."

My heart broke and my stomach turned as I listened to everything Iyana was saying. He hadn't given me a ring in ten years, but this bitch showed up and in six months she won his heart and was pregnant with his child. Images of her perfect body flooded my mind. Was that what had won his heart? Was I too fat to deserve his commitment, loyalty, or hand in marriage?

I jumped up from the couch and ran for the bathroom. I made it just in time to empty the contents of my stomach into the toilet.

TRUE

"So..." my mother said hesitantly. "How did he take it?"

Her question made me cringe as I recalled Coop's anger just a few hours ago. "Not well." I avoided her eyes as I felt her staring at me from across the booth in the Olive Garden.

"You told him *everything*?" she asked with a raised eyebrow.

I swallowed hard, answering, "Yes." I dropped my fork in my chicken Alfredo. I didn't even know why I had ordered it. I knew I needed to eat since I hadn't done so all day. But no matter my stomach pangs, I didn't have an appetite.

Satisfaction left my mother's body in a huge sigh of relief. She put her fork down in her nearly-devoured salad and sat back. "Well, thank God. *Finally*."

My eyes rolled slightly. "Glad *you're* happy that I told him, because he's not, and neither am I."

"Of course, he's not. You're having his baby when you're... You're..." She paused and shook her head, unable to finish her sentence.

"Dying," I whispered, finishing it for her.

She visibly cringed. Her eyes darted at Joy, but I had already known that she was too deep in the cartoon app on my phone to had have heard me.

"Don't say it like that," my mother hissed.

I shook my head, holding it with the tips of my fingers. "Mama, that's what's happening. I'm *dying*. You can say it."

"I don't want to."

I had come to grips with this long before my mother ever would. She most likely would never accept my fate. I had already come to terms with it while I was sure my mother would still be waiting for a miracle even as I took my last breath. She had never overcome my stepfather's death. She was still hurting and mourning him. She had yet to recover. And now she was going to have to bury the only other person in her life close to her besides her grandchild. She didn't want to face it. When she had to, it was like this; with reluctance and a false sense of reality.

"C'mon on, Ma. Let's go," I insisted as I pushed the pasta away from me.

Concerned, she asked, "You're not feeling well?"

"No."

On bad days, the tumor made me feel weakness, world-stopping nausea, and headaches beyond imagination. But, today, I was sadly using my illness as a sympathy card to get out of a very uncomfortable conversation.

My mother paid the bill while I gathered Joy and her things. As she signed the credit card receipt, I stood and brought Joy out of the booth.

It had been a long day. Dealing with Coop's rejection was hard, but dealing with my mother's inability to face reality was making this all so much harder.

She must have seen it on my face because before walking away from the table, she grabbed my hand and smiled into my eyes. "I'm sorry. This is just really, *really* hard, True."

"I know," I agreed, watching the oh-so familiar tears filling her eyes. "I'm trying to make this as easy for you as possible."

Her lips pressed together tightly as she shook her head. "You're so worried about me, when this is about you."

"Mama, I'll be gone before you, so nothing is about me. I won't be here. This is about you and Joy. This is why I am having this baby. I want you to have as much of me here to remember me by."

A tear slid down her cheek. "Thank you. I'm old and—"

"You are not old," I insisted. My mama was only sixteen years my senior, but she swore she was an old lady.

"Yes, I am." She weakly smiled. "But if this is what you want to do, then I will raise that baby to that best of my ability. Thank you for giving me this gift."

I reached up and wiped her lone tear away.

"So..." She paused and rubbed my stomach with a weak smile. "How many months are you?"

Relieved that she was finally on board, I smiled, "Almost two months."

"I hope it's a boy." The smile on her face was finally free from sadness. I stood admiring it. She caught me and snatched me into an embrace. Right there in the middle of the restaurant she stood holding me so tight. Many people watched us oddly, once the embrace started to last longer than normal. She held me as if it were last time, and soon, it would be.

So, I let her.

9

COOP

-TWO MONTHS LATER-

I was leaving an after-hours spot alone. At four in the morning, it was already a hot and sticky, July morning. Seventy-fifth Street was abandoned. The only souls floating in the darkness were the lost ones who were either homeless, high, or both. Yet, I was lost too. Since True had told me her truth, I had been lost, not knowing what the fuck to do or how to deal. I cared about True more than I wanted to. I wondered about my child she was carrying in her womb, but I was too much of a pussy to reach out to her because I couldn't stand having *that* conversation again; the one about her dying.

As my life had been for the last two months, I was once again drunk off my ass. I had spent the last several weeks trying to mask the pain of losing someone I loved with 1738. This was the very reason why I had been staying clear of giving a fuck about anyone since the moment I realized there was no one to give a fuck about me when I was a shorty. Shit, the pain of losing parents I had never met had hurt so deeply that I wasn't trying to even care about another person. But two people had climbed over that wall; Rakim and True.

I hadn't lost Rakim, though. He had surprisingly survived his gunshot wound. But nearly losing him and learning that True was dying on the same day had been devastating enough to cure me from ever getting close to another human being again. Though I hadn't lost him, it had taken him two months to start speaking again. Since the shooting, the attempts on my life had ceased. I'd spent a week looking for Prince before I heard he had taken Issa and left Chicago. He was a punk, but that motherfucker wasn't stupid.

I *had* lost True, however. We hadn't spoken to one another since the day I kicked her out of my crib. Before Rakim got shot, I had been contemplating whether I was right or wrong. But, after watching Rakim take breaths we thought would be his last, I knew I had to let True go. There was no way that I could stand being around her knowing she was dying and I would lose her. I had to walk away from her. Two months later, I was still pissed that she had played me like that; lying with me and watching me fall for her, knowing she was dying. I had been a game to her, some fun for her to enjoy before she died.

I wanted nothing more than to be there for my child, but, despite my anger, I was still feeling True. Therefore, there was no way that I could watch yet another loved one leave me.

Not again.

My fear was outweighing my need to be a father, and, no matter how hard I tried, I couldn't shake the fear so that I could be there for my child. Suddenly, I had new compassion for the parents that I never knew. Before now, I never considered their situations when I was born, the reasons why they hadn't been there for me. Maybe they had been in situations like I was now; their hands tied, too afraid to be parents.

"Fuck her," I spewed as I walked to my ride. I faulted True for putting me in this position with my unborn child.

However, no matter how much hate grew in my heart for True playing me like that, there was still love in my heart for her that I forced myself to ignore. But, if I had to be honest, I missed shorty like I would miss my next breath.

"You're leaving so soon?"

Caught off guard, I jumped a bit and spun around. My guard was instantly down when my eyes landed on a pair of beautiful hazel eyes. I had heard about black women with light eyes, but I had never seen one before in real life. Baby girl was chocolate with eyes as bronze as a setting sun. Her curves could be seen even in the darkness. She was built just liked I liked my women; tall and thick. Her curves weren't natural at all though. Shorty had to have ass and hips that were over fifty inches in width. But her waist was extremely tiny, her stomach was flat, and her breasts were perky. She had definitely gone to the Dominican Republic and got her body done. Every woman returned from the island with the same look, and shorty had that signature body. I preferred natural curves, but for a quick nut, I was down for whatever. Her hair was from overseas as well. It was long, curly, and draped down to her ass. The curls fell into her amber face, cascading over slanted eyes that were heavily outlined with those expensive mink lashes that I often overheard women talking about.

I looked her up and down slowly. My drunken eyes took in her spandex tube top dress tightly covering her curves and the gold, Louie sandals wrapped around her pretty, feet.

"Aye, shorty," I said, licking my lips. "You shouldn't be out here so late alone."

TRUE

"I got you, baby. Let it all out."

I could feel my mother pressing a cold towel on the back of my neck as the contents of my stomach expelled into the toilet.

I was now going on four months pregnant and feeling every single, solitary prenatal symptom. Yet, because of the chemo treatments I'd undergone, I was used to nausea and throwing up. Vomiting was like a walk in the park at this point. Unfortunately, the symptoms of pregnancy were much like the symptoms of my brain tumor, so my mother had been a worry wart for the past two months. However, because of my pregnancy, I had been getting brain scans on a regular basis to monitor the tumor's growth. Since becoming pregnant, it hadn't increased in size.

Finally finished, I sat back on my butt on the cold tile floor. My mother handed me a towel to wipe my mouth. After doing so, I stood slowly and walked over to the sink.

"You okay?" my mother asked.

I sighed. "Yeah."

"I'll go get some breakfast started for Joy."

"Thank you."

As she left, I looked at my small pudge that had started to

protrude. I had managed to gain a few more pounds, but that pudge was still the biggest thing on my body.

After brushing my teeth, I slipped on a robe and left the bathroom. I prepared myself to face the day. Mentally, I had prepared myself to die, but I was in no way ready for this. I had decided to have this baby regardless of how Coop felt, but I had not prepared myself for him to be totally out of the picture. I hadn't heard from him since he kicked me out. I refused to call him because I did not blame him for deciding not to be a part of this. Shit, I was a part of this and didn't want to be so how could I expect him to? I had selfishly made this decision, so it was his right to choose not to be involved. However, despite his hardcore, mean demeanor, I knew Coop cared for me. I knew there was a soft spot for me in his heart somewhere. I hoped it would eventually bring him to be able to be a part of this baby's life, but so far, no luck.

Just then, the doorbell rang. So, I hurried out of the bathroom.

"I'll get it, Ma!" I shouted toward the kitchen where I could smell bacon frying.

"Good morning, Mommyyyy!" Joy sang from the floor in front of the TV.

"Good morning, baby. Scoot back. Why are you sitting so close?" Just then I peered through the peephole. Imagine my surprise when I saw Jameel standing on the other side. "What the hell?" I snatched the door open, glaring through the small opening that I peered out of. "What the fuck do you..."

This motherfucker barged into the house like he still lived there.

"Jameel!" I shrieked. "What the hell?!"

"Where is my daughter?"

I was on his heels as he charged through the house towards Joy. I ran past him and scooped her up from the floor.

"Are you fucking crazy?! You're *not* taking my daughter!"

Jameel lunged at me. He grabbed Joy's tiny waist and attempted to rip her from my arms.

"No! Let her go!" I screamed as Joy started crying. We were playing tug of war with our own daughter. "Let her go, Jameel!"

"Give her to me!" he hissed.

Using all of the strength I had, I clung to Joy with one hand, reached for Jameel's face with the other one, and swung. As I made contact, he stumbled back, holding his face.

My mother came running out of the kitchen. But when she saw Jameel, she quickly turned around and went back inside.

I wondered why she was running away as Jameel spewed, "This is illegal. You can't keep my daughter from me."

Clinging to Joy, I spat, "I don't trust you! You didn't want her when we divorced. Why do you want her now? You may take her and never bring her back. I don't have the type of time to take that chance."

"You can't do anything for her. She needs a parent that can raise her." His hostile words ejected at me through his disgusted frown.

"Does she look like she needs anything to you?!" I challenged.

"I want full custody of her."

I laughed. "Are you crazy?! *That's* why you can't have my child! You want full custody of your money. That's what you want!"

He was glaring into my face so closely that I could feel the rage coming off of his skin. "You're not a good role model. You've got a disease that's killing you, yet you're still out here fucking and getting pregnant."

A smile crept on my face as my eyebrow rose. "Jealous?" I taunted him. "Why do you give a care anyway? You left me, remember?"

His finger jabbed towards my face. "I left *you*, not her. Not my daughter."

Suddenly, a vision of my mother running from the kitchen with a knife grabbed my attention. When my eyebrows rose, Jameel spun around to see what I was looking at. We both stared at the fire in my mother's eyes as she charged towards Jameel with the butcher knife in midair.

"Mama, no!" I shrieked as I ran in front of Jameel. Suddenly, all of that bite he'd had was gone. He cowered behind me like a bitch. He deserved to die way more than I did. Yet, I was dying while he was still here to wreak havoc on me and the next woman he chose to terrorize once I was cold and in the ground.

However, I knew my mother's potential. I knew her life before my stepfather had come along and whisked her away out of the projects on his white horse. I'd heard the stories of her savagery. And I needed my mother here to take care of my children, not in prison.

She stopped midstride, nostrils flaring. "Move, True."

"No, Ma. He's not worth it," I pleaded with her.

Still standing behind me like a punk, he threatened, "I'm calling the police on you bitches. My daughter doesn't need to be around this shit."

"Get the fuck out!" my mother shouted as she ran towards us.

I jumped out of the way to protect Joy, who was clinging to me.

I watched, fearfully as my mother ran up on Jameel and held the knife to his neck. The tip of the blade made an indention in his throat, and he cringed, standing perfectly still. "I suggest you leave, motherfucker. I don't feel like I have shit to lose at this point in my life. I'll do time when it comes to defending my babies. Now, *get the fuck out.*"

Biting down on his lip, Jameel glared between Joy and my mother as if he were considering risking it all. "I'm going to get full custody of my daughter. True is dying, and you're not her biological parent. *I'm* her father. I have a right to have my daughter."

My mother's eyes turned into angry slits. A demented fire was dancing in her orbs. She pressed the knife deeper, causing his hands to shoot up in surrender. "A'ight, a'ight," he chanted. "I'm out."

He started to walk slowly towards the door. When he saw that my mother was allowing him to leave without slitting his neck open, he started to walk faster until he disappeared. My mother jogged towards the door, slammed it shut, and locked it tight.

"Motherfucker," she cursed.

I collapsed on the couch with tears in my eyes. I rarely let my condition bring me to tears until it came to my mother and Joy.

"Mama, you can't let him get my baby," I cried.

That was my biggest fear, not being here to protect Joy from Jameel. He had never turned his aggression towards her, but I wondered the possibility once I wasn't here to be his punching bag. I already felt so much guilt for not being there for her eighth-grade graduation, the onset of her period, her prom, or her first boyfriend. But the guilt of not being here to protect her against evil was heartbreaking.

I clung to her as I cried on her shoulder.

Her little voice consoled, "It's okay, Mommy." I cried even harder for her.

ANGEL

♫*Your hands on my hips pull me right back to you*
I catch that thrust, give it right back to you
You're in so deep, I'm breathing for you
You grab my braids, arch my back high for you
You're diesel engine, I'm squirting mad oil
Down on the floor 'til my speaker starts to boil
I flip s***, quick slip, hip dip and I'm twisted
In your hands and your lips and your tongue tricks
And you're so thick and you're so thick and you're so

Crown royal on ice, crown royal on ice
Crown royal on ice, crown royal on ice♫

I bobbed my head slowly to Jill Scott's angelic voice as I swallowed the mixture of Don Julio and lemonade. I allowed it to slide down my throat slowly, enjoying the burn and how it instantly eased my mind. I smiled and looked towards Russell. "Thank you. I needed this."

Finally, after two months, I had taken Russell up on his invitation for a night out. But, instead, after today's drama, I had opted for a night with him in his house. As soon as I walked into his three-thousand-square-foot home, I felt comfortable and safe. It was a brick, two-story, four-bedroom, two-bathroom home in on a quiet block in Matteson, Illinois. I felt right at home as soon as I walked into the warm voluminous foyer, which was adjacent to the formal dining room. A casual breakfast-dining area divided the kitchen from the open layout of the family room where we were sitting at his bar. From what I could see from where I sat, his home was decorated with a mid-century modern feel; refined lines, minimalist silhouettes, and natural shapes. His furniture and décor were clean, sophisticated and inclusive.

"It's nice to see you." Russell wore a charming grin as he looked down on me. "I'm glad you finally took me up on my offer."

Suddenly, I felt anxious under his intense gaze. I had managed to age gracefully, so I didn't feel as if I didn't deserve the praise his eyes were giving me. Plus, to feel like more of a woman than I had felt as of late, I had put on some makeup and a form-fitting maxi dress. I didn't have many curves. Worrying and sadness had left me without an appetite most days. But I had enough of a figure to catch a man's attention.

However, Russell made me nervous. He wasn't like the strangers I had allowed to court me while knowing full well that they would never get as much as a kiss from me. Russell knew me. He had lived in the Gardens back in the day, and he so happened also to have been an associate of my late husband, Darnell.

Blushing, I nervously played with my hair. "Thanks."

"Honestly, Angel, I've had my eye on you for quite some time, but I didn't know how to approach you."

I stared at him blankly. I was truly caught off guard. I had known Russell for over twenty years, and he had never even blinked an eye at me. But considering that Darnell would have killed him, I wasn't surprised that he hadn't spoken of his attraction to me until now.

"Had your eyes on me?" I quizzed.

"You know what I mean. I'm attracted to you. I'd love for the chance to get to you know."

The way he licked his lips made me press my thighs together tightly. While Darnell was alive, I had been so committed to him that I had never even considered another man. But as I saw Russell at events and in passing back in the day, I could not deny how attractive he was. He was the textbook definition of tall, dark, and handsome. His build was slim, but he had packed some tone and definition on it over the years while doing a few bids here and there in prison. His chiseled jawline was draped with the signature, thick beard that many men were wearing nowadays. He had a set of deep dimples that beautified his otherwise rough appearance. Tattoos decorated his dark skin, some old and amateur because he had gotten them at such a young age. The others were decorative and pure artistry. There were specks of grey in his beard and curly-top fade, but not enough to age him. And his brown eyes were so lively and bright that I could not even guess his age if I needed too.

"I haven't seriously dated anyone since Darnell," I warned him.

He shrugged as he sipped slowly from his cognac. "I'm open to just seeing where it goes."

I raised an eyebrow, saying, "I also haven't had sex since Darnell." After that revelation, I waited for his response.

"I said I wanted to get to *know* you, not have *sex* with you."

His dominance made me blush and squirm like an inexperienced virgin. He smiled at the way I hid my blushing behind the back of my hand.

He took that same hand and kissed the back of it softly. "*Angel...* a.k.a the Angel of The Streets."

Instantly, I pulled my hand away from him. "Don't call me that."

Lifting his hand in surrender, he smiled, "Aye, that was your name. You were a G. You were the best at moving cocaine."

I cringed. I hadn't had anyone bring that up in years.

Darnell had worked for Metra, but he had also sold weight up until his death. I had kept that part of our lives deeply hidden from True because I was ashamed about the things I had done and the results my actions had caused.

"Can we talk about something else?" I asked.

Russell studied my sudden discomfort and sadness. "Aye, look at me."

I couldn't. I turned away from him, but he softly grabbed my chin and brought my eyes to his.

"Look at me," he demanded again in such a sweet, sultry voice that my eyes obeyed against my will. "You didn't kill him."

My eyes lowered in embarrassment. "Yes, I did."

I felt his arms around me. Needing the hug, I hid inside of his embrace.

I had not only been Darnell's Bonnie, I was also his partner and his right hand. I was supposed to have been there to have his back, but I wasn't. And because of me, he had lost his life four years ago.

We had been selling weight successfully for twenty years. We had never been on the radar of the Feds or thieving niggas in the streets. Many people had no idea that Darnell was the man behind a lot of the cocaine floating around the city because he kept a low profile and he continued to work his nine-to-five. The only people who knew about his position in the drug game were a few friends, Russell and his other buyers, and of course, me.

Darnell had been successful in his position until he met me.

He had asked me not to go out that night. But being a woman, I sassed him and refused, wanting to spend a night out with my girls. I had slipped, not paying attention to my surroundings on the way home from the club and led two niggas right to my front door. They bombarded me as I let myself into the house. They held me at gunpoint while they awakened Darnell from his sleep. After robbing us blind, they shot him right in front of me.

I had protected True from our lifestyle when she was a child. I continued to, even though she was now an adult. Darnell was my hero. He had rescued me from the projects and showed me a life that only queens lived. He had accepted the father role for a child that wasn't even his blood, loving her unconditionally.

I had lost the love of my life. And now, I was losing another.

10

REMI

-Three months later -

I had been told so many times that it would get better. Everyone had said to just get over it. Many had suggested that I find a new man to mask the pain. None of that bullshit inspiration had worked. I was truly depressed. A week after Banks had ignored my calls and text messages, he had moved out of our home while I was at work. The motherfucker hadn't even had the decency to face me.

Not only had I lost my mind, but the entire city had witnessed him wife a smaller, more modelesque woman than me. I was a laughing stock. She paraded their engagement and pregnancy on Facebook like it was the second coming of Jesus.

I had finally managed to lose some weight, however. Since I had no appetite, I had lost about fifteen pounds.

I had never felt this low in my life. I had distanced myself from everyone, including my friends and especially, my mother and sister. I couldn't stomach their judgmental stares or their constant I-told-you-so chants. I buried myself in my house, only coming out to work because I couldn't bear to lose my job on top of losing my man.

Currently, I was lying wide awake in the bed that my patient's family had given me in their spare bedroom. This particular patient was dying from Melanoma. I had switched to the third shift. That way, I was able to sleep during the day when most of the bullshit occurred that reminded me of my heartbreak. But during the wee hours of the morning when I couldn't sleep, I found myself browsing social media, the source of most of my pain.

"What the hell?" I sat straight up as I stared wide-eyed at the picture on my Facebook timeline. Tears pooled in my eyes as I clicked on it to zoom in. Banks was pictured in a white Louis Vuitton tux. His sandy brown eyes were the happiest I had ever seen them. The light in them was undeniable. His colorful tattoos creeped out of the collar of the suit jacket, causing a great colorful contrast to the all-white suit. His big smile shot through his gleaming beard like a beam of light. His tall frame towered over Iyana and Niyah, who were in the picture with him dressed in their Sunday's best.

My heart started beating so fast that I felt faint. I had blocked Banks and his bitch of a fiancée on Facebook, but Iyana and Niyah had been tagged in these pictures, so I was able to see them. I clicked on the person's page that had tagged them and instantly felt a rush of fire soar through my body. I was both mad and devastated, sad yet full of rage. These pictures were of Banks and Brandi's wedding. They had gotten married the day before on a beautiful, sunny, Saturday morning in a wonderfully decorated church. The theme was romantic with soft hues of cream and pink, delicate lighting, and an array of flowers.

I couldn't stomach looking at the pictures, but just like a woman, I continued to. I kept scrolling and investigating, until I found more people with more pictures. I saw Brandi and Banks holding hands at the altar. I saw how beautiful she was in her strapless, lace wedding gown and pregnant belly. There were even videos of their vows and first dance.

I was sick to my stomach. My mouth watered because of the

oncoming vomiting, but I kept looking, signing my own death certificate.

"Remi?"

I jumped and quickly wiped my face free of tears as Mr. Holmes' daughter peered into the room, causing a beam of light to peer in. I quickly looked at the time to see if I had missed the alarm to check my patient's vitals.

I hadn't.

"Is everything okay?" I asked, trying to maintain some professionalism.

"I...I think it's time." Her voice croaked. "His breathing is really shallow, and his hands are cold."

"Oh... Okay." I jumped out of bed, grateful to have someone else's grief to focus on, yet ashamed for feeling relieved. "I'm coming."

COOP

"You Jurassic Park-mouth, motherfucka," I barked out of the window. "Take that thick-ass jogging suit off, Bill Cosby."

Henry, a hype from the hood, sucked the few teeth he still had. "Man, c'mon, don't do me like that, young blood."

"Do you like what?" I chuckled, taunting him. "You the one at my window asking me for shit."

Leaning into the window, he begged, "C'mon, man. Let me get a couple of dollars."

I backed up because his stankin' ass was too close. "Get the fuck away from my car with that late 90's FUBU jogging suit on."

Before I could punch his ass, the light turned green, so I sped off.

Vanessa was giggling in the passenger's seat. She was the bodied-up shorty I had met at the after-hour spot three months ago. She had let me smash that night. I had taken out all of my anger and frustrations on that pussy, and had been once a week ever since.

Shorty wasn't a THOT, though. She was just an older woman who knew what she wanted when she saw it and went after it. She was thirty-five, eight years older than me, and a pretty successful real estate agent. Her business kept her busy, and she was married to a dude with a whack dick game that stayed on the road as a truck driver. However, he kept her happy in every other way, and she loved her husband. So, she only wanted the dick from me, and I was good with that.

"Urgh! Damn it," she cursed as she tossed her phone onto her lap.

"What's wrong?" I asked.

"I was supposed to show a client this spot tomorrow, but he canceled. I was banking on that sale. It's such a nice place. Someone can do so much with it. It used to be a huge gym."

My eyebrow rose. "Oh word? Where is it?"

"Right off of 83rd and State across from the bank."

My eyebrow arched even more with interest. "For real?"

"Yeah." She looked at my interest curiously. "Yeah. Why? You interested?"

I shook my head. "Naaah."

"You sure?" she pried.

"I mean, I *had* been thinking about starting something like a rec center for boys."

"Really?" she asked, surprised. Those hazel eyes got big as hell.

"Yeah. Why that face?"

"Your mean ass don't seem like the type to wanna help anybody." She giggled, shaking her head.

I smirked. "Fuck you."

She laughed me off. By now, she was used to my crass demeanor. For some reason, that made women want me more. "Seriously, though, you speak of it as if the thought is past tense. Why not make it happen?"

Suddenly, a knot formed in my throat thinking about True. Swear to gawd, she was the only woman who brought me to my knees, shut me up, and made me think twice. Shorty had had me thinking about all types of different things back when we were messing with each other. She had me wanting to get out the game, change my life, and make a difference only for her to end up being calculating and shadier than the hustlas in the street along with me. Five months later, I still felt as if she had set me up.

"Hellooo?" Vanessa suddenly intruded my thoughts.

I sucked my teeth. "Man, would you mind your own business?"

She shrugged. "I was just asking."

"Ask about this *dick*," I spat as I started to unbuckle my belt. "Ain't that what you came for?"

She smiled, revealing perfect white teeth. I had a feeling those were fake too. They were a little too big and too white. I was sure they were veneers.

I pulled my dick out, and she started to salivate. Even soft, it was long and thick. It wouldn't be soft for long, however. Grabbing the top of her head, I pushed her down into my lap. I soon felt her warm mouth as I pressed the gas and headed to a telly.

ANGEL

♫Hello, it's me
I've thought about us for a long, long time
Maybe I think too much but something's wrong
Something's here that doesn't last too long
Maybe I shouldn't think of you as mine, but I can't help it baby
Seeing you, seeing anyone as much as I do you
I take for granted that you're always there
I take for granted that you just don't care
Sometimes I can't help seeing all the way through, baby♫

The Isley Brothers played in the distance as Russell sat me down at his lavish dining room table. There was a delicious-looking meal sitting before us. I knew he hadn't cooked it. He had been honest and told me he had purchased the meal from Vivere. My dish was clam toasts with pancetta. He was feasting on cioppino seafood stew with gremolata toast.

"This is *so* nice, Russell," I gushed as I took in the beautiful place setting and centerpiece made up of pink roses.

"It's all for you, baby."

I blushed. For the last three months, Russell had been courting me heavily. We had spent so many days walking downtown We had attended shows, plays, and concerts, and dined at five-star restaurants. He was so active that I could barely keep up with him, but I appreciated him. Dating him was a brief vacation from my agonizing life at home. A month into dating, I had shared True's diagnosis with him. Because he had known her since she was so little, he shed tears with me as I'd confirmed that many doctors and specialists had said there was no hope for her. As everyone had asked who knew, he asked had we talked to cancer experts. He offered me money to find the best oncologists that specialized in her type of cancer. But I had already done that. Darnell had left me with a substantial amount of money and life insurance, and I had spent a good bulk of it finding experts that could help my daughter. But there was not enough money to stop cancer. However, I was still praying for a miracle.

Because he was so familiar with me, Russell knew not to press me when it came to my abstinence. Therefore, he never tried to persuade me to commit my body to him. He simply got to know *me*. He catered to me and nearly worshipped me, which was honestly, making my body feel things it hadn't felt in years.

"So, how is the new grandbaby doing?"

I looked up with a huge smile. "He's doing great."

"*He*?" Russell asked.

"Yep, *he*." I smiled, thinking of the moment True and I saw his ten fingers and toes in the 3D ultrasound. "We found out a few days ago that she's having a boy."

Russell smiled. "Whaaat? Why didn't you all do some big gender reveal like I've been seeing people do?"

I shrugged. "She didn't want all of that fuss."

Russell nodded. "Understandable. How many months is she now?"

"She's nearly seven months."

He left it at that. He hated to see me in tears, so he never asked me about True's illness or how her health was affecting her pregnancy.

I was so proud of True. Not only was she handling her illness with immense strength, she had also been handling this pregnancy with the same. Even with the absence of Coop, she had managed to enjoy this pregnancy, just as she had been making sure to enjoy every day as if it were her last, since they truly were.

♫*It's important to me*
That you know you are free
Cause I never want to make you change for me, babe (don't change, don't
change)
No, I wouldn't change you, change you for the world (don't change, don't
change)♫

I sat my fork in my plate and started to snap my fingers as I swayed to the music. I couldn't hold it in any longer. "This is my soooong."

Russell sat across from me, looking as if he was in complete admiration of the sight before him. I had tried to look as beautiful as possible that night. I felt a lot of pressure when I was with Russell. He was forty-two. Yet, he was a very *young* forty-two. He was still in the game, and a lot of people knew it, particularly *women*. Whenever we were in public, women flocked to him and looked past me as if I weren't there. And those women were young with nice bodies, both real and fake. I had been so consumed with Darnell's murder initially and then True's diagnosis that I had forgotten all about my appearance. My once regal and modelesque appearance had been downgraded by stress and worry. I had bags underneath my eyes, and worry lines streaked my face in certain places. I had lost my curves because I was too consumed with mourning a daughter, who wasn't even dead yet, to eat. I had cut off my long natural hair when True lost hers during chemo, so I was rocking a short, curly look like Eva Marcille.

Yet, Russell still looked at me like I was a contestant on America's Next Top Model.

As Russell gazed at me, I caught his difficulty to keep his eyes on me, rather than my cleavage. It was a cool October evening, so I was wearing a very low cut, black sweater, with high-waist jeans and black, knee-high boots.

"Come dance with me," he requested as he stood up.

I giggled. "We're eating."

His strong shoulders shrugged. "I have a microwave."

He glided towards me, and suddenly, I wasn't hungry anymore. I rested my fork on my dinner napkin, scooted back, and took his hand.

I admired his masculine scent as it infiltrated my nostrils and molested me. It was filled with oud note, Blackberry, and Golden Wood. I enjoyed the feel of my cheek pressed against his hard chest. The feeling of his hand on the small of my back was so intimate. It was sensual contact that I hadn't felt in a very long time. Because he was six feet, he had to bend slightly to slow dance with my 5'5" frame.

I felt some guilt since he was one of Darnell's associates back in the day. However, it was the only relationship I could feel comfortable with in order to experience this. I needed somebody who knew me, truly sympathized with me, and was familiar enough with my past lifestyle to cater to *me*. This was what I had been missing; this type of attention and care. It was what Darnell had given me so freely.

I looked up with a smile as Russell began to step with me.

"Oh, you don't wanna step with me," I warned him.

"C'mon, now. You know I know how to step."

We stepped effortlessly to the beautiful melodic tone of the Isley Brothers until the song changed to "Lately" by Anita Baker.

♫*I can't imagine life*
Without you by my side
This is love that I'm feeling
I'm hoping you're feeling the same
Things tend to slip my mind
Like how you love to wine and dine me, baby
(I know romance is important)
Important to the way that we feel♫

He pulled me close to him again. I could feel his steely hardness against my stomach as we swayed to the love song that expressed my true feelings. After all this time, I *finally* felt like I was falling for another man.

> ♫*Don't you think twice about my love*
> *I say these things because*
> *Because I love you baby*
> *But it's hard to explain*
> *I'm hoping you feeling the same*
> *You know all that I feel inside*
> *Verbally, I tend to hide, baby baby*
> *Sometimes I tend to forget*
> *How much L-O-V-E really means*♫

11

TRUE

A month later -

"Awwww! These are sooo cute! What do you think, True?"

I squinted as the severe pain in my head pulsated so strongly that I felt I would fall off my feet. I held on to the clothing rack nearby for support. Luckily, my mother's back was turned, so she didn't see how I was struggling to remain standing.

I closed my eyes and took slow and steady deep breaths as my mother gushed at the Ralph Lauren Polo onesies. "We should definitely get a few of these." Finally, she noticed that I hadn't responded. She turned with concern etched all over her face and looked at me. I instantly swallowed the agonizing pain I felt from the excruciating headache and forced a smile on my face.

She asked, "You okay, baby?"

"Yeah, Mama, I'm fine," I lied.

"You sure?" she pressed as she stepped towards me.

"Yep," I insisted. Then I gave my attention to the onesies in her hand. "I like those. Get the red one too."

My mother smiled and tossed more than a few onesies in her cart and kept going to the next rack of newborn clothes in Macy's.

Mama was enjoying this much more than I was. Joy was in daycare, so I would have much rather spent that day in bed. All I had been doing as of late was sleeping whenever the headaches allowed me to.

I was now eight months pregnant with a baby boy. I had been expecting this pregnancy not to be the easiest because of my condition. Yet, for the last few days, I had been feeling exceptionally ill. I had been having difficulty walking. The dizzy spells were unnerving. My arms and legs were weak. My headaches had been very severe and more persistent than ever. Sure, I was eight months pregnant, but I had been pregnant before. I knew my body, and I knew my cancer. These symptoms were from my tumor, not my baby.

The doctors had prepared me for this. I had read all the pamphlets and done the research. So, I knew what this was. I was nearing the end stage.

Just thinking about it made my hands shake with a fear that no one will ever be able to put into words. Sure, we all knew that life was short. We all knew that one day we weren't going to walk this earth anymore. But I did not have the comfort of knowing that I would live to grow old. I knew my end was near. And that was so frightening until it made me blind with so many emotions. When I looked at my daughter, I thanked God that she was so young that she may not remember losing me once she got older. But when I looked at my mother, my heart went out to her. She had barely survived losing my stepfather. I feared for her sanity when the day came when would I take my last breath.

"Oh my goooosh!" my mother once again squealed. It was as if she was experiencing having her own baby, and I was happy for her. I forced a smile as my mother ran towards the Adidas section. "Do you see all of these Adidas onesies? He is going to be so fly."

I gritted through the headache pain, telling her, "Yeah, he is. Get those too."

My mother was so excited. For a year, she had been crying uncontrollably and sulking. I loved seeing this smile on her face. Therefore, I hadn't told my mother how I had been feeling. I blamed my nausea and sleepiness on the baby.

I did want to tell Coop, however. Knowing that I would be dying soon had led me to live a very honest life. I didn't want to die with anything on my conscience. But for the past few months, Coop had been on my mind. I worried and feared that I had ruined him and turned him back into that careless savage that pushed anyone who could love him away because love had escaped him all his life. I knew this child wasn't going to be born into the ideal situation for Coop. I knew his past. I knew he wanted to raise his children in a two-parent household to keep them from ever experiencing any of the pain and disappointment he had as a child. I was already ruining his child, making him face a motherless world. But I felt like this baby would fix Coop and teach him how to love. I really wanted him to give this child a chance. I wanted him to love his baby boy and help my mother raise him with my sincerest apologies for lying to him and hurting him.

With a deep, nervous breath, I fished my cell from my pocket. I swiped through the apps until I got to Coop's contact information. I gushed at the picture I had saved under it. I missed that hard and serious yet handsome face.

But, as I had done every time I'd picked up the phone to call him, I cowardly put it down. I locked the screen and returned it to my pocket. I had never seen him so livid as I had the day he kicked me out of his house. I didn't have to know him for that long to know that look in his eyes. I had hurt him after he had opened himself up to me against his will. I had made his biggest fears come true for my own selfish reasons. I knew, for that, he would never forgive me, and even though I had the courage to face death, I did not have the courage to face Coop's wrath.

COOP

"I'mma give you two minutes to explain that outfit."

Rakim stared down at the tight fit like he didn't know it was whack. "Man, f-"

"Shut up. Times up," I barked through a chuckle. "That outfit don't even deserve two minutes. Walmart-shopping-ass boy. You look like you been a freshman in high school for eight years."

That bullet to the neck had messed up my homie's sense of style. I didn't know what he was attempting with this tight plaid shirt and nut-hugging skinny jeans, but whatever it was, he had failed.

"You through getting on me, bro? I thought we were here to celebrate?"

I grinned as I handed him a shot of 1800. "It *is* a celebration, motherfucker. Welcome back."

I picked up my shot of 1738 from the desk and toasted Rakim before we threw the shots back. We both cringed as the alcohol burned on the way down. We were seated comfortably in the big, black leather chairs that reclined in my new office. I leaned back and kicked my feet up on the huge desk.

"Real talk." I swallowed hard, letting down my hard shell. "It's good to see you back at it, my dude."

After six months of rehabilitation, Rakim was back at my side. He had had to learn to walk all over again. I was relieved that he was back. I hadn't felt quite the same without him.

Looking around, Rakim held an admirable look on his face. "I'm proud of you."

"Whatever, motherfucker."

"I'm serious. This is a good look."

I had to look around and take it in myself, even though I had been in the rec center day in and out watching the construction crew like a hawk during the renovations.

A month ago, the rec center had come up again during a conversation with Vanessa. She was complaining that no one had put a contract on the property when it was such a good spot. I had driven past on my own. Instantly, I knew it was what I had been thinking of when I talked about it with True. As I looked at it, I thought of her and the man she had turned me into; the man she felt like I should be. I had bought the building with her in mind and started the renovations. Although it was what I wanted, it had been sitting empty for a year and needed a lot of cosmetic and technical work. I had a crew remodeling the place, installing a basketball court, pool tables, and multiple flat screens with game systems installed. There would also be classrooms and a gym. This rec center would be fully equipped to house the males of the inner city after school and on the weekends to keep them safe and occupied. During the summers, it would be open the entire day. I would also have trained counselors and educators to teach classes to those who need those services. It would also be free of charge to any boy who wanted to come in. I planned on funding it with my own money and grants.

It was the exact type of place I had needed when I was out on the streets alone. There had been nobody to help me, but I hoped to help hundreds of boys in this neighborhood. And if this rec center was a success, I planned to open up many more.

I could feel Rakim giving me this goofy grin, but I ignored it as he said, "True dug a soft spot in that cold heart of yours."

My eyes darted toward him. I was caught off guard just hearing her name.

I turned my nose up as if I didn't know what or who he was referring to. "Fuck you talkin' 'bout?"

Rakim held his hands up in surrender. "Aye, man, I ain't been so sick that I didn't see you were hurting."

"Hurting?"

He lightly tapped my leg as he sat up and leaned forward. "I'm your right hand. I'm your brother. I know you. You miss her."

I grimaced, but I didn't bother to argue with him. He was right. He *was* my brother, the closest thing that I had to it. He knew me better than I knew myself sometimes.

"What happened? Where she at?" Rakim pushed.

"How you know she ain't around? You've been in the hospital and the crib recovering."

Rakim laughed as if he were purely answering to entertain me. "You haven't said anything about her."

Stubbornly, I simply shrugged.

"And that big, goofy-ass grin you had on your face when she was around is gone. I saw you with Vanessa. That shit ain't the same."

I waved my hand dismissively. "Of course, it ain't. I'm just fucking Vanessa."

Rakim smirked coolly. "You were supposed to have *just* been fucking True too, right?" I wanted to smack that smile off his face.

I wanted to be stubborn, but I felt like I was in a counseling session. The way Rakim was looking at me sincerely, pulling the truth to the surface was annoying.

"Nah," I had to admit. "True was different." I was relieved to say it out loud. I had been dealing with this on my own and trying to walk through my days like nothing was wrong with me, like a part of me wasn't missing.

"So, where she at? What happened?" Rakim pried.

Leaning back further, I ran by hands over my face in frustration. "Maaaan..." I had been avoiding telling Rakim this. For weeks, he couldn't talk. Then for a few more weeks, he struggled with depression while the doctors operated on his spine over and over again to give him the chance to walk again. Then, once he finally had the mind and mental strength to go to rehab, I didn't want to be selfish and talk to him about my bullshit.

"What's up, bro?" Rakim asked as he poured us up another shot.

I took my foot off of the desk and grabbed the shot that he was handing me. I would need it to talk about this. As I threw it back, and the 1738 burned my throat again, I wished it would burn away any memory of True.

After six months, I was still thinking about that girl, missing her presence in my life, and wanting her more than ever. But every time I remembered that even if I reached out to her, she wouldn't be here for long, I couldn't bring myself to do it. I figured I would rather take the time to get over her betrayal because getting over watching her die would be remarkably worse. Then I thought of my child and figured I should at least be there for it. I wanted to be the father that I never had. But every time I was reminded that being a father right now would mean having to watch True die, I couldn't do it.

"She's pregnant."

"Oh shit." As Rakim studied my expression, he asked, "So, what? You mad?"

I leaned back again and folded my arms across my chest. "I wouldn't have been... had she not told me that she was dying."

Rakim blinked a few times in shock. "What?"

"She has cancer."

I sat there watching Rakim go through every emotion in a matter of seconds. He sat there, his mouth agape as he stared at me, seemingly waiting for me to take back what I had just said.

"Real shit?" Rakim asked.

I nodded with a grim look in my eyes. "Dead ass. A brain tumor. It's stage 3. She only had like a year to live when she told me."

Rakim covered his mouth in disbelief. He had never met True, but he had heard me talk about her so much that he felt like he knew her. "Is she sure?"

I sadly nodded my head, rethinking the last conversation I'd had with True. "Yeah, she's sure. She's gone to multiple doctors and specialists. It's nothing that can be done."

Rakim still couldn't believe it. "So... She's dying?"

His constant questions didn't give me the usual irritation. I had asked myself the same over and over again as well.

I nodded. "Yeah."

"Sooo... So... Sooo, why is she having the baby?"

"That was my question. That's what pissed me the fuck off. Not only did she let me fall for her knowing she was dying, but she's bringing a baby into this. She knows I didn't grow up with my parents, and she knows I don't want any of my shorties to ever go through what I went through. And even though my baby would have me, I can't stomach watching it beg for its mother like I did."

Rakim continued to slowly shake his head with doubt. "If she's going to die, then why is she putting herself through having a baby?"

I shook my head slowly. She had told me her reasons. I felt her, but I didn't understand it for the life of me. "She said she doesn't feel right taking a life when she's begging for her own. And I can't knock her for that."

Rakim nodded. "Facts."

Then I cringed. "But I did."

"Huh?" he asked, confused.

Remorsefully, I told him, "I *did* knock her. Man, I snapped. I was pissed. I was thinking about my own feelings and my kid. I felt like she was being selfish by having this baby, by fucking with me. She told me that I was just supposed to have been fun, and I lost it."

"Damn."

I held my forehead. "We haven't talked since."

"Damn, man, when was that?"

I lowered my head. "Like six months ago."

His eyes bulged. "Six months? So, you don't know if she's still pregnant, still alive, or nothing?"

"I've been stalking her social media pages. She's alive and very pregnant as of two months ago when I could bring myself to look at it last."

Rakim sat up with a bleak stare. He poured us two more shots and pushed mine towards me. He threw his back and told me, "Aye, man, this ain't you to have some kid out there that you aren't taking care of. You always told me you would do better than your parents."

I groaned. "I know, man, but I can't be there to watch her... to watch her... *die*. Man, that's fucked up. I was just getting to know shorty, starting to like her, and now *this*? I can't do that, man."

Rakim leaned forward, looking me dead in my eyes. "I know you aren't close to a lot of people because of what you been through in the past. I know you don't like emotional shit, but you gotta do this. How will you feel about yourself if you don't?"

I sucked my teeth and shook my head. Groaning, I mumbled, "Maaan..."

"What's more important?" Rakim grilled me. "Sheltering your feelings now like some punk-ass bitch or feeling like a punk-ass bitch later when she's gone and you can't fix this?"

I sucked my teeth again, face bawled up, frustrated that I was even dealing with this bullshit. Every time I felt this frustration, my anger towards True grew. But as I threw my last shot back, I knew that after six months, my feelings for her had outgrown my anger so much more.

REMI

♫Hold up, get right witcha (I'ma get right witcha)
Bad bitches, fuck 'em then dismiss em (bad, woo)
I ain't really here to take no pictures (flash)
Middle finger up fuck the system (fuck 'em)♫

"Ayyyye, that's my shit!" I started to sway my hips to Migos as I maneuvered through the tight crowd at the President's Lounge. It was a Saturday night, so the club was bussin'. People were packed in that bar like sardines, and I could barely get through the crowd back to my seat at the bar. I was actually having a good time, but that was because my misery had been masked by the countless shots and drinks I'd had that night. Tonight, I would dance and laugh like my heart hadn't refused to mend its broken pieces.

"Fuck!" I heard a guy bark in my ear.

I whipped my head towards him and saw that he was wiping himself down. He glared at me and spat, "You knocked my drink out my hand."

"I'm sorry." I wanted to help him wipe down his Gucci shirt with my napkin, but his glare was full of drunken rage, so I backed up.

Despite my apology, he snarled. "Fat ass."

My eyes narrowed. "What did you say?" I asked, as if I hadn't heard him.

Biting his lip furiously, he stepped closer to me. "I said *fat ass.* Gawd damn, your big ass needs to watch where you goin'."

People around us started laughing as they looked my large body up and down. I cringed inwardly, tucked my tail, and continued to make my way through the tight crowd. Now, I was purposely pushing my way through.

"What's wrong with you?" Gigi asked me as I appeared next to her at the bar.

I knew I was wearing my emotions on my sleeve. I had already been feeling insecure and embarrassed. The littlest things set me off and turned on the tears. I could feel them pooling in my eyes as I snatched my purse and coat off of the barstool I'd been sitting on.

I threw my purse over my shoulder. "Let's go."

"Whyyyyy?" Gigi whined. "We just got here, and that fine dude over there keeps sending me drinks." She looked a few feet away towards the end of the bar where an average-height guy with a thick, Rick Ross beard and bald head was gushing at her and licking his lips. She was right. He was fine. But every man in this world annoyed the shit outta me at the moment, fine or not.

I rolled my eyes as I threw on my Moncler puff coat. "Fine. Whatever. I'm leaving."

Gigi dramatically tilted her head to the side. "Are you serious?"

I smacked my lips. "Yes!"

Instead of copping the same attitude as I had, Gigi looked at me with concern. "What the hell is wrong with you?"

I took a deep breath, trying not to give my sister an attitude that wasn't meant for her. I was also trying to keep the room from spinning. All of those shots of 1800 were catching up with me. I wasn't sure whether it was the liquor or the fact that the guy in the Gucci shirt had called me fat that had me ready to throw up on Gigi's Ugg boots.

"Nothing. I'm fine," I lied.

Gigi pulled me closer to her, giving me a sincerely concerned stare. "Sissy, it's been months. Let that nigga go."

That made my blood boil. I was sick of people telling me to get over it and let Banks go as if I was supposed to get over my man of ten years leaving me for a bad bitch and flaunting her all over social media as easily as kids got over colds. It wasn't that fucking easy!

Despite my clear annoyance, Gigi went on, "Sis, he's moved on, so you should too. You're letting him affect your good time when he's not letting you affect him at all."

I lightly pulled out of her grasp. "I'm out, Gigi."

Regretfully, she nodded. "Are you good to drive?"

"Yeah, I'm fine."

"Well, I'm staying for a little while longer. Call me when you make it home."

I nodded as I turned to leave. Luckily, the door was right next to us, so I was able to scurry out without anyone seeing the tears streaming down my face. By now, it was January. The air was cold and crisp. As my hot tears slid down my face, they froze against my icy cheeks. I struggled to stay on my feet, fighting with my drunkenness and the black ice that covered the uneven sidewalk.

As I hopped into my car, I was hot on the inside despite the wintery temperature. I was enraged, mad at myself, and mad that Gigi was right. I *was* allowing Banks to affect me when he had not stopped one part of his life because of me. He was moving on, having a baby, and enjoying the newlywed life, all without having looked back at me once. Yet, I was stuck in a rut, drinking more than I ever had before, losing friends, isolating myself, and burying myself in my work.

At the beginning of the year, I had sworn that the New Year would mean a new start for me. I wanted new friends since my old ones had been disloyal and attended that wedding. I wanted to lose weight. I wanted to get a man who would love me unconditionally. But all I had managed to do was overwork my liver.

Inside my car, I turned the engine. To pass the time it took to warm up, I reached behind the driver's seat for the bottle of 1800 that

I kept on the floor. I removed the top and drank from the bottle until my throat burned.

Slow tears slid down my face as I finally started to feel the heat. I threw the car into drive and pulled out of the parking lot, not even looking at my surroundings. Horns honked violently as cars swerved around me. I blinked to force myself to be able to see the road through my drunken haziness.

I was floating, anger guiding me. I saw my anger, instead of the streets. I was ignoring every stop sign and light, only paying attention to my hurt and the rejection... until a light flashed brightly, blinding me and a sound blared so loudly that I was forced to stop focusing on how Banks had hurt me and focus on the road instead. I blinked, hearing the blaring sound over and over again so blaring that I winced.

"Shit!" I gasped as I realized I was approaching train tracks at ninety miles an hour on an icy, slick road. The train was barreling towards the intersection at an even faster speed than I was driving. I had a split-second choice between stopping and causing my car to spin out and most likely, hit the trees that lined the street or barrel into the train.

The train's horn continued to roar as if the engineer saw me coming but couldn't stop. Cars on the street were blowing their horns as well.

I struggled with the decision of what to do when it suddenly hit me that it wouldn't be so bad to hit that train dead on. Why continue to live with this heartbreak and misery? Clearly, I wasn't good enough to love or to be chosen for a wife.

Death felt like a relief at the moment.

12

ANGEL

Russell and I had only been dating for about six months now. However, he had put in more work than any other man that I had ever experienced except my late husband. But I truly believed it was because he and Darnell were of the same caliber. Both were real men from the hood who knew how to stake claim on the woman that they wanted to become histheirs. He knew how to court me and sweep me off of my feet with the same swag and confidence Darnell had. Russell and I had yet to discuss the details of a committed relationship. I believed it was because he knew that I had yet to even consider being with another man after Darnell. Yet, Russell had been so successful at changing my mind that my body had been yearning for his intimate touch for weeks.

"What are you thinking about?"

I jumped slightly at the sudden sound of Russell's voice as if I weren't lying in his bed right next to him. Nervously, I ran my hand over the back of my head through my tapered hair as I ignored the throbbing sensation between my legs.

"Angel..."

Shit. He was so dominant, so masculine.

"H-huh?" I stuttered.

When he chuckled, he was so undeniably handsome. "Baby, what's up with you?" Before I responded, he reached over, placed his hand on my waist, and turned me towards him. "Talk to me."

I had shared a bed with many men since Darnell, even in one of their T-shirts, as I currently was, but I had never felt such a need to be touched and loved.

I needed it. I had needed it for quite some time. I had just never felt comfortable enough to get it from anyone until now.

I just lay there smiling at Russell, stuck between wanting him to fuck all five years of abstinence out of this pussy and not wanting to regret it.

He matched my smile, and we lay there in the darkness, the light from the television bouncing off of our faces.

Then he leaned over to kiss me, which wasn't unnerving, because we had kissed so many times before. But, hell, I was forty years old, and I wanted him to do more than just kiss me. Finally, I wanted a man to make love to me. Russell had never pushed me any further than what I was comfortable with, but this was the first time *I* would do the pushing.

As we kissed, his hand held the front of my neck softly. I took my hand and placed it on top of it and slid it down, past my chest and over my breast. His breathing became labored as he sensed what I wanted. He started playing with my breasts beneath his Nike shirt, and then my breath became heavy as well. I leaned into him, pressing my covered breasts to his bare chest. His tongue traced my lips as his hand started to hungrily caress my hips and ass. My fingers went into his hair, gripping his curls.

Then my phone rang.

When he hesitated, I begged him, "Don't stop."

He smiled into our kiss, then left my lips and began to kiss his way down my neck.

I let out a raspy moan.

After my phone finally stopped ringing, Russell's hand disappeared under my shirt and began to caress my back, before he pulled me to him. I arched my back, pressing myself against him. I moved my leg up his body, hugging him with it. I felt him hardening against my thigh. I began to rub my sex against his, like some virgin teenager, and he groaned. He began to claw at his shirt that I was wearing, tearing it off.

I giggled at his anxiousness as he threw it behind us on the floor.

"You sure you wanna do this?" he asked.

I nodded as I nibbled on my bottom lip. "Yes, I'm sure."

He gazed at my breasts as I stared at him. "Beautiful," he whispered as he leaned forward, pushing me on my back, and climbed on top of me. He began to tongue kiss my neck. Wrapping my legs around him, I squirmed from the sensation while attempting to kiss him wherever my mouth could reach. Our breaths were so heavy that they began to drown out the series that we had once been watching on Netflix. Continuing to kiss my neck, he rested on his side and started to play with my pussy.

But he only played with it long enough to realize how soaking wet it was. "Shit," he groaned at the touch of the lake between my thighs. He reached over me towards the nightstand. He opened a drawer, and I could hear the fumbling of plastic. He then rested on his knees between my legs. I snuck a peek at his dick as he placed the condom on it. I was satisfied with his above average size, but, considering how long I had been abstinent, I wasn't picky. Yet, as he leaned over and slowly penetrated me, I gasped at how thick it was.

I opened my legs wider to allow him full access. He rested completely on me and started to kiss me slowly as he fully thrust inside of me.

"Fuck," he grunted as he started a series of rhythmic thrusts.

My eyes began to roll to the back of my head. My mouth lay agape. I couldn't form any moans or words. The way my pussy had stretched around his dick, gripping it, milking it, and hugging it as he thrust perfectly inside me was orgasmic.

"Ahhh," I finally moaned and bit his shoulder lightly. "Yesss..."

He reached down and cupped one of my legs, causing me to open up and him to fill me up even more.

"Shiiiit!" I hissed, just as my phone began to ring again. "Fuck," I groaned in frustration.

He left me, and I reached to bring him back. But he chuckled and continued his journey away from me towards my phone that was continuously ringing on his nightstand. Looking at it in his hand, his eyes widened a bit as he thrust the phone towards me, saying, "It's True."

I grabbed it and answered immediately. "Hello?"

I heard panting... lots and lots of panting. "Mamaaaa!"

I sprang up, nearly pushing Russell off of me. "What's wrong, baby?"

"I'm having contractions, Mama," True forced out through heavy breaths. "The baby is coming!"

TRUE

"Should she be throwing up like this?"

My mother was hysterical as I vomited into a bucket for the fifth time. I clung to it in the hospital bed, heaving as nothing came out because literally nothing was left inside me. The cold towel my mother had applied to the back of my neck gave me no relief. Exhausted, I lay back, gasping for air as I stared up at the ceiling.

"Here comes another contraction," the nurse announced.

I could feel my mother's overly concerned eyes on me as I struggled for strength. I had been immensely exhausted for the last two days. It had been a struggle to walk or stand. The vomiting had gotten worse. If I wasn't vomiting, I was sleeping. Some days, I'd found myself delirious. Yet, I had been hiding it all, blaming it on the baby. I had even struggled with Joy that night so that my mother could spend some time with Russell who I felt like was a godsend. He had even refused to leave the hospital, hanging out in the waiting room and offering to tend to Joy. I was so happy my mama had found someone to love her and be there for her.

She was going to need it.

"Okay, True, breathe," the nurse encouraged as the contraction began to tear through me.

"Aarrrrrrrrrrrgh!" I bit down, breathing, gritting through the intense sharp pain for a few agonizing seconds until relief filled me so heavily that I threw myself back on the bed, gasping for air.

Again, I could feel my mother's concerned eyes on me, but I was in such intense pain that I could no longer front. I allowed the headache pain to take over. I squinted and fought to see, tears coming to my eyes. Exhaustion was consuming me.

My mother stood above me, holding the cold towel to my forehead now, as I looked up at her, my eyes begging for help that I knew she couldn't give me. She stared at the look at my eyes and tears came to hers. "You're okay," she tried to convince me. "You're doing good, baby."

I watched as the nurse stared with concern at the monitors. "Doctor Shaw, her blood pressure is still rising."

He rushed over to gage my vitals. "Prepare for C-section."

"*C-section?*" my mother asked with concern in her voice. I, too, was concerned, but I was too preoccupied with pain to question it.

"Yes," Dr. Shaw confirmed. "Her blood pressure has been high since she arrived. At this point, I don't want to risk a vaginal delivery. We need to get this baby out *now*."

My mother's eyes darted towards me. "You need to call Coop."

"No, Ma—"

"True!" she barked, interrupting me. "He needs to be here. This is his child just as much as he is yours."

"Mama, please," I said through labored breaths. "He doesn't want to be here. Just please..." I couldn't utter another syllable. My tears spoke for me.

I was tired...*so* tired.

ANGEL

I fought to keep myself from breaking down in uncontrollable sobs as I marched towards the waiting room. Through the glass, I could see Russell entertaining Joy at a desk full of coloring books and crayons. Hearing my heels clicking against the tile, he looked up. As soon as he saw my face, he stood with concern in his eyes. He said something to Joy that I couldn't hear. She nodded with a smile and went back to coloring as Russell met me in the doorway of the waiting room. As soon as he was in reach, I collapsed in his arms, sobbing.

"Babe, what's wrong?"

I couldn't speak through the pain. It hurt like nothing I had ever felt before. When I buried Darnell, I felt like nothing could ever top that pain ...until I was told that I would have to bury my daughter.

"Angel, baby, talk to me," Russell urged as he rubbed my back.

But I couldn't say a word. The tears were arresting me, taking my body into captivity. I buried the sobs into Russell's chest to keep Joy from hearing my fear and pain as I clung to him.

"Angel, you're scaring me. Is everything okay?"

I finally found my words. "No," I cried.

I could feel Russell's heartbeat intensify. "What happened?"

Sobbing, I whispered. "She's not okay."

"What's wrong?"

"She-she..." Tired of sounding like a babbling fool, I took a deep breath and tried to get my words together. "She has to have a C-section."

He seemed relieved. "Oh, babe, women have C-sections all the time. You know that. I'm sure it will be fine."

"No, Russell," I corrected him. "I'm not talking about that. She's *sick*. She's getting sicker."

He finally realized what I was saying, fully understanding the meaning behind my words. His eyes squeezed together briefly before he opened them again and asked, "How do you know?"

"I can just..." I wiped my face, trying to get myself together for Joy and True. "I can just tell. I see it in her eyes. I know my child."

"Come here." He brought me back into his embrace, holding me tightly, allowing me to claw at his back as I fought with the stinging heartbreak. "You gotta be strong for her. You need to be in there with her. She can't be in there alone."

"I know," I cried.

He took my chin into his hand and lifted my eyes to his. "I got you. You can be thinking too much into this."

Russell was a man. With him, I rarely had to think of anything. He took care of me. I could trust him, but in this particular situation, he was wrong.

REMI

"You could have killed yourself, Remi!"

I tore my eyes away from my mother. I couldn't take her judgmental stare. Who was she to judge me? She had been too stubborn to allow herself to love a man in years.

Yet, I still could not take those condescending eyes of hers. I pouted and recoiled under the hospital blanket.

"Unt uh!" my mother snapped, tearing the blanket back. "You're going to listen to me, and you listen to me good."

God. At the moment, the last thing I needed was to hear my mother's mouth, but at least I was still alive to hear it.

I was in the emergency room at The University of Chicago Hospital. An ambulance had brought me there, and for that last twelve hours I had been under observation, tested, and scanned.

As I had sped toward that train, I had contemplated allowing it to run me over and end my misery. I was sick of feeling like I wasn't good enough, as if I had eaten myself into being a woman that no man would ever want. I was so tired of comparing myself to every fat girl I saw that had a man beside her that loved her, rolls and all. For years, I had psyched myself out, making myself think that Banks loved me unconditionally because he still had sex with me with every pound that I had gained. No matter the little bitches that he had cheated on me with, he still was with me, fucking me, claiming to love all of this. Now, I had been truly humbled, brought down to my knees to stoop in my embarrassing truth. I couldn't hide behind that facade anymore. He had finally chosen, and his choice hadn't been me. I could no longer deny that for all these years, he had not, in fact, loved me how I deserved to be loved. I couldn't front like he was the perfect man anymore. I could no longer stunt like we had been happy. My truth had been revealed for the world to see, and I just couldn't take it anymore. At the time I had wanted it to be over.

However, I had chickened out, hitting the brakes. My car had spun out on the black ice covering the pavement. I went head-on into a tree, totaling my Benz. The impact had caused a few facial lacerations and broken a couple of ribs.

"You're lucky to be alive," my mother fussed.

I didn't feel lucky. But I dared not encourage more of my mother's chastising by saying that.

"It's not that serious," my mother insisted.

"Exactly," Gigi added. I slightly rolled my eyes and just stared at the ceiling as she drove the judgmental knife into my back deeper. "You're gonna let this nigga kill you while he ain't even with you? Get your shit together, Remi."

That was easy for her to say. I had given Banks most of my life. At this point, I was not lovesick. I was embarrassed and disappointed in myself. I felt like less of a woman for allowing someone who did not even know my man like I did to swoop in and save him from clearly a woman who he felt captive with... until he met her. She obviously gave him the strength to finally shit on me so bad that there was no turning back.

13

TRUE

Keyes was born a healthy seven pounds even. I'd named him that because with a mother named True and a sister named Joy, he had to have a unique name. Keyes was the Hebrew version of Caius, which meant rejoice. And my baby boy had definitely given me something to rejoice about during such dark days.

He was now a week old and out of the hospital. Yet, my mother had been catering to him as I remained a patient at the hospital at the insistence of my oncologist, Dr. Sabi. He had run a series of tests to determine the status of my cancer while medicating me so that I was able to deal with the pain and other symptoms that were crippling me.

Yet, I didn't need the tests to know what was going on. As he looked at me, I also could see it in his eyes, that there hadn't been a real need for him to run the tests to know either.

However, he still wasted the time and money to run them, and now my team of doctors were standing around my bed with looks in their eyes that only meant one thing.

Dr. Sabi had the most distressed look in his eyes, eyes that he couldn't bring to look directly into mine. The oncology residents surrounding him had white skin that had flushed red. The one sistah resident was the only one who had the balls to look me in the eyes, but her stare held so much sympathy for me.

Finally, when the tension in the room became too obvious, Dr. Sabi cleared his throat and forced out, "I honestly don't know how to tell you this, True."

I took a deep breath, preparing myself to hear what I already knew in my heart. "Just tell me," I insisted.

Dr. Sabi nodded and regained his professionalism. "The cancer is progressing ... *fast*."

I bit the inside of my jaw nervously. "Stage 4?" I asked, knowing his answer.

He nodded and sadly answered, "Yes."

"How much time do I have?"

Again, Dr. Sabi's professionalism went out of the window. He had been quite caring since becoming my oncologist nearly two years ago. He thought I was so courageous for battling this disease while going through a divorce and giving birth to Keyes. He had come to admire me.

"Dr. Sabi, it's okay," I insisted with a smile.

He cleared his throat and nodded again. He walked around the foot of the bed and took a seat. With a light hand on my leg, he told me, "Three months at the most."

My eyes bucked a bit in shock. I had known I was getting sicker, but hearing that had hit me so hard that I was speechless. My eyes shut tight for a quick second as I nodded slowly. Yet, I swallowed hard in an attempt to maintain my composure.

With a loving pat on the knee, Dr. Sabi told me, "It's time for Hospice care."

COOP

♫*She calling my phone, all in her feelings*
Wanna ask me where I'm at, ayy look bae you tripping
See I'm coming in lil late or I might not come in
Cause I'm tryna turn your Honda Accord, into a Benz
Aye I'm tryna get it lil baby, I'm tryna get it
Aye I'm tryna get it lil baby, I'm tryna get it
Aye I'm tryna get it lil baby, I'm tryna get it
Aye I'm tryna get it lil baby, aye I'm tryna get it.♫

"*You know I like spending lil' baby. So, I gotta get it lil' baby. Never had shit. All you know is get it when you come up from the trenches, lil' baby.*"
I was cruising through the city as I rapped along to "Lil' Baby" by Money Bagg Yo. I had just left the rec center that was coming along good. It looked dope on the inside. I would be ready to open the doors in a few weeks. I was too turnt up to finally see one of my few dreams coming to fruition. "*Sending texts, thinking I'm fucking off with other bitches. She crazy. Take the R out of free, you get fee. If I do fuck with them, just know they gone pay me. I'm 'bout to stretch a whole 9. I ain't lying. I'm bout to whip it like slavery'.*"

I was doing eighty on the Bishop Ford on my way to pick up

Vanessa. Her husband had left town, and she was feigning for the D. Since she knew so much about real estate and connections, she had been a tremendous help as I renovated the rec center. She had hooked me up with many of the contractors and had even gotten me connections with a few schools in the neighborhood where I had gone to tell the male students about the center. They seemed excited, and so was I. The only dark cloud over this excitement was that True was missing. Unbeknownst to her, she had birthed this idea within me.

Just thinking about her left the usual ball in my stomach. It had been eight months. I wondered if she had given birth yet. I wanted nothing more than to wash away my feelings for her so that I could be there for my child, but no matter how hard I tried, I still had mad love for shorty.

However, that day, I was full of so much excitement that I really only wanted to share it with True. She was flooding every thought I had. I hated that she wasn't there to witness what she had instilled in me.

As I exited the expressway, I reached for my phone in the center console and swiped through the screens until I reached my Facebook app. I searched for True's name and clicked on her page. She still hadn't posted in months, but her mother had tagged her in a picture of a baby boy. Approaching a red light, I stared at the baby boy who was surprisingly already chocolate. Yet, his ears were darker than the rest of him, so I smiled, realizing he would be dark like me. His eyes were closed, and he didn't have any features yet, so I couldn't tell who he looked like yet. But staring at him, I knew he would be the spitting image of me. He was mine, my son.

I closed the phone. I couldn't stare at him any longer. Looking at my son gave me an even more unusual feeling than I had started feeling for True. It was unconditional love. Just looking at that picture, I felt love and connection to a person that I didn't even know or hadn't even held.

"Fuck," I cursed as I gripped the steering wheel. Reluctantly, I picked up my phone again and unlocked it. It was still on her page.

Luckily, her mother had tagged which hospital they were in. So, even though everything in me was telling me that this was something I should run far away from, I headed to the University of Chicago.

~

I was still feeling some reluctance as I went to knock on True's hospital room door. I lifted my arm, knuckles ready to knock, but I stopped myself. I was a gangsta, the hardest of them all, but I didn't have the heart to do this, to raise this baby without her, to have to tell my son how wonderful his mother was because all he would have of her were the memories that True's mother and I would share with him.

However, Rakim's words had been ringing in my ears since he'd said them to me. *"Aye, man, this ain't you, to have some kid out there that you aren't taking care of. You always told me you would do better than your parents."*

I *had* always said that. I wanted to be better than my parents. This wasn't the way I wanted to do it, but regardless, I was now a father. And I had already broken a promise to my son for the eight months his mother had carried him and then birthed him into the world.

Biting down on my bottom lip, I knocked on the door and then let myself in. I walked through the door slowly, not knowing what to expect or how True would respond. But as I walked past the bathroom and entered the room, I instantly regretted it. Her mother was sitting on her bed. They had been in an embrace that her mother was letting her out of now knowing that someone else was in the room. They both quickly wiped their eyes, still not looking in my direction, but I could see that they had been crying. I noticed Joy lying on the couch under the window fast asleep.

Finally, True looked up and nearly jumped out of her once-bright skin when she saw me. My heart broke as I looked at her. Most pregnant women gained weight, yet she had lost even more. She was so thin that she was nearly only skin and bones. Her color had left her beautiful face. But I knew I loved her when she still looked so beautiful to me.

"C-Coop," she stuttered, lashes fluttering repeatedly.

I walked towards her slowly, as her mother watched me curiously. That's when I noticed that small, brown baby in her mother's arms. But instead of being wrapped in the usual hospital blanket and onesie, he had on a Ralph Lauren onesie, hat, and booties. My little man was very handsome as he slept.

There was fire in her mother's eyes as she watched me. I had never met her before. I only knew who she was because I had been stalking True's Facebook page. I figured True had told her how I had responded to the news about her pregnancy.

Regardless of how she was eyeing me, I smiled and extended my hand. "Hi, I'm Coop."

She eyed my hand, glaring. I could see that tears were still in her eyes. She looked back at True, whose eyes were begging her mother to be nice.

Her mother looked back at me and shook my hand weakly. "Hi," she spat curtly. "I'm Angel, True's mother."

I smiled, revealing my dimples, and she gushed despite her reluctance. True smiled as well as her mother cleared her throat, stood, and smoothed out of her sweater dress.

"I'll give you all some privacy," she announced as she put my son in True's arms. She then stood and took her purse from the nearby chair. "True, I'm going to the cafeteria for some coffee. Do you want something to eat?"

"I'm not hungry, Ma." In response, Angel gave True a stern look, so True sighed. "Fine. Bring me a cheeseburger." True shook her head behind her mother's back as she marched out of the room.

I slowly walked towards the chair near her bed and sat, staring at my son. "Can I hold him?" I asked, hopeful that True didn't harbor so much resentment against me that she didn't want me close to my son.

But in genuine True fashion, she smiled sincerely and said, "Sure." Then she handed him to me.

He squirmed as I took him into my arms, but he didn't wake up. "What's his name?"

True smiled at the sight of me holding him. In my large arms, he seemed to disappear. "Keyes."

My eyes darted at her. "What's his *real* name?"

Her mouth dropped. "That *is* his real name!"

My head cocked as I glared at her. "Why you name my son that shit?"

"It's nice! It means rejoice. It's different," she insisted.

I groaned, shaking my head. "You already signed the birth certificate?"

"Yes." She chuckled. "He's a week old."

"Well, you need to change his name," I fussed. Her mouth lay agape again as I continued to bark, "He needs a name he can get a job with. Some shit they don't let people know that he's Black as soon as they look at his résumé. Something like Jackson or Steve."

"Your name is Coop," she reminded me.

"No, because those white folks at the group home had sense enough, my name is *Cooper*, not no ghetto shit."

Insulted, True clutched her chest. "Barack Obama was the *president*, and his name is ethnic."

"And he graduated from Yale. You don't know whether this little motherfucker is gonna graduate from *high school*, let alone college."

True giggled. "I hate you."

I reached over with a smile and pinched her side: "No, you don't."

As she laughed and swatted my hand away, I realized how much I had missed her. I knew I had missed her, but being there with her let me know exactly just how much I needed her. This felt real. She filled gaps in my life that I didn't even know needed filling. She made me feel like my head was in the clouds even though I knew damn well that my feet were on the ground. Looking at her and being in her presence was like the first warm, sunny day after a brutal Chicago winter.

I felt lost. This territory of feeling and loving was so unknown to me. Yet, I felt lost in the right direction.

"I'm sorry." It was that simple. There was nothing more to say. "I'm *so* sorry."

True's shoulder sank as sympathy filled her eyes. "I'm sorry too. I should have told you the truth from the beginning. I just never expected for us to get so close so fast, and I never, *ever* considered getting pregnant."

I smirked playfully. "Yeah, you were treating me like a fuck buddy."

She giggled. "Yeah, that was my only intention."

"It was mine too. I'm not going to lie."

True laughed. "I know."

"That's why I pushed you away when you told me about Keyes and your cancer. I wasn't strong enough to be in love with you and watch you die."

Her eyes filled with admiration as we stared at one another. "In *love* with me?"

I felt like a bitch. I felt soft and weak, but it was my truth. And I had been letting my ego keep me away from my son and True for way too long.

"Yes," I confessed.

That confession made her feel guilt that poured into her eyes, instead of the happiness I expected. "Well, I am..."

"Huh?" I asked curiously. "You're what?"

Sitting back, she sighed long and deep. Swallowing hard, she looked up at the ceiling. "I am dying. *Soon.* It's getting worse. I only have three months at the most. There's nothing more that can be done for me."

My eyes closed for a second as I fought to keep my composure. I didn't want to be selfish and show her my reaction. I needed to be there for her. I would deal with my hurt on my own. Leaning forward, I reached for her tiny hand and kissed the back of it, fighting to swallow the huge lump in my throat.

"I'm getting released to Hospice care tomorrow," she told me as she stared blankly in front of her. It was as if, even though she had been told that this would happen, she still couldn't believe it. "You can walk away now, and I would totally understand. And in three months, after I'm gone, you can come back and take care of your son."

I squeezed her hand to make her look at me. "Nah, I ain't gon' do that."

14

REMI

A week after my accident, I was back to work. I was getting a new patient that evening, so I was preparing myself to be more hospitable and personable than I felt. I had been going through all the stages of grief when it came to Banks and Brandi. Now, I had returned to the stage of anger. I was pissed that he had wasted so many years of my life and had left me so broken that I may never love again. He had just left me alone to put myself back together.

However, I was going to put myself back together, and I was going to start by blocking out elements of Banks and Brandi that would trigger any ill feelings. So, I had blocked all those motherfuckers from my social media pages. I tried my best to stay off of social media as well. The last thing that I needed to see while trying to get over this was a picture of their baby, which I was sure had been born by now. I had also completely separated myself from Niyah and Iyana's messy asses.

"Fuck him," I muttered as I pulled up in front of the home in Morgan Park on 108th and Talman.

I killed the engine on the rental. My car had been totaled out. I was waiting on the insurance check so that I could get me a new ride.

Luckily, I had gotten away with blaming that accident on skidding on black ice, and they hadn't given me a breathalyzer test. So, I hadn't been charged with a DUI, and I had not been found at fault.

It was approaching eleven at night and it was the end of January, so it was cold. The sidewalks were icy. I grabbed my bag from the back seat, closed the door, and rushed towards the two-story brick house with my hands in the pockets of my Moncler.

Before I could ring the doorbell, my cell phone surprising started to ring inside my purse. I paused before ascending the steps of the front porch and fished it out of my purse.

Looking at the screen, I gasped, as I stared at the contact that read "Husband." I still had Banks' number saved in my phone as what he was supposed to have been, even though he'd ended up stepping into that role for another bitch.

"Hello?" I answered slowly and curiously.

"H-hey," he stuttered, as if he were surprised that I had answered. "H-hello..."

We were both stuttering over our nervousness. I knew why I was nervous, but I wondered first, why he was calling and second, what the hell he had to be nervous about. I was the one he had left broken-hearted without an explanation, not the other way around.

"How you doin'?" he asked me casually.

Leaning against the banister, I lied, "I'm okay." I wanted to ask him so many questions, but I was tongue-tied. All that came out was, "How are you doing?"

"I'm straight," he answered half-heartedly.

Something was wrong. I had been with him for most of my life. I knew everything about him. I knew his moods, and I knew how he sounded when he was in those moods. I wondered where his bitch-ass wife was and why he wasn't somewhere asking her how she was doing, but I kept that sass to myself for the sake of trying to keep my composure.

"That's good to hear," I forced myself to say.

"It's good to hear your voice." I was shocked to hear the sincerity in his deep, sultry voice. "I've been thinking about you."

Curiously, I pressed, "Have you?"

"Yeah."

Suddenly, a light came on inside of the house near the front door. It looked to be in the living room. I looked at my phone and saw that it was two minutes after my starting time.

"Banks, I have to go. I was actually on my way into a new patient's home."

"Oh... Okay." He sounded regretful. But then hopeful as he asked, "Can I call you back?"

"Yeaaah, I guess," I answered slowly.

"All right. Have a good night, Remi."

"You too."

"Hit me if you need something."

"O-kay." My face bunched with confusion as I quickly hung up and climbed the stairs. I had no idea what that call had been about, but it honestly made me feel so much better that after all this time he had finally thought of me. The possibilities of what that call meant swam through my mind as I rang the bell. I honestly was smiling for the first time in so long as the door opened. Then my smile dropped when the massive figure appeared in the doorway. His appearance would have instantly frightened me. His stance was tall and wide, and his bulging arms and legs looked dangerously strong. He would have been scary-looking had he not been so strikingly sexy. His presence snatched away what little professionalism I had left after Banks' call. Suckable, pouty lips curved up into a smile, beaming white teeth shining through his full, luscious beard, but there was so much sadness in his cognac, cat-like eyes that I saw right through the happiness in his grin.

"H-hi." Once again, a man had me stuttering. "This is the home of True Jenkins, correct?"

"Yeah. Come on in."

I hadn't even noticed that he was carrying a small infant until the baby started to make small, whiny noises. The baby looked so tiny against his huge chest. He began to turn his face, revealing his cuteness beyond the blue, fuzzy baby blanket that he was wrapped in. I gushed at him as the guy let me in.

"Awww, he is so precious. How old is he?"

"Just two weeks. His name is Keyes." He started to talk to the baby. "Say hi, Keyes."

I melted at how he cooed at the baby. "Hi, Keyes," I cooed, playing along. "I'm Remi." I looked up into the gentleman's eyes and asked, "And you are?"

"Coop. I'm his father," he answered as he closed the door, shutting out the wintery wind. "You can come this way."

I followed him into the beautiful home. There was no evidence that anyone was dying inside. The home was full of so much life and smelled of Febreze. But this was usually how homes felt when I first arrived. It was still full of so much hope. The family members forced themselves to smile, to laugh, to keep moving until the day came that the death of their loved one was inevitable.

He led me into the kitchen where an older woman was seated at the kitchen table. She didn't offer me the phony smile that Coop had. She looked up at me, sadness overflowing from her eyes. She stood slowly and reached out to shake my hand.

"Hi. My name is Angel. True is sleeping."

As I shook her shaky hand, I offered, "I'm sorry to meet you under such circumstances. But I promise to make this as easy for your family and True as I possibly can."

That was the speech I had been taught to give family members. But I already knew that no matter what I did, watching their loved one die would never be easy.

AN HOUR LATER, I was administering some pain meds through True's IV. She was still asleep, which was to be expected after her mother had explained her condition to me. After learning so much about True, I instantly felt such embarrassment for how I had been acting for the last year. I had been crying over a man, nearly killing myself with depression and sadness. When this young woman, two years younger than me, was fighting through something so much worse. I was used to having older patients. True was one of the first younger ones I could see myself in. I still had a life. I still had the chance to fall in love again and make babies. But she didn't. She was being forced to leave her children and family, and it was so unfair. But she was doing it. She was facing it bravely, so who was I to complain and feel like anything I had endured was unfair?

Instantly, I was grateful that I had been led to this patient. I had yet to even get the chance to meet her personally, but I was so grateful to have met her already. I suddenly realized how much I had to be thankful for, but I had yet been so ungrateful. My stomach turned as I felt her frail arm in the palm of my hand. She was literally skin and bones.

After administering the drugs, I swallowed the lump in my throat. I forced myself to maintain as I stepped out of the room because Angel was still wandering around the house. She had told me that she often couldn't sleep at night so I might hear her every now then.

I tiptoed through the house. I grabbed my coat out of the kitchen and headed out of the back door, onto the patio with tears in my eyes.

COOP

"Why you always trying to fuck with funny-looking bitches?" I laughed into my cell phone as I hit the blunt. I was sitting outside on the patio, taking a smoke break before I headed inside to get a nap before Keyes woke up again.

I had been spending every day at True's house, only leaving to take care of much-needed business. I wanted to be able to spend every waking moment with her and Keyes as much as I possibly could.

"Funny-looking?" Rakim asked on the other end. "Man, she ain't funny-looking."

I looked at the phone, wondering what the fuck was wrong with my homie. "Did you catch a bullet to the eye too? Because you gotta be blind."

"What's wrong with her?" Rakim pressed.

"Her fat-ass back is what's wrong with her."

Rakim started cracking up. "She ain't got no fat back."

"Her back looks like a turtle shell." I started barking in laughter at my own joke just as the patio door opened. I jumped and hid my blunt, thinking it was Angel. But it was Remi.

Even in her coat, I could see that fabulous figure of hers. When

I'd opened the door for her earlier, I saw how beautiful she was. But when she took her coat off, as Angel spoke with her in the kitchen, I was floored at how she was built. She was exactly how I liked them, tall and thicker *than a motherfucker.*

Remi had the type of look that no matter what was going on around him, a man couldn't keep his eyes off of her. So, I had to get my ass up out of there. I wasn't about to let Angel catch me gawking at her daughter's Hospice nurse after I had just gotten back in good with True. I had disappeared into Keyes' room to put him to bed.

"Oh, I'm sorry," she said when she saw me.

I could see the weariness in her eyes as I told her, "Nah, it's cool." Then I told Rakim, "Let me call you back." I hung up before he could say anything. "You cool?"

As she took a deep breath, it exited from her mouth in a big fog due to the cold air. Then she shook her head slowly. "No, I'm not." Her voice cracked as she hid her face in her hands. She plopped down into an empty chair and wiped her face free of tears. "I'm so sorry. This is very unprofessional. I've never had a patient affect me like this. She's just so... So young..."

I sighed and sat back in my chair, hitting the blunt. "Yeah, I know."

Remi gasped and instantly looked at me with regret. "Oh, my goodness. I'm so sorry. I'm probably making you feel so much worse."

I assured her, "You're good, and you're right. Being here is sobering than a motherfucker."

"Yeah." She nodded as she stared off into space. "It is."

"You wanna hit this?" I asked with a chuckle as I offered her the blunt.

She stared at it as if her mouth was watering. "I shouldn't while on duty."

I shrugged. "I won't tell."

She looked behind her into the house.

"Angel isn't going to come out here," I reassured her. "She hates the cold."

Remi stared at the blunt for a few seconds before shrugging and taking it from me. She hit it softly, and then handed it back. The weed exhaled slowly from her mouth as she sat back shaking her head. "I feel so bad."

"Don't feel bad for her. She is actually handling it well. Feel bad for those of us who'll be left here when she's gone, missing the hell out of her." Even while sitting there, I felt the pain of mourning for True already. She was still physically with us, but day by day, I could see her slipping away. I thought I had been strong prior to this, but this situation was teaching me strength and manhood that no father could have ever taught me.

"Are you two married?" Remi asked.

"No. We're... Um... It's complicated."

Remi chuckled and nodded, giving me a judgmental smirk. "It's 'complicated', huh?" she mocked me.

"It's not like that," I reassured her. "We were messing around. It was supposed to have been just casual. Then she got pregnant and told me about her condition. I just came back around."

Even more interested now, Remi sat up a bit and asked, "Just came back around?"

"Yeah. I was pissed at first." Quickly, she gave me a judgmental look, so I explained, "I was raised in group homes. I never had parents. I was out here on my own. Always have been, besides my homie, Rakim. I didn't want to ever have a child in that situation. That's why I never had any kids. I was pissed that she was having my baby, knowing she wouldn't be around to be his mother. Plus, I'm not used to having feelings for anyone. I only previously gave a fuck about Rakim. I had never loved anybody. Never cared. So, to fall for her and then learn she was dying fucked me up. I just couldn't bring myself to watch her die. I still can't, but I now know that I don't have a choice because I will hate myself more for not being here for her."

"You don't know how many patients I've had who have been forced to do this alone. She's lucky to have you." She looked at me and smiled. "Even though it's 'complicated'."

"Aye, don't judge me. I love her. I would love for her, my son, and me to be a family, but..." I chose not to say it since it was evident. "I just want to make sure I'm here to love her for as long as she has left."

"That's sweet, but..." She slightly rolled her eyes. "You men and your 'complicated' statuses..."

"What's *your* status then?"

She chuckled sarcastically. "No complication there. I'm single than a motherfucker."

"Damn, why you say it like that?"

"Because it's a lot."

I shook my head. "Nah, I told you all my dirt, so tell me yours."

Laughing half-heartedly in my opinion, she explained, "Well, I was with this guy for over ten years. He proposed, but the ring was too small, so he was getting it fitted, or so I'd thought. One day, I went to the bar that he promoted and saw one of the bartenders with my ring on." My eyes bucked as she went on, "The ring was actually hers. It was meant for her all along. She was his fiancée. I left him broken-hearted and embarrassed, and, now, they're married with a baby on the way."

My eyes stayed widened as I stared off into space. "Woooow."

Again, she chuckled with obvious cynicism. "Right."

"Well, then, you were wrong."

Her perfectly arched eyebrow rose as she asked me, "How so?"

"That *is* complicated," I laughed.

Remi thought about it for a few seconds. Then she finally smiled and agreed, "Yeah, you're right. It's *extremely* fucking complicated."

15

TRUE

a month later -

"True..."

I looked up at my mother and was immediately cautious. I didn't like the look in her eyes as she looked down at the papers in her hand.

"What, Mama? What's wrong?"

She nervously bit her nails as she stared at the envelope in her hand, reading it. "Ummm... This letter was in the mail for you. It's from family court."

I cringed as she walked towards me, handing it to me. As I tore it open, I prayed that this wasn't "it." I hoped that Jameel hadn't finally done what he had threatened. I didn't want to have to spend the little time I had left worrying that he would win custody of my daughter and erase every good memory of me that she had.

But as I removed the forms from the envelope and read them hesitantly, my stomach ached but not only from the disease; it was from disappointment as well because Jameel had indeed finally followed up with his threats and filed for full custody of Joy.

"Shit," I cursed as I slammed the papers down on the bed.

"Is it...?" My mom was too afraid to finish her sentence.

My lips pressed together tightly as I nodded.

My mother shook her head as she plopped down in the chair next to me. "When is the court date?"

"The end of June," I whispered. "He waited until I wouldn't be here to fight for Joy." Tears filled my eyes. I had come to grips with the fact that I was hurdling towards death faster than I had ever expected. I had made my peace with God and asked Him to accept me into the pearly gates. Of course, I didn't want to leave my kids, my mom, or Coop, but I had come to accept that I didn't have a choice in the matter. But, knowing that Jameel would have my daughter was something I could never come to terms with.

As tears slid down my cheeks, my cell phone rang. I quickly answered when I saw that it was Jameel. "What?"

I literally had no strength to listen to whatever foolery he was about to say, but I hoped that allowing him to speak his piece would prevent him from running down my battery. He had been calling since Keyes was born. Of course, his excuse was that he wanted to see Joy, but I knew that was a lie. He wanted to take my baby. And since I only had weeks left with her, the last thing I was going to do was give Jameel the chance to take my child from me.

"Did you get the papers?" I could hear the evil smirk in his voice.

"You will never get custody of my daughter," I hissed.

"Why won't you just die?" he slurred disgustingly. "It would best for Joy and me if you would just die already."

"Don't worry, Jameel. You don't have much longer to wait." I hung up before his sorry ass could say anything else.

"He is a monster," my mother hissed as she shook her head. "He'll never get custody of Joy, True. I won't let it happen."

Thank God I hadn't had the phone on speaker. Otherwise, my mother would be in an uproar. And, since there was no chance for me, I was spending my last days protecting her, Joy, and Keyes.

Even Coop. He had been trying so hard to be strong, but I knew his big ass was a teddy bear. Every time he looked at me, I saw the sadness in his eyes. I had to be strong for him and my family.

Just then, Coop appeared in the doorway of my bedroom that had been turned into a freaking hospital room. "What you want to eat?"

"Ummm..." Now that I was on so many medications to eliminate the pain and manage my other symptoms, I had an appetite again. "I want a gyro cheeseburger and fries with mild sauce." I looked at Remi, who was sitting in a chair in the corner on her tablet. She was so quiet and sweet. Coop had told me about what she'd shared with him on the balcony a month ago when she had first started caring for me. My heart had gone out to her. I knew how heartbreak felt. It damn near felt like death. She may have felt like I was in a worse situation than her, but she and I were still in the same pain. "You want something, Remi?"

For the last month, I had grown closer to her than I had my other nurses. Since we were so close in age, we spent a lot of time laughing and hanging out during her shift. We talked a lot about her ex, Banks. Most nights, it had been Remi, Coop, and I staying up, shooting the breeze, until I drifted off to sleep. Often times, I could hear them still conversing in my sleep.

"Uh... Sure, I'll have something." She shrugged. "What all do they have? Is there a menu?"

I laughed. "Not online. He's going to a hood spot. Why don't you ride with him?"

She shook her head. "I'm good."

"Please?" I begged. "I don't want him in the streets alone at this time of night."

"I can't leave you unattended during my shift," Remi warned.

"Pleeeease," I begged. "I won't tell."

She contemplated for a few seconds. As she did, I gave her puppy dog eyes. While I did so, Remi smiled and shook her head at me.

Finally, Remi shrugged and stood. "Okay. Let me get my coat."

I smiled. "Thank you."

Coop looked at me strangely as Remi left out to get her coat. I ignored his questioning stare, telling him, as I put my attention into my phone. "Hurry up. I'm hungry."

I MOANED as I rolled over and cuddled in Coop's arms. He was lying in bed with me as he often did whenever Joy and Keyes were sleeping. The CNA had run out to do some grocery shopping for me, and Russell had finally convinced my mama to get out of this house and enjoy herself.

I sighed with relief. "I'm so glad my mother is gone."

I could hear Coop's deep chuckle in my ear as my face lay pressed against his chest. "Don't do her like that."

"I need the air," I grumbled. "She's been hovering around me for weeks."

"Of course, she has. Can you blame her?"

"No, I can't, but she needs some air too. I'm glad Russell came to get her. I'm so glad she has him."

"I'm glad to have you."

I looked up into his eyes and smiled. "Look at you being all sweet."

I hadn't had the chance to be alone with Coop until now. Since being released into Hospice care, my mother hadn't left my side. I understood, of course, and appreciated it, but I desperately wanted some alone time with Coop now that he had come back around.

I reached for his face, brought it down close to mine, and kissed him. I moaned into his mouth because I hadn't felt any affection like this since the last time we had made love nearly a year ago.

If our kiss had a voice, it could have been compared to the angelic sounds of H.E.R.

I spoke into his mouth. "Does my breath smell like gyro?"

He started chuckling heavily. "Yeah, but mine does too."

We smiled into each other's eyes like hopeless romantics, except this was far from a fairy tale.

I cupped his face and asked, "Will you make love to me?"

He pulled back and looked into my eyes. "For real?"

"Yes," I practically begged.

Despite my efforts to exude as much sex appeal as I could, he still asked, "Am I going to hurt you?"

I giggled. "The tumor is in my head, not down there, silly."

He was still cautious. "But you just had the baby."

"I gave birth by C-section, remember? And it's been six weeks."

Still, he pressed, "You feel up to it?"

I cringed. I was dying, but I hated being looked at by him like I was. I wanted him to see someone sexy, the mother of his child, someone beautiful. Not a dying, cancer patient. And I wasn't stupid. I knew what he actually saw when he looked at me. I was skin and bones. My eyes were sunken in. I was weak. Most of the time I was asleep because of the meds. When I was awake, I sometimes had difficulty breathing. Yet, I was still a woman, and I still wanted to feel like a woman.

I looked longingly into Coop's eyes until he finally gave in. He carefully pulled the covers back and carefully hovered over my frail body. I closed my eyes and allowed his scent to overwhelm me. I seemed to disappear under him, much like Keyes did whenever he was in Coop's arms.

To take his mind off of things, I once again cupped his face and kissed him deeply. He put all of his weight on one elbow as he pushed my college shirt up with his free hand. He cupped my breast softly. Finally, the reluctance in his face was gone, and pleasure had replaced it.

As soon as he took my nipple into his mouth, I gasped and opened my legs wider. Still, with his weight on one arm, he started to play with my pussy as he kneaded my nipple softly. His large fingers in my pussy were orgasmic. His thumb rubbing my clitoris was euphoric.

"Fuck me," I begged. "Fuck me please."

He leaned forward, nibbling on my neck while pulling his dick out of his basketball shorts. He pressed his large head against my opening. He cupped my butt cheeks as he slowly pressed his way inside me.

"Sssss," I hissed as I felt his huge erection slide into my slippery walls.

He started to move, slowly and steady. He was loving and careful.

"Don't fuck me like I'm dying, Coop. Fuck me like you used to."

His gaze turned intense, and then he flipped me over. He brought me up on my knees and forced my face down and ass up. He arched my back perfectly. Then I felt him grab my waist and dig into me.

"Ahhhh," I moaned with a smile. "Yes, Coop."

It was rough and nasty just like I wanted it, just like I needed it. He let go of one side of my waist, reached around, and played with my clitoris. I instantly started shaking and panting as I felt the oncoming of my orgasm.

I came, finally feeling as if I could truly be at peace with dying. And that time death was barreling towards me. I could feel it. I had barely lived, but I was thankful that I had been able to experience much more than many had been lucky to. I had children who loved me unconditionally and a mother who adored me. I had had a stepfather that loved me better than any biological father could. I was able to die with my family knowing that I loved them. I was able to die with no regrets. I had had time to say my piece. I had been in love. I knew how it felt to be loved. I had no questions for God. I was secure in knowing my part in His plan. I had served my purpose. My time on the earth was coming to an end.

I came, knowing that it would be my last time.

COOP

That night, Rakim came over to True's to meet his godson and his mother for the first time.

"Yo', look at lil' homie." Rakim smiled down at Keyes as he slept in his crib.

Keyes was a good baby. He almost slept as much as his mother did. Sometimes, I wondered if he felt her exhaustion since infants had such a strong connection to their mothers.

"He's a handsome lil' nigga. Too bad he don't look shit like you," Rakim joked.

I laughed. "Whatever. Yes, he does."

After a month, Keyes was turning into me right before my eyes. Since I had been bounced from house to house back then, I had only seen two pictures of myself as a baby. As the weeks went by, my lil' homie was turning into his dear ol' dad.

"He definitely got your color, though," Rakim joked as he looked down on Keyes with a shake of his head. "Black ass..."

I smiled. "Stop hating. Black is in."

"He got a head full of hair, too."

"Don't he?" I smiled down and rubbed my son's full head of curly locs. "C'mon," I said, tapping Rakim on his side. "Let me take you to go meet True."

As Rakim and I left the nursery, I could hear Joy laughing and giggling in her mother's room, so I knew this was one of the rare moments that True was awake. As the weeks passed by, she slept more and more. Remi had explained to me that extensive sleep came with the onset of her demise. I was happy that she had felt up to us having sex earlier that day. I had wanted to feel her at least one more time, but I didn't want to be so selfish as to ask her for something like that. I was happy that she had asked me, though. She had wanted it to be raunchy, and I had given her that only for a while. Watching her for the past few weeks, I knew she didn't have much more time. Therefore, I knew that that sexual experience was our last one ever. So, I eventually slowed it down and turned her over so we could look in each other's eyes. I told her I loved her over and over again.

Before walking into her bedroom, I tapped on the door. She had already been expecting Rakim, so she was dressed.

"Come in."

I pushed the door open, and Rakim followed me inside. My smile was big as I introduced them. "True, this is Rakim. Rakim, this is True." I was finally introducing the two out of the three most important people in my world to each other.

True smiled as Rakim bent down and hugged her after she sat up in bed.

"Nice to meet you," he told her.

"No, it's nice to meet *you*," True insisted. "The infamous Rakim..."

"Nah, you're the infamous one," he told her. "Glad to finally meet you."

"Hi! I'm Joy!" Joy cut in with her high-pitched, squeaky voice.

Rakim smiled and bent down to shake her hand. "Nice to meet you, beautiful."

For the next thirty minutes, we sat and made small talk. Rakim and I mostly did the talking because True's shortness of breath made it hard for her to speak at times. Rakim and I told True of our old hood stories from back in the day until she became too tired to keep her eyes open. Joy had fallen asleep for her afternoon nap next to her mother, so once True fell asleep in mid-conversation, I quietly escorted Rakim out.

Once out on the porch, he took a deep breath of the brisk, biting February air. He stared blankly at nothing. I knew that look. Many people had had it after visiting True. You always heard about what cancer can do to the body, but seeing it firsthand was mind-blowing and earth-shattering.

"Man, dawg..." Rakim said as he shook his head and stuffed his hands into his pocket.

"I know," I replied without him even saying.

"She doesn't even look like the pictures you showed me, anymore."

"I know."

"Cancer is a bitch."

When he sniffed, I looked down at him. I would be surprised at seeing such a gangsta like my nigga, Rakim, brought to tears. Yet, I had been brought to those same tears many times after leaving out of that room, so I felt my homie's pain.

Just then, a car pulled into the driveway. I didn't recognize it, so I focused on the driver's door as it opened. I was surprised to see Remi climb out.

As Rakim wiped his tears away, he asked, "Damn, who is that?"

I chuckled. "Stand down. That's one of True's Hospice nurses."

Rakim's eyes squinted as they took in the sight of Remi walking towards us in her traditional scrubs. Today, she was wearing blue scrubs with pink flowers all over them. She made scrubs look like they should be worn on a runway.

"Damn, she fine," Rakim groaned.

"Yeah, she is."

His voice was full of lust as he damn near moaned, "And she thicker than a motherfucker too."

"That she is," I agreed as she looked at me and waved with a smile.

"Ooooh weee," Rakim sang under his breath.

He made more obscene sounds as Remi approached, switching without trying to, all that ass being clearly seen from the front.

"Hey, Coop." She reached up and gave me a long embrace. Outside of being True's nurse, she had gotten acquainted on a personal level with True and me over the last four weeks. Outside of being beautiful and wonderfully-built, she was truly a sweet girl and her heart was surprisingly as beautiful as the outside.

"What's up, girl? What you doin' here?" I asked her as she released me.

"The second-shift nurse had to take off, so I offered to do some overtime."

"Awwww," I taunted her. "You missed us that much."

She grinned. "Of course, I did."

Staring at the temp tags on the BMW she had climbed out of, I asked, "You finally got a new ride?"

She stared back at it as well with a smile. "Yeeeah."

"Good shit." I nodded.

She prepared herself to go into the house, asking, "How is she doing today?"

I shrugged nonchalantly, but the moment I was stroking that pussy ran through my mind. Luckily, I had put on jeans, so the sudden erection wasn't showing. "She's having a good day."

Remi smiled wide. "Good." She obviously felt Rakim's eyes on her and blushed. Then she quickly made her exit. "Let me go start these sixteen hours."

"I'll be inside soon."

Rakim, finally able to look at her ass, watched it with bulging eyes as Remi disappeared into the house.

Once she closed the door behind her, he excitedly hit me in the side. "Maaan, hook me up."

I sucked my teeth hard and long. "Nigga, please. You know you only like ugly bitches; the ones whose mamas' got tickets for littering when they dropped those ugly hoes off at school."

Rakim glared. "Fuck you, dawg."

I laughed, happy to have something to laugh at even if it was Rakim. "Bitches so ugly that when they take their kids to the zoo, the security guard thank the kids for bringing them back."

REMI

I looked at the phone, wondering what I should do. I had heard from Banks since he had suspiciously called me a month ago, but it was random and friendly. I honestly had been trying to tell myself not to think too deep into it because he was married and, after ten years, he had married a woman other than me.

"What are you going to do?" True asked. From her bed, she looked at me with wide eyes as Coop sat beside her, looking at me with questionable ones.

Over the last few weeks, the three of us had really gotten to know one another, so they were aware of everything Banks and I had gone through.

"Hellooo?" True pressed me.

I looked at Banks' text message, which asked me could he bring me some lunch, and shrugged. "I don't know."

"Do you want to see him?" Coop asked me.

I shrugged again, whining, "I don't know."

"Maybe he realized he made a mistake," Coop said.

"And?" I shot back with a frown. "He's *married* now. I'd be damned if I go from his main woman to his side bitch."

Coop smiled at me and nodded. "Good girl."

"That's right," True cheered me on. "You deserve better than that... But get the free food."

Coop and I started cracking up.

"Let him see you winning," True added. "Ask him to bring me some too."

"What you want?" I asked her.

For her, I would do anything. I had never felt so close to a patient before. I was sure it was because we were closer in age and had more in common. It was definitely because witnessing her approach death made me so much more appreciative of what I had and care less about what I didn't. After meeting True, I dared not have the nerve to complain about simple things like a man or my weight. Looking at her, those things seemed so trivial now. In a sense, she had fixed me.

"I want Italian Fiesta pizza with sausage, pepperoni, onions and green peppers." As she rattled off her order, she closed her eyes as if she was savoring the taste already. She had been ordering all of her favorite foods, but once it got to her, she could only take two or three bites before she couldn't eat anymore.

"Bet." I went ahead and sent Banks a text with the order and True's address. As soon as I had pressed send, I felt the nervous bubble gut. I started to play with the new bob that I had gotten cut into my natural hair a few weeks ago with an attempt to start anew.

"You look fine, Remi," True insisted. Then she nudged, Coop. "Doesn't she look pretty?"

When Coop looked at me, I instantly looked away, giving my attention to my phone. True often brought my beauty up to Coop. I hated when she did that and wondered why she insisted on doing it. I already found Coop super attractive. Watching him love on True and Keyes only made him more irresistible. It was clear that he loved True, and I adored her. So, there was nothing to my attraction to him, except admiration. But when she often insisted that I ride along with him and constantly asked him if I was pretty, it made me uncomfortable.

"Yeah, she's gorgeous," Coop said, and the hairs on the back of my neck stood straight up.

Nervously, I stood and announced, "It's time for your meds. Let me go get them ready."

I walked out without looking at either of them. I hated that I got so flustered around Coop and hoped my feelings didn't show. I couldn't help my nervousness, though. He was the epitome of a good man. During the last month at True's, he had shared so many stories with her and me about how ruthless he was, but all I saw was a gentle giant.

~

True's eyes widened as my text notification sounded. I reluctantly pulled my phone out of the pocket of my scrubs.

"Is he out there?" True pushed.

I read Banks' text and nodded. "Yes."

"Okay, so go," True insisted.

Coop laughed and asked True, "You ain't sleepy?"

Again, Coop chuckled as True replied, "No, I'm hungry, so hurry up." I nervously toyed with my hair, and she insisted, "You look cute. Just put on some lip gloss."

"She ain't gotta put on no lip gloss for that nigga," Coop fussed.

True elbowed him in his side. But her small elbow probably felt like a dull needle in his large side. "Yes, she does. He needs to see what he's missing and what he'll never get again."

I dug into my pocket for my MAC lip gloss and applied it before I walked out.

"Talk loud so that I can hear!" I heard True order.

I laughed and shook my head as I approached the front door. I smoothed my clothes over before opening it. Banks stood on the opposite side. Over the aroma of sausage and pepperoni, I could smell his hypnotic cologne. I took a deep breath, taking in the physical sight of him after all this time. He was wearing a black leather blazer with a mink collar that exuded money and power. His tattoos crawled up his neck out of the fur. His butter skin had lost its tan in the winter months. He was once again pale. Yet, his once cocky frame had lost some weight. He was still draped in diamonds, however. He had clearly lost weight but not money. His tapered fade was now a curly fro.

He smiled and licked his full, pink lips as he looked down on me. "Hey, baby."

Instantly, I was like putty. It was as if all the pain from the last ten months had withered away. All I had needed was for him to smile at me like this and call me baby.

I blushed. "Hey."

I took the pizza from his hand, telling him, "Be right back."

I purposely switched hard as hell as I left the doorway and rushed the pizza into True's room. She was still sitting up in bed with wide eyes.

"What he say?!" she whispered harshly.

"Nothing yet," I rushed to say. "Be right back."

I hurried away. On my way towards the door, I grabbed my coat from the couch and slipped it on. Once at the door, I calmed down and walked out of it smoothly, closing it behind me.

On the porch, Banks watched me with a smile as I joined him. "You look great. Did you lose weight?"

I cringed at him mentioning my weight, but I forced a smile. "I did. You did too."

He shrugged. "But not on purpose."

"Then why?"

"Stress, man," he grunted, shaking his head.

I wanted to pry into that, but I told myself that it was no longer my concern. "*Sooo...* what's up?"

Looking at me, he actually appeared sincere as he said, "I wanted to see you."

"Why?"

He leaned against the banister with the same love that I had seen prior to him breaking my heart. "I miss you."

I was mute, not knowing what to say to that. I became even more speechless as he walked closer to me. "I owe you an apology."

I instantly wanted to stop him. I had finally made it off of this emotional rollercoaster. I had finally stopped crying and wondering why. I had finally been able to make it through the day without questioning how good of a woman I was. I didn't want to backtrack. "Banks, I—"

"Listen. Let me explain." He grabbed both of my hands. I bit my lip reluctantly and let him finish. "I owe you this and so much more. I'm sorry for hurting you, baby." I closed my eyes, relief bringing tears to my eyes. Sometimes, a simple apology, a simple acknowledgment of wrongdoing, can heal so many wounds. And as he continued, he was healing mine. "I was a fool to do you like that. I was stupid."

I tried to pull away, but he let go of my hands and cupped my face. He brought his close to mine and took my mouth with his. I melted as he kissed me, slipping his tongue into my mouth. I reached up and lay my hands on top of his, and that's when I felt the hard steel wrapped around his left ring finger. I was reminded that he was married, and that realization made me sick to my stomach. I was reminded that he'd had the baby with her that I so desperately had wanted to give birth to.

Just as I was about to pull away, his phone rang. He reluctantly stopped our kiss, but I was relieved. He reached into his coat pocket for his phone. He looked at it, and instant annoyance ran through him. I saw her name on his screen and a huge ball of regret formed in my throat.

"I gotta go," he told me as reluctance filled his eyes. "I'll call you, okay?"

I said nothing. I just stared at him, wondering why I was so weak for him and why had ten months passed of him completely ignoring my hurt just for him to show up and continue to treat me like I was second best. He bent down and kissed my cheek, and I still said nothing as he left the porch. I stared at him as he walked towards the Range Rover, paid for in cash that I had helped him get the money to pay for by taking bricks of cocaine over city limits so many times.

As he climbed in and drove away, I slid down and sat on the top step, my embarrassment leaking out of my eyes in tears.

16

COOP

"He pulled off?" True asked anxiously.

"Yeah, nosy," I taunted True as I discreetly peered out of the window.

"And she's still out there?" True pried.

I sucked my teeth. "Yeah."

"Then go check on her."

I left the window. "Why? Maybe she wants to be alone."

True's eyes narrowed at me. "Go check on her."

I laughed at how her tiny ass was trying to force me to do something.

"A'ight. Sheesh. Pipe down." But I was gon' do it to please her.

She smiled. "Thank you, baby."

I gritted discreetly as I walked out of her bedroom, grabbing my jacket off the back of her door on the way out. True was always forcing me to be around Remi when I was trying my best to keep a platonic distance between us. I couldn't deny her beauty, but I respected True. Yet, it was as if True was insisting more and more that I be around this woman and form a bond that I felt was unnecessary.

I opened the door and slid into the cold, bitter air. Remi was still sitting on the top step with her face in her hands.

"You want some company?"

In response, all I heard were her sniffles. I walked towards her and sat beside her on the top step. I put my arm around her, and she leaned into my chest.

"What he say?" I asked. I felt my chest rising. I wanted to protect her from these tears and him.

"He apologized," she mumbled.

"Then why are you crying?"

She sat up, wiping her tears. "Because I feel so stupid. His presence just reminded me that I'm not good enough."

I frowned at the thought. "How aren't you good enough?"

Her weeping eyes looked up at the sky. "He was with me for years and never married me. Then he gets with that bitch with a perfect body and marries her after not even a whole year. Now, he pops up here, kissing on me, but still goes home to her."

Goosebumps full of envy covered my arms when I heard that he had been kissing her, and I immediately felt guilty for even giving a fuck.

Remi grimaced as the events replayed in her mind. "I'm just some fat bitch he was ashamed of."

My head whipped toward her. "Fat? What?" I took her chin into my hands and lifted her eyes to mine. She stared into my eyes with tears pouring from hers. "You're dope."

She sucked her teeth and tried to shy away from me, but I held her chin tighter and made her look at me. I couldn't deny the tension between us as we stared into each other's eyes, but I respectfully pushed it away.

"Listen to me," I told her. "Seriously. You're dope as fuck. I think you're gorgeous. That nigga is stupid. I may have fallen for True's skinny ass, but I love a thick woman. And if that nigga don't, then he stupid. Fuck him."

We stared into one another's eyes for a few seconds longer. Her beauty shone through her tears, and it rattled me. I let her chin go as she told me, "Thank you."

"No need to thank me, Ma. That's real shit." I stood to leave. I could feel her watching me as if she wanted me to stay, but I couldn't. "I'm gonna go inside before True falls asleep on me. Don't stay out here too long and catch a cold."

She said nothing, but I could feel her eyes on me as I opened the door.

I walked back into the house feeling guilty for not being there for her. From what I had learned about Remi, she didn't deserve a punk like Banks. However, True didn't deserve for me to be lusting after another woman while she was facing death. And I was definitely lusting after Remi. It wasn't on purpose, though. No one could deny her beauty, not even True. And because Remi was so down to earth and sweet, she was truly hard to resist. But I managed to because my love for True outweighed any attraction to another woman.

Always would.

True was still sitting up with wide eyes when I walked back into her bedroom. The pizza box was on the nightstand. As expected, she had only eaten one slice. Her appetite was decreasing as the days passed. A part of me was hoping for a miracle, but the more I was forced to watch her expire, I was coming to the harsh realization that this particular miracle wouldn't occur.

"What happened?" True pressed.

I closed her bedroom door behind me. Then I climbed into bed with her. First, I ensured that the baby monitor was on. Then I spooned with True and turned on her TV with the remote that lay in my spot.

"She's crying." True immediately tried to spring up, but I held her down. "Mind your own business."

True fussed, "Go back out there. She shouldn't be out there by herself."

"Why are you so worried about her?" I asked.

"Because she's in pain, and I know how that feels."

I kissed the top of True's head. "Well, I'm here to comfort *your* pain because I'm in love with you. I'm not here for Remi."

She rolled over and looked me in the eyes. "Do you really think you're in love with me?"

First, I looked strangely at her question. Then I nodded confidently. "Yes."

For once, I didn't feel weak for admitting that. I was proud to feel this way about her. When first learning about her condition, I was pissed that she had allowed me to fall for her. But, now, I felt honored to be the man here for her at this moment. God had obliviously chosen me for this reason. For what, I was still learning.

Though I was sure, True wasn't. "No, you're not."

"How are you going to tell me?" I questioned.

"Because... We didn't know each other well enough or long enough for you to *truly* fall in love with me. I'm sure you love me, but loving somebody and being *in love* are two separate things. You wouldn't know the difference because you've rarely or have never done either."

She was right. I had never loved a woman. I only knew that how I felt about True was different than anything I'd ever experienced. She had been married before, she had been in love before, and since everything else she'd told me had been right so far, I believed she knew the difference.

I shrugged. "Maybe you're right. But I know I will never love any other woman the way I love you. You were the first, and you'll be my last."

True held a humorous smirk. "Just like you opened up to me, you will open up again to the right person."

I grunted. Loving True had been the best and worst thing that had ever happened to me. It was a fairy tale that would end in a nightmare. No way was I ever going to fall for another woman.

I sucked my teeth, grunting more. "The next woman I fall in love with, I'ma tase her ass."

True started cracking up. "You're gonna tase her?" she repeated.

I shrugged. "Yeah, she's getting tased."

True looked scared to ask, "Why?"

"So, we can both be shocked."

The way True started to convulse with laughter made me laugh heartedly at my own joke. Even though I had been teasing with her, I was still serious as a motherfucker. This love shit had hurt too bad. I wasn't giving it to anyone else but my son.

"Seriously, though," True insisted. "There will be somebody that you'll have a stronger connection with than we have. This is preparing you for that. I believe that."

I started to get frustrated and feel that usual ball of fear in my stomach when she talked about life after she was gone. "Why are you telling me this?"

She held me tighter around the waist as she stared into my eyes. "Because I want you to find someone you can truly fall in love with who'll raise my son how I would."

My face became stern as I stared at the TV behind her while I tried to ignore that ball of regret and terror my stomach. But she tugged on my shirt to get my attention. I reluctantly looked her in the eyes as she ordered, "Promise me you'll do that. Give my baby a good mother."

My lips pressed firmly together, and my nostrils flared with frustration, having to even think about this.

True knew it. She saw my frustration, so she lay her lips on top of mine, saying, "Promise me."

Tears welled in my eyes as I kissed her back. "I promise."

ANGEL

"Does that feel good?"

My eyes rolled to the back of my head as Russell's thumb massaged the arch of my foot. I lay back on his couch barefoot, dressed in one of his shirts since he had convinced me to stay the night. My head lay back on his couch as I moaned, "Mmmm, yes, it does."

"And how is your drink?" he asked just after I took a sip of the Jack Daniels and Coke. I smiled. He was so fucking attentive that it almost seemed planned.

I briefly closed my eyes as I enjoyed the burn as it slid down my throat. When I opened them, Russell was gazing at the way I was enjoying the intoxication.

I smiled. "It's perfect."

Every day, I thanked God for sending me Russell. He had come just in the nick of time. I didn't know how I would have ever survived watching my daughter die had I not had someone to lean on, especially someone as strong as Russell. He had been the ideal man as he stuck by my side while I went through so many bipolar moments. I was an emotional wreck on an emotional rollercoaster. Most of the time, I neglected him completely because I wanted to spend every moment that True had left, with her. At times, I would take my frustrations out on him without even realizing it. Most of the times, when he was able to pry me away from True's bedside, I was in tears.

Every time we ended a phone call, I felt like that would be the last time I would talk to him. Every time we left one another's presence, I just knew it would be the last time we saw each other. Russell was attractive, and he was a hustla with lots of swag. Any twenty to thirty-something teeny bopper with the perfect body would crawl to him on his knees as soon as he snapped his fingers. He didn't need me and my issues. Yet, every time I assumed we were over, he would call again. He was in my presence again, caring for me and holding me down without me even asking.

So, that night, being one of the rare moments we had been able to spend time together, I wanted to be a desirable woman instead of the mourning mother I had been since we reunited.

As he sat massaging my foot with his eyes on the basketball game, I slid it out of his hands. He looked at me questionably. His interest piqued when he saw the lustful smile on my face. I crawled towards him, and when I straddled him, his eyes bulged.

I hadn't been in a sexual mood since True had been under Hospice. But with the help of the Jack Daniels, I was able to temporarily leave my horrible reality and slip into a happy, loving space with Russell.

Our mouths met sweetly with caring pecks and thoughtful kisses. As our tongues started to play, my fingertips roamed through his beard that smelled of argan oil.

His hands ran up my thighs and onto my waist. I tingled all over, feeling goose bumps spread all over my body. I felt the unfamiliar feeling of my pussy pulse with wanting.

We began to kiss deeper. One of my hands wandered down between his legs, feeling him stiffen inside his pajama pants. Then I began to nibble on his ear. A deep, masculine moan left his lips, which gave me motivation.

I climbed off of his lap, sliding down on my knees between his legs. He licked his lips, and I saw anxiousness in his eyes as I clawed at the waistband of his pants. He lifted his hips to help me pull them down to his ankles. His beautiful piece of vein-covered steel pointed directly toward me. I took it into my mouth slowly, and he sucked in a sharp breath. I sucked him in deep. I got him sloppy wet with my tongue.

He became very theatrical as I took him down my throat. I had never heard a man give such throaty praises.

"Fuck. Baby, yes. Your mouth feels so good."

I moaned as I sucked, and he hissed, "Ssss."

I couldn't take anymore. I wanted him. I pulled him from my throat and climbed on top of him.

He watched my anxiousness with a smile on his face. "You want this dick, huh?"

I nodded eagerly.

His eyes bore into mine with pure sexual desire glossing his orbs. In a deep voice, he asked, "You need me to fuck you, baby?"

I could have cum simply from his words.

He lifted his lower body, pushing his steeliness against my wet lips. "Answer me."

"Yes," I whispered. "*God*, yes..."

I rose on my tiptoes, and he brought the head of his dick up to my sopping wet opening. He pushed his girth into me. I sucked in a breath as he entered me slowly until he was buried all the way up to my cervix. I squirmed a bit from being spread beyond my limit. It filled me completely. Now that he was totally immersed in me, he began to thrust while stripping me of the DePaul Demons shirt.

We kissed passionately as our hands roamed over each other's bodies. His hands lingered over my breasts, and mine lingered over his shoulders and beard.

"Damn, you're so wet for me, baby." We rocked in a steady rhythm. As we rocked, he watched me so intently, and groaned, telling me, "You look beautiful."

He then took control, standing up. I wrapped my arms tightly around his neck as he laid me down on the couch. He took both of my feet in one hand and brought them together. Then he turned me to the side and pushed his way back inside of me. The curve of his dick was now rubbing against my front walls, causing an incredible sensation.

I began to moan as theatrical as he had earlier. "Shit!"

He increased the pace of his thrusting, using my hip and sides as leverage. My breathing started to come in gasps in concert with his thrusts. He was panting for air. I could feel him pulsating inside of me. He was hurtling towards the edge.

He started thrusting at an unhurried pace, slow and long. Soon, we were both moaning and grunting in unison. He kept speeding up and slowing down, as if he was slowing down to keep from cumming, making sure that it lasts.

My body started to thrash and whimper under him. I could feel my skin glowing with perspiration. He was dripping with sweat. My moaning was drowning out his grunts by now. I was close too. Soon, I tensed up. Then I yelped out sharply before burying my face in one of the couch pillows.

But he yanked it out of my hands. "Unt uh. Let me hear you cum, baby."

His dominance caused my oncoming orgasm to explode. "Oh! Shiiiiiit!"

My pussy went into spasms around his dick. At the sight of my quivering body and the feeling of the wet heat of my sex, he couldn't hold on much longer. He collapsed on top of me as he came hard, groaning into my neck. His dick twitched and pulsated inside of me.

I breathed in his scent as we shared our climax. I felt electric, long after our breaths slowed down.

He fell to the side, snaked an arm around, me and brought me as close to him as I could be. I turned my head towards him, and we kissed long and passionately. We lay spooning, reveling in the feel of each other's flesh and sweat.

I pulled away from his kiss and wrapped my arm and leg around him. "Hold me please," I begged.

I needed to feel his love.

17

REMI

After Banks left that night, I cried for thirty minutes straight. By the time my anger toward myself had subsided, and I had moped back into the house, True's door was closed. I figured I wouldn't bother her and Coop. Besides, I wasn't hungry anymore anyway. I went into the guest bedroom and thought about Banks between the times I had to administer care to True.

Like a fool, I checked my phone all night for a text or call from Banks. I wasn't sure what I expected because nothing would have made me feel better. He could have sent me text messages with a thousand sweet nothings or called me and professed his love. Either way, it wouldn't have made me feel like anything other than a second choice or a plan B and not good enough.

Every time I eased into True's room and saw Coop holding her, I got emotional. I wanted that, a man who would love me so much that he would never leave my side.

I had felt the tension between Coop and me on the porch that night. There was no denying our attraction to one another. But there was also no denying his love for True and my respect for her. And the more he ignored his attraction to me, the more I admired him. He was a man's man, and True was so lucky to have him. And every time

I felt that twinge of jealousy, every time I felt like True was lucky even though she was dying, I felt like a fool.

During the night, Keyes would cry, and as usual, Coop's figure would lumber sleepily past the bedroom where I slept. I admired his dedication to Keyes and True as well as the attention he gave Joy and Angel. I wondered if that was the same dedication Banks gave Vanessa and their child. And, all night, I wondered why he'd never felt that way toward me. I didn't want Coop, but I damn sure wanted a man just like him.

My last time going into True's room before my shift ended, I found her and Coop wide awake. Coop looked as if he had just finished getting dressed.

"I'm going to check on the rec center. Then I'll be right back," he told True.

"Good morning," I greeted them.

Coop only looked at me briefly and replied, "Morning."

True smiled up at me as she lay in bed. I felt a pang of regret looking at her. I could see that her breathing was more abnormal than the night before. Her eyes were sunken in deeply. Her cheeks had caved in too. She was looking more and more like a skeleton each day.

"Good...morning...Remi," she replied through gasps of breath. She turned her attention to Coop while I got her meds ready. "Is...the rec center...ready?"

It obviously pained Coop to watch her struggle to breathe. "Not quite ready. And if I want it to be ready in two weeks for the opening, then I need to go up there and show my face to put some fire under those contractors' asses."

"My mother...should...be here any minute," she told Coop as he walked towards the bed.

"Cool." He bent over and kissed her forehead. "Let me go check on Keyes."

"It sounded like he and Joy were still asleep when I walked by their rooms," I offered.

Before anyone could reply, we heard Angel rushing into the house. "I'm here!"

True giggled. "She sounds guilty as..." She gasped for air yet again. "...hell."

Coop and I laughed as he left the room.

True took a deep breath before saying, "I know she got some dick last night."

I giggled again. "If she did, that's good for her."

She chuckled and ended up coughing a few times before catching her breath. "You're damn right. Have you seen Russell?"

I gave her a side eye. "Hell yeah, I've seen him with his fine ass."

Just then, Angel popped her head into the room, looking like she was about to take the walk of shame. She had on the same jogging suit she'd worn the night before, and her usually perfect hair was all over her head.

"Hey, boos!" she greeted. "I'm going to get breakfast started for Joy." With that announcement, she rushed away.

"Yeah, she definitely got cracked last night," I mumbled.

True started cracking up, causing her to cough terribly due to shortness of breath.

Regretfully, I told her, "It's time for you to be on oxygen, True."

"I know." She looked up at me. Her tiny hand reached for mine. Holding it, I felt nothing but skin and bones. "Will you go to the rec center with Coop?" She instantly saw the reluctance in my face and continued, "I know you just got off...and you're probably tired, but I really...want to see how it looks. Coop...doesn't know how to take pictures and videos to show...me everything."

I didn't want to go. For the life of me, I couldn't understand why True kept putting Coop and me in the same space. There was nothing between Coop and me, except an attraction that neither one of us would ever disrespect True by acting on. But, because of that, I really didn't want to be around Coop more than I had to be.

But she begged, "Please?" as she smiled up into my eyes.

I couldn't say "no" to her, so I sucked my teeth. "Fine."

~

"Wow, this is really nice." As I stared up at the building, Coop met me at the curb. I had trailed him so that I could go home after the tour.

"It's dope, right?" he asked with a smile.

I was impressed. The outside of the building was landscaped with beautiful greenery. The front of the building was completely made up of tinted glass. A bike rack lined the entryway. It was modern, clean, and a great addition to the Chatham neighborhood.

I smiled up at him as he stood next to me. "It's *really* dope."

"C'mon." As he led me up the entryway, he explained, "It's not fully finished yet, but you'll be able to see its potential."

As Coop pushed open the big glass doors, I was overwhelmed. For a street hustla, he had truly done his thing and had done good for the community.

I followed him with eyes full of admiration as he gave me the tour. There was an Olympic-size swimming pool, fully equipped gym, basketball court, game room, a hall available for party rental, a kitchen-cafeteria area, and classrooms for training and educational programs. Behind the rec center was a football field and bleachers. It reminded me of the recreational center on the campus of my college. For it to be in the middle of the hood was breathtaking.

Along the tour, I had been taking pictures and recording videos of everything and sending them to True's cell.

At the football field, Coop sat on the bleachers with such a look of pride. I had the same pride in my eyes for him as I stared down on him. "This is really nice, Coop."

It was a state-of-the-art facility that would provide boys under the age of eighteen with a productive and safe recreational environment. It would also stay open until midnight to keep teens entertained in a secure atmosphere.

"Thanks. I got a couple of homeboys who know a few NFL and NBA players who are willing to do camps in the summer. I've also got the hookup with a few music artists and entrepreneurs who're gonna slide by and give speeches and lend their support."

"That's dope," I gushed.

"Thanks." He smiled proudly.

"Seriously," I insisted. "Most hustlas put their money into clubs or car lots. But this will help so many young boys in this community."

He exhaled deeply. "It's all because of True, so I can't front. She talked me into being a better person, straight up. Now, everything she told me makes sense, and I just want to make her proud, ya know?"

I only nodded, because watching this man's admiration for True left me amazed. The thought had left him speechless too. He stared out onto the field with a blank expression, but his eyes were saying so much.

"You will most definitely save so many lives," I finally said.

"That's what I'm hoping for. When I was a shorty, I would've loved to have had a place like this to escape to." With a deep breath, he continued to admire the field. "Back then, all I wanted was for somebody to give a fuck about me and teach me something I could use to help me survive. I wanted a place where I could eat decent food and enough of it so I wouldn't have to steal." My heart went out to him as he went on. "There's no telling how I would have turned out if I'd had just a little help."

"I don't think you turned out bad at all."

When Coop looked up at me, I felt that usual nervous tension instantly appear between us. I anxiously stuffed my hands into the pockets of my leather blazer and tore my eyes away from his magnetic orbs.

"Well..." I sighed. "I should get out of here so I can get some sleep."

"Yeah, I need to go in here and curse these motherfuckers out anyway."

I chuckled. "Cool. See you tonight."

I turned, to quickly walk away. I shook my head at the tension between us. Even though there was nothing physically to feel bad for, I still felt so guilty for even being attracted to him.

Just then, I felt my phone vibrate in my pocket. I reached inside and pulled the phone out, expecting to see responses from True, but instead, it was a text from Banks, which stopped me dead in my tracks.

"You good?"

I jumped out of my skin, not realizing Coop was behind me.

"Yeah, I'm good," I rushed to assure him.

"A'ight. Be careful." He strolled through the side entrance of the rec center.

I unlocked my phone with shaky hands and read Banks' text message: *Let's have breakfast together.*

"Arrrghhh!"

I hoped Banks was cumming. No sooner than he had stuck his dick in me, I felt stupid.

He had come over with takeout from Chicago Chicken and Waffles. Funny how he'd always had comments about my weight, but he was constantly feeding my fat ass. I ate quietly as he talked about everything that had been going on in his life since we'd last spoken, everything, except Brandi and the baby.

He was still manipulative and keeping the full truth from me. I sat there eating my emotions and wondering why I couldn't be blessed with a love like True and Coop's, but I reminded myself to be grateful for a life that True wouldn't have much longer. I tried to hype myself up to think that there must be some love in Banks' heart for me that kept him coming back. So, when he hugged and kissed me goodbye, I kissed him back hungrily, needing him to want me, love me, and need me.

Plus, I wanted to get that bitch, Brandi, back. I wanted to fuck her man like she had fucked mine.

But as soon as he stripped me from my clothes and thrust inside of me as I bent over the couch, I became ashamed. Most likely, after laying up with his woman all night, he'd left that morning as soon as his exit time was reasonable to his wife so that she wouldn't suspect him of being with another woman. He still wasn't shit. He hadn't changed. He was still a dog. And I was rewarding him with *me*? Still? I was still giving him my love and my body? Why?

"Damn, this pussy is making me cuuuuum. Fuuuuck," he growled as he pushed off of me.

I sat back on the couch as he hunched over, holding his dick as he ejaculated into the condom. He had on a condom and had *still* pulled out. He had been fucking that bitch for only a year, and it was okay that *she* got his last name and his baby. But he'd be damned if I got either.

I shook my head as I went to redress quickly, covering my body shamefully. I couldn't even look him in the eyes as he plopped down on the couch out of breath.

"I... Um... I have some errands to run," I lied smoothly. "I need to take a shower. You can let yourself out."

I turned just as misunderstanding showered over his expression. "Oh... Okay," he said slowly.

I couldn't look at him as I left the couch, but I could feel his questionable eyes on me. With my head down, I shuffled into my room and closed the door. I then hurried into the master bathroom and closed that door too. I ran the shower so that he wouldn't hear me sobbing and prayed that he would leave without question.

A man who truly loved me would have kicked down that door to be with me, to question my mood. He would be able to feel my sadness.

Yet, over my tears, I soon heard my front door close shut.

COOP

♫*Came through drippin' (drip drip)*
Came through drippin' (drip drip)
Came through drippin' (drip drip)
Diamonds on my wrist, they drippin' (ice)
Give me little something to remember (Cardi!)
Tryna make love in a Sprinter (yeah)
Quick to drop a nigga like Kemba (go)
Lookin' like a right swipe on Tinder (woo)
Shit on these hoes (shit)
Light up my wrist on these hoes (wrist)
Now I look down on these bitches (down)
I feel like I'm on stilts on these hoes (woo)♫

"Naaah! Unt uh," I snapped at Remi playfully. "You said you didn't have any more hearts! You reneged!"

Her mouth dropped as she danced to the beat of Cardi B in her seat at the foot of True's bed. "Who played a heart?"

Remi looked at her partner, Angel, and Angel shrugged with an amusing smirk.

True's head tilted to the side. Her smirk was hard to take seriously, with the oxygen tubes coming from her nostrils and wrapping around her head. "I led with a heart. Stop playing, ya'll."

"When?" Remi asked.

I overturned the books that True and I had won in Spades and found the heart. "Right here! True played the ace of hearts. Angel and I dropped hearts, and you played a spade," I told Remi.

"Mmm humph..." True smirked.

With a guilty expression, Remi laughed. "Okay, okay. My bad."

"Nah! Unt uh, I wanna trade partners," Angel expressed, and we all laughed. "True, you know you always my partner. You traded me in for Coop."

True simply shrugged with a smile as she stared at her hand, squinting. My heart filled with remorse every time she fought to simply see or speak clearly. It was another sign that she was passing, and each sign broke my heart. True was a trooper, though. She was a soldier. She never complained. There was no fear in her eyes. The only time I saw sadness was when she looked at her children. She didn't even look at me and her mother with regret. In her eyes, her passing would be relief to her mother and me. She wanted us to finally continue on with our lives without having to worry about her.

That night, she wanted to have a party. So, we were playing Spades and listening to some music. We had promised that we wouldn't say a word to the agency if Remi had a drink. Remi accepted that with no problem. As soon as she had walked in for her shift that night, it looked like she needed it. And, ever since, Remi had been throwing back shots. She and I were drinking some 1738 together, which wasn't Angel's thing. She had some Jack.

Just then, True's phone started to ring. She paused from playing her hand and picked it up. Visibly agitated, she ignored the call and tossed her phone on the bed.

"Who was that?" Angel asked.

True sneered. "Who else? Jameel."

Angel groaned.

"Mama, please don't let him get custody of my baby."

Angel shook her head and looked at True as if she were speaking another language. She insisted, "I would never allow that to happen."

"He hates me and will fill my baby with so many evil lies about me." True's voice was filled with sadness as she finally played her hand.

I leaned over and kissed her forehead. "I'll kill that nigga before he takes Joy anywhere." True had told me how verbally abusive Jameel had been since she'd been diagnosed. Luckily for him, Jameel was so fucking insensitive that he hadn't shown his face since she'd gone into Hospice care. If he had, that motherfucker would be dead right now. I wanted to pull him apart with my bare hands. Fuck a gun.

We played a few more games before True got tired and we called it a night. I turned off the radio while Angel went to check on the kids. Remi administered True's meds before she was fast asleep.

In the kitchen, I found some leftovers. After a fifth of 1738, a nigga was ready for some food. There was still Italian Fiesta pizza from the night before, so I was on that.

I was standing at the microwave waiting for the slices to finish warming up when Remi stumbled into the kitchen. She was doing a horrible job of carrying a heavy load of red cups, plates, and other garbage. I drunkenly went to help her and only made matters worse. As I attempted to take some things from her, I fumbled, and everything fell to the floor.

"Shit," I cursed softly.

We both bent down to pick it all up, laughing at our clumsiness.

"Oh God, we are drunk as shit," Remi whispered with a laugh.

We squatted, trying to pick things up, but just kept dropping stuff everywhere. We just sat there laughing, hands on each other's knee for support. My hand slid up her thigh a bit closer, just for support, but she stopped laughing and looked at it. A bolt of electricity struck between us as her eyes came up to meet mine. It was the sort of electric, tightrope feeling that you get between you and another person. It felt like looking over the hill of a rollercoaster you're about to go down when the rollercoaster does the little fake-out stop at the top. It was teasing and even a bit scary, but the ride was laid out in front of me, and I was *riiight* about to go over the hill.

The electricity was pulling us towards each other despite our reluctance.

Then... the microwave started to wail, causing us both to jump to our feet.

I sighed deeply and broke the eye contact as I stood up. "Why don't you go sleep off that liquor before you have to do some real work? I got this."

She laughed nervously as she stood as well. She nervously ran her hands over her scrub pants. "You're right. Thanks."

"Good night, Remi."

She turned bashfully and disappeared down the hall after sweetly saying, "Good night."

18

ANGEL

Two weeks later, the party was over. Life had completely left True's home. All I felt was death surrounding us. Her end was near. She mostly slept. Whenever she was awake, she experienced delusions. Her weakness had become profound, and she was having trouble even moving around in bed. She had less and less interest in eating. She had trouble swallowing her medication. She was often confused about time, places, and people. Her legs, arms, and face often twitched randomly with involuntary muscle spasms. She was quickly losing her senses. Her vision was so blurry that many times, she could not see at all. When she would speak, often, it was slurred.

That tumor had squeezed nearly all functionality from my daughter's brain, and I felt helpless. I was her mother. I was supposed to be able to help her and protect her from the boogeyman and monsters. But I could *not* fight this monster off of her.

Nobody could.

I sat in a chair next to her bed, rubbing what little hair she had left as she stared at the TV.

She started to struggle, trying to speak.

"What's wrong, honey?" I asked.

"Where...are the...kids?" she struggled. "I want to...see...them."

Behind her back, I cringed. Joy couldn't see her like this. We had been keeping her out of the room for the last few days, only allowing her to see her mommy whenever True was sleeping. Anything else was too hard to explain.

"Coop took them to the park."

Finally, it was March, and there had been a break in the weather. Spring was coming. The sun was finally out and shining. It was still only about fifty degrees, but Coop had bundled the kids up in jackets and hats so they could finally enjoy some fresh air and sunshine.

I couldn't tell whether True was sighing with relief or if she was struggling to breathe. "Remi went with them, right?"

"Yes." Remi was a sweetheart. She had grown so attached to our family that she had been offering to do double shifts. I believed she wanted to be sure to be here during True's transitioning.

True nodded. "Good."

Then I shook my head in bewilderment. "What's your obsession with that girl?"

True smiled. "Nothing."

I continued to watch her oddly as she reached under her pillow. She pulled out an envelope and handed it to me. "Here."

"What's this?"

"It's a letter, but I don't want you to open it until a week after I'm gone. Promise me."

I looked at the envelope in sheer confusion. "What? True, what are—"

"Ma, just promise me."

I sighed, shaking my head. I slipped the envelope on the dresser behind me as I nodded my head. "I promise."

I yearned to know what was inside that letter. However, everything that True wanted was the law. I would never defy her, so I obeyed her wishes.

As I looked at her strangely, True placed a hand on one of mine. "And, Ma?"

"Yes, baby?"

She struggled to speak. "I don't...want...an open cask—"

I instantly cut her off. "True..."

But she stopped me by squeezing my hand with the little strength she had. "Mama, please? We have to...talk about this." Tears burned my eyes. My thin lips pressed tightly together as I allowed her to go on. "Don't have...an ...open casket. I want people to remember me how...I used to look, not...like...this."

A tear slid down my face as I nodded. "Okay."

"And make sure it's..." She coughed and forced out, "...a party. No sad songs. No crying. Just...happy memories of me with...joyous music. Okay?"

Sadly, I complied, "Okay."

"Just dancing and singing..." She reached up and began to wipe my tears away, which only made me cry even more because her hands felt so cold.

REMI

Coop had been in a solemn mood all day. For the past two weeks, he had been managing to keep a smile on his face around True, her mom, and the kids. But today, it was as if he just couldn't do it anymore. From the moment he woke up, he had been wearing his emotions on his sleeve. And with a big man like him moping angrily around the house, everyone felt it.

It had been so hard for him to focus on his rec center's grand opening that was set to take place in two days on Friday. Rakim had had to step in and do a lot for him because Coop could hardly focus on anything except True.

Once at the park, he pretended to be happy as he played with Joy while I held Keyes, but I could tell his heart was heavy.

Beyond watching his sadness with so much empathy, I did enjoy my private time with Keyes. I was twenty-seven years old and childless. I wanted a baby so bad. But having lost the love of my life, I no longer saw that in my future. I didn't know when I would ever love again. It would take years possibly; probably when I was so old that I no longer wished to have kids.

"You ready?"

I looked up from Keyes' drooling smile and into Coop's ever-present sorrow. He looked ashamed to even be showing me his weakness. I gave him a weak smile so he would know it was okay.

Then I nodded. "Sure."

I gathered the baby bag and my purse and then followed Coop as he moped towards his car hand-in-hand with Joy.

I got Keyes into his car seat. He was now two months old. His features made him an exact replica of Coop. He was a gorgeous baby and already a very handsome boy.

As Coop buckled Joy into her car seat, I heard him grunting. I looked up and saw him struggling with the buckle. Keyes was in tight, so I shut the door and went around the car to assist Coop, who looked like he was ready to punch a hole in something.

Once on his side, I lay a hand on his shoulder, and he jumped. He spun around with such a threatening look in his eyes that I stepped back with concern. He instantly felt remorse. Suddenly, he broke down in sobs. I was taken aback. The way his tears were tumbling down told me he had been holding this breakdown in for quite some time. I wrapped my arms around him. He was so tall that he had to bend down to hug me back. I wrapped my arms around his neck and rocked him from side to side.

"This shit hurts," he cried.

Hearing such a huge man express his pain through tears instantly triggered mine. "I know."

"I'm not ready," he confessed. "I can't do this."

I continued to rock Coop gently and slowly as I told him, "No one can ever be ready. But you have to be strong for True. You can cry all you want after she's gone, but you can't scare her with your anger. You don't want to make her worry about you. Please stay strong until the end. You can do this."

At the moment, I was being a caring nurse, talking to my patient's loved one, but in such a short amount of time, I had also become Coop's friend. I had created a bond with this family that went beyond our professional relationship. True truly was not just a patient, and Coop wasn't just my patient's loved one. They were my support as well.

"Why *her*?" he cried into my shoulder. "Why does it have to be her? It's not fair."

"Cancer... Dying... None of it is fair," I answered as I rubbed his back, trying to soothe him.

"I thought she had more time," Coop sobbed.

"With cancer, we can't predict the exact time that a patient will go."

He cried into my shoulder, "I can't breathe watching her go," and my heart broke for him. "I can't breathe."

Once back at True's, Angel put Keyes to bed. She allowed Joy a few minutes to sit with her mother. But it was only brief because that was all the time True could handle with Joy's excessive, toddler energy. I took her to put her to bed while Coop crawled into bed with True and spooned her thin body.

When I returned to her bedroom to administer her meds, I expected her to be fast asleep, but Coop was the one who had finally fallen asleep. For the last few days, he had been restless and had been up with me during my third shift. We spent a lot of time talking about any and everything to get his mind off of True's transitioning.

As I stood by her bed, I noticed her looking up at me with a smile.

I matched hers, happy to see it. "How are you feeling?"

"Have you talked to Banks?"

I giggled at the stern look in her eyes. Neither she nor Coop felt like it was healthy that I talked to Banks. They had been so transparent with me that I had shared with them my drunken, failed suicide attempt and depression over the last year. However, they didn't know about me and Banks' sex session that had come with breakfast.

"That's not what I asked you. How are you feeling, True?" I pressed.

She smiled. "Have you talked to him or not?"

I folded my arms across my chest. "Why?"

"I don't want to talk about how I feel. *This* is what I want to talk about."

I shuttered from embarrassment. Giving in, I sat down in a chair close to her bed and answered, "No."

That wasn't a total lie. I hadn't talked to him since stupidly sleeping with him two weeks ago. He had been calling me randomly ever since, but I was too pissed at him and myself to answer. I had nothing to say to Banks. As far as I knew, he was still a married man with a newborn.

My fat ass didn't fit anywhere into that equation.

"Do you still want to be with him?" True asked.

"I think it's beyond that. It doesn't matter whether I want to be with him. Regardless of what I *want*, I don't *need* him."

"Are you scared to love again?" she pressed.

My eyebrows curled at her question. "Why?"

"Don't be," she simply said as her eyes fluttered shut and she drifted off to sleep.

I giggled. "Good night, True."

I went to stand, but suddenly, her arm darted out and grabbed my wrist.

I looked down at her strangely.

She looked up at me, saying, "Seriously, Remi, don't be afraid to love again."

19

REMI

"I'm not going," Coop refused. I had never seen him be so stern and cold when he talked to Angel.

Standing behind Coop, I looked at Angel, shaking my head. She had a hell of a fight ahead of her.

"Coop, you've been waiting for this for months. You *have* to go," Angel fussed.

"I don't have to do shit." Angel's eyebrow rose, and Coop immediately apologized for his obscene remark. "No offense."

With her finger pointed at him, she stepped into his space and pressed her acrylic nail into his chest. "Oh, *you're going*, because if my baby finds out that you didn't because of her, she's going to feel horrible."

Coop couldn't argue with the tears in Angel's eyes.

He simply nodded. "Okay."

It was admirable the way Angel had made this giant fold so quickly.

She then looked at me, and I instantly felt regret for what she was about to say next. "And you're going with him."

I gasped. "What? Why?"

"Because she'll want pictures and video footage of him. Besides, she would want you there."

Inwardly sighing, I replied, "Okay."

Angel nodded sharply, made an about-face, and darted out of the room towards True's bedroom.

"Will she even know if I am here or not?" Coop asked me with reluctant eyes as he waited for my answer.

Remorsefully, I told him, "Honestly, she won't. But her *spirit* will."

At this point, True was only responsive randomly. She had been having delusions. Her breaths were so sporadic that we wondered if the next one would come. She hadn't talked in an entire day. She had only responded to us in moans and groans, so we knew she could hear us.

"I don't wanna miss..." Coop struggled. "I don't wanna..."

I lay a hand on his shoulder to stop him. I knew what he wanted to say, but he found the courage to ask, "How long does she have? Keep it real with me."

I chewed on my bottom lip and forced myself to be a professional, instead of a friend. "A day... Maybe two...*Maybe*" He gritted and walked towards the kitchen counter, leaning on it for strength. I walked towards him cautiously. When he didn't push me away, I lay a soothing hand on his back. "She has enough time for you to go to the opening, come back, and spend every minute with her that she has left," I assured him. "Angel is right. If she even feels that you missed that opening because of her, she'll be upset."

He whipped around and looked at me with fear in his eyes. "'Enough time for *you* to go? You're coming, right?"

I sighed. "I don't think Angel left me with much of a choice."

"Good." He exhaled with relief. "I need you there."

As Coop walked away, I stood there shocked at where I had ended up. I wondered how I had become so involved in this family, but I appreciated the experience. They had taught me so much about gratefulness and true love in such a short amount of time. For that, I would be forever grateful for True.

◠

♫*I drink 'til I'm drunk (yeah), smoke 'til I'm high (yeah)*
Castle on the hill (well damn), wake up in the sky
You can't tell me I ain't fly (you can't tell me I ain't fly)
I know I'm super fly (I know), I know I'm super fly (I know)
The ladies love the luxury (yeah)
That's why they all fuck with me (woo)
Out here with the moves (yeesh) like I invented smooth
You can't tell me I ain't fly (you can't tell me I ain't fly)
I know I'm super fly (I know), I know I'm super fly♫

THAT AFTERNOON, Coop stood on the makeshift stage in the center of the lobby of his rec center. He looked exceptionally handsome in a Gucci button-up and matching jeans and shoes. His jewelry was more exquisite than the five thousand dollars' worth of fabric he was wearing.

He looked good, but as I focused on him through my phone's camera while recording him, the sadness in his eyes was undeniable. He was physically there but mentally checked out as he took the mic from Rakim and the deejay cut the music.

All eyes were on him, and the crowd began to clap, cheer, and chant his name. From what he had told me, in the crowd were politicians, teachers, a few of the Bears and Bulls players, and parents and children from in the neighborhood. But, since I was once the wifey of a dope boy, I also saw some hustlas that he probably ran with and bitches that had gotten wind of his opening and had come dressed scantily, hoping to get his attention.

"Speeeech!" Rakim bellowed from behind him on the stage.

The crowd agreed with Rakim and started encouraging Coop to speak with more cheering.

Everyone around him was happy and excited, but he wouldn't even crack a smile. But from what I had learned about Coop, most in attendance assumed it was just his norm. Only Rakim and I knew he was suffering emotionally.

Coop cleared his throat and began his speech by first saying, "I want to thank everyone for coming out today for the grand opening of the Keyes to Joy Recreation Center. Shout out to the contractors and my partner, Rakim, who helped make this all possible. This center is for the young men in this community who want to do something positive with their lives. I was raised in the system. I ended up in the streets, and I am a product of my environment. But thank God I didn't end up dead or in prison. This center was established so that I can keep a lot of other young men out of the penitentiary and the grave, especially those in the system." The crowd broke out in thunderous applause. Coop held his hand up for them to quiet down, and they did. "I want to also give a very, *very* special thank you to a beautiful soul and the mother of my baby boy, Keyes. His name means to rejoice, and every time I think about his mother, my heart rejoices." The crowd interrupted him with a series of aaahs and Coop fought tears to speak over them. "She... Um... She can't be here today." His voice cracked. I held my breath, wondering if I should go run up there to console him. But Rakim quickly stood by his side and placed a soothing arm around his shoulders. Coop cleared his throat, stopping the emotion that was threatening to pour from his eyes. He forced out, "She can't be here today, and I'd like for anyone in here that believes in any higher being to say a special prayer for True Jenkins."

He quickly gave the mic to Rakim and headed off stage, so I stopped the recording. As the deejay started the music again, I wiped a lone tear from my eye and made my way towards the open bar.

♫*I was born to flex (Yes)*
Diamonds on my neck
I like boardin' jets, I like mornin' sex (Woo!)
But nothing in this world that I like more than checks (Money)
All I really wanna see is the (Money)

I don't really need the D, I need the (Money)
All a bad bitch need is the (Money)
I got bands in the coupe (Coupe)
Bustin' out the roof
I got bands in the coupe (Coupe)
Touch me, I'll shoot (Bow)♫

I BOBBED my head to Cardi B as I waited in line at the bar. I had been downing 1738 since I'd been at the opening.

So much was on my mind. Banks had called once again while I was getting dressed for the grand opening. Every foolish part of me wanted to answer my phone, but my common sense *finally* outweighed my lust and weaknesses. Then, I was stressed out about how to dress. I kept thinking of Coop seeing me out of my scrubs for the first time and then feeling like shit for even having that thought in mind. Because of that, I had snuck into the opening late without even letting Coop know I was there. And then there was True. She was on my mind heaviest of all. For the first time, I was having a battle of my faith when it came to death and disease. I wondered how and why something like this could happen to such a loving and caring family. My heart truly went out to them.

The bartender saw me as I stepped up to the bar and asked, "1738. Neat, right?"

I smiled. "Yes, please."

He smiled at my choice and poured it quickly. He handed it to me, and I quickly got out of the way for the many other attendees that wanted to take advantage of the free drinks.

"Remi?"

I spun around with the wineglass at my lips. There stood Coop close behind me with so much wonder and amazement in his eyes as he looked down on me, perusing me over.

"Well, damn, you dress up nicely."

I cowered under his intense gaze. I smoothed out the fitted, floor-length, long-sleeve, emerald green dress that slightly draped the floor. It was casual enough for the daytime event but had enough elegance to catch eyes. It fit every one of my curves that I wanted to spotlight with its mermaid fit. A good pair of Spanx was slimming down the lumps and bumps that I wanted to hide. I had paired the dress with a pair of black pumps that brought me almost eye level with Coop. I had curled the layers in my bob and parted a heavy bang into it that covered my eyes. It was also his first time seeing me wear makeup. I had used green eyeshadows from a palette from the Crayon Case, minimal highlight, and contour, and a clear gloss. But I had used enough gold glow in the right spots where the light hit my face to make me shine like a penny.

I smiled and eyed him up and down. "You do too. Let me get a picture for True."

He stepped back and allowed me to take his picture. As soon as I snapped it, Rakim pulled him away. "Hey, Coop, I need you for a minute."

Hesitantly, he looked at me. "I'll be right back."

"Take your time," I insisted.

Just as he walked away, my cell phone rang. I was shocked to see that it was Niyah calling. I hadn't heard from her or Iyana in months, and I hadn't been upset about it. It seemed as if they had gravitated towards Banks' new circle with him and his wife. And they had completely lost me when they'd attended the wedding.

Out of curiosity, I decided to answer the phone. "Hello?" I answered dryly.

"Bitch, I see you at the grand opening of Coop's new rec center."

I rolled my eyes. "First of all, hi."

She rushed, "What's up, girl? How you doin'?" Then, before I could answer, she pressed, "So, what the fuck you doin' at Coop's opening?"

I groaned inwardly and started thinking of a way to get off of the phone. "How did you even know that I was here? Where do you see me?" I asked, looking around.

"He's broadcasting it live on his Facebook page."

"Oh…"

"Don't just *oh* me, bitch. What you doin' there?"

Just then, I caught Coop's eyes on me. He was talking to two white men in suits, but his gaze was on me. I turned my back and began to walk deeper into the crowd to hide from him.

"Helloooo?" Niyah pushed.

My face balled up with irritation. "He's a friend of mine."

"Umph. Banks is going to *haaaate*," she sang.

My eyes rolled up to the ceiling. "Banks shouldn't care since he's married."

Niyah sucked her teeth and grunted. "Not for long."

That piqued my interest. "Not for long? What you mean?"

"Giiiirrrrl," she drawled the way women did whenever they had some piping hot tea. "Brandi's grimy ass got caught up."

My eyes bulged. "What?" A grin crept across my face as my heart began to pound with excitement.

"Yeah. Banks got robbed about three weeks ago in a home invasion. They took a couple of hundred thousand dollars in money and dope. Come to find out, Brandi had set the whole thing up with her brother and cousins—"

My rage drowned her out. Three weeks ago was when I'd finally received my long overdue apology, breakfast, and dick. *That's* why I had gotten the apology. His number-one choice had broken his heart.

"Niyah, I gotta go," I interrupted her.

"Wait!" Niyah stopped me. "So, what's up with you and Coop?"

I hung up on her, seeing nothing but red. I instantly sat my cup down on the nearest table and started to bolt towards the door. As I made my swift exit, my phone started to ring again. I answered without looking at the screen, praying that it was Banks because I had so much to say to him this time.

"Hello?"

"Remi…" a soft voice called so low that I barely could recognize it.

"Angel?" I asked.

"Yes, it's me." She then sighed deeply. "You and Coop need to come back… It's… It's True… It's time."

My heart dropped to my stomach. I made an about face and nearly bumped into Coop.

"Remi, where are you going?" he asked.

"Okay, Angel." I regretfully looked into his eyes, as I spoke into the phone. "I'll let Coop know."

It was as if Coop could feel what was happening, as if he'd read it in my eyes. What little composure he had conjured up to get through this event had left his body. His shoulders sank, and his eyes started to beg me not to say it.

My eyes pooled with tears as I gently looped my arm through his. "We have to go. It's time."

COOP'S MIND was idle as I drove him back to True's house. He stared blankly out the window, not making a sound. He had only managed to unlock his phone so that I could send Rakim a text message, explaining what was happening. Rakim had quickly replied, letting us know that he would take care of the rest of the opening in Coop's absence.

Once in the driveway of True's house, I turned off the car. As I was getting out, I noticed that Coop was just sitting there paralyzed.

I gently placed a hand on his arm. "Coop, you have to go in there."

He grimaced. "I can't."

Sadly, I tried to encourage him. "I know you don't think you can right now, but you will regret it if you don't. You don't know how much time she has left."

I climbed out of the car, closed the door, and walked around to his side of the car. I pulled his door open, grabbed his hand, and pulled his heavy body out of my car.

I was rushing inside, my feet moving a mile a minute, but Coop was literally dragging behind me. I let his hand go, darted up the stairs, and rang the bell. By the time Russell opened the door, Coop was behind me. We hurried inside, and that's where we saw Angel on the couch, holding Joy, and rocking slowly with a tsunami of tears flooding her weary face.

"What's going on?" I asked as I rushed to her side.

Angel didn't look at me. She sat staring at True's bedroom door and continuously rocked slowly. "Tammy said it's time. She is in their checking her vitals."

I turned on my heels and rushed towards True's room. I pushed her door open. My eyes rested on her body that was surely lifeless. Tammy had the stethoscope on her chest, but when she saw me, she stopped. Her eyes were full of sympathy as she looked at me. She was a part of my agency, so she knew how much I had grown to love this family. She removed the stethoscope and handed it over the bed to me.

"Thank you," I cried as I looked down on True.

Tammy nodded and exited the room.

I leaned over to check for a pulse. As I did, my tears fell on to True's pajamas. Her pulse was faint, but it was there, although barely. I touched her arm, and she was cold to the touch. While she *was* looking at me, her eyes were blank. There was nothing in them. They might as well have been closed. She only took a deep heavy breath every thirty seconds or so.

I sighed heavily, bent down, and kissed her cheek. "Thank you for changing my life. Thank you for making me better," I told her as I rubbed her hair. "I love you."

I kissed her cheek again and hurriedly left to give her loved ones, time to be with her for the short time she had left.

When I walked out of the room, Russell, Angel, and Coop looked at me with so much hope, but I had none for them.

Sadly, I announced, "It's time to say your goodbyes."

Angel broke down. Russell rushed to her to console her as Joy looked at her, wondering what was happening. I didn't know whether to go to Joy or Coop, but Coop then quickly rushed into True's room. I went for Joy. I took her out of Angel's arms as Angel sobbed into Russell's chest while he tried to coax her to go into the room to say goodbye.

I shuffled towards Joy's room, telling her, "I need you to be a good girl and watch a movie for me, okay?"

As we walked past Keyes' room, she nodded. I peeked inside, thankful that he was asleep in his crib.

Once in Joy's room, I turned on Netflix and picked the first kid movie I saw. Over the sounds of the usual Disney Pixar movie introduction, I could hear Angel wailing, and I flinched. There was absolutely nothing like hearing a mother cry for her child. It was gut-wrenching, chilling, and gnawing to the bone.

"Are you hungry, baby?" I asked Joy, trying to fight my own tears.

When she looked up at me, I could see that Joy felt the despair that was tightly wrapped around her. "No. Is Grandma okay?"

She was a child, but she could sense that something was wrong. I could see the fear in her eyes.

"Grandma has an owie. But you remember that I'm a nurse, right?"

She smiled and nodded.

"Well, I want you to be a good girl and watch this movie while I go and fix your grandma. Okay?"

Again, she nodded. "Okay."

"I'll come back and check on you soon," I assured her. Then I rushed out. I no longer heard Angel's cries, so I rushed into the living room, wondering what was going on. Everyone had disappeared, so I rushed to True's room. I stopped in the doorway when I saw Angel at True's side, her face resting on True's belly as she gripped the sheet that covered True. Her sobs were muffled by the bedding. Russell was behind her with his hand soothingly on her shoulder.

Coop was on the other side of True laying with her, his face against hers, tears falling from his hard eyes.

True let out a long moan but her mouth lay agape, and her eyes remained fixated on nothing in particular.

To give them privacy, I backed out of the room and closed the door slightly. Yet, I peered inside through the small crack that I'd left, waiting on the moment to call time of death.

"Don't go," Coop cried against her face in a whisper. True's gasps of breath were heard over his words as he begged her to stay even though he knew he was indeed saying goodbye. "We're the air that each other is supposed to breathe. You changed me." As he cried, his tears rolled into his mouth as his lips pressed against her cold cheek. "You saved me."

20

COOP

A week later, I was walking out of Great Saints Church in Oak Lawn. Keyes was nestled in the crook of one of my arms. Joy was holding my free hand as Angel held her other. We followed True's casket being pulled by her pallbearers out of the church. Russell was on the other side of Angel, holding her other hand. I could feel Remi behind us, where she had been since True had taken her last breath. She'd never left us since True had passed away last Friday. I had been consoling Angel as much as I could, helping her make the funeral arrangements, and Remi had been unconditionally there for me and Angel. Angel hadn't needed to lift a finger. Remi had even accompanied me as I purchased True's burial outfit. Even though her casket was closed, I had refused to let my baby be buried in anything but the best.

Russell and I watched Angel intensely as True's casket was placed into the hearse by her male cousins and uncles. We waited for her to have another breakdown. We had waited during the entire funeral, but she had held her own during the hour-long service. The funeral hadn't really brought out any sadness in any of us. Everyone had been given stern instructions to give uplifting remarks and tell loving, funny memories of True to keep the style of a happy and lively homegoing that True wanted. The service had been upbeat and had instilled hope in all of those in attendance.

Angel had let go of Joy's hand as many family members started to surround her and extend their condolences. Russell eyed me, silently asking me if I had Joy, and I nodded, letting him know that she was good.

"You need some help?" Remi asked as she took Joy's hand.

I shook my head, and asked her, "Are you riding with us to the cemetery?"

Remi gazed at Keyes as his eyes bounced around lively. A sweet smile spread across her face as she reached and softly brushed a finger across his cheek. "No, I'm going to drive."

"Nah, fuck that. You can get in the limo." I had felt like Remi should have been in that limo on the way to the funeral. To me and Angel, Remi was family. She had gone over and beyond her call of duty before and after True's death, more than her own family had. She deserved to be recognized for that.

REMI

Coop immediately went into control mode. He turned and went towards one of the drivers, but I grabbed his elbow. "Coop, no. It's okay," I insisted.

He frowned. "You family. Fuck that."

I continued to pull him away from the limo, saying, "But she has *real* family here. There's no room for me. It's okay."

Coop grimaced with a clenched jaw. "You deserve to be in there. You were there for her more than any of them other motherfuckers were."

"Coop," I warned with bucked eyes.

"Fine. Then I'm riding with you."

Using his body, he forced me towards the parking lot, and I didn't argue. I just shook my head. Since True's death, Coop had been absolutely nothing to fucking play with, let alone argue with. He had been a wall. Emotionless. I had recalled how True had told me how he used to be when they'd first met, and this was it. However, I remembered the gentle and caring man who had held her and cried until she took her last breath. And he had remembered me, as I sat next to him on the couch holding him until the funeral home had come for True's body. Therefore, I didn't take his crassness personal at all.

As we approached my car, I realized, "We don't have car seats."

"Shit," he cursed. "Here. Hold Keyes. I'll get their car seats out of the limos."

He forced Keyes into my arms before he turned around. I thanked God he had, because he came face to face with who appeared to be an extremely angry man.

"Who the fuck are you, and why do you have my daughter?!" he barked at me as he tried to see over Coop's shoulder.

Realizing it was Jameel, I pulled Joy back. I fumbled with my key fob as I tried to open to the passenger's door.

"Give me my fucking—" That's all he got out before Coop's fist connected with his jaw. I immediately screamed as I saw the side of Jameel's face cave in as he hit the ground. I was finally able to pop the locks as Coop started to pummel Jameel.

"Bitch-ass nigga! Give you who?" I heard Coop taunting Jameel as I heard his fist crack against his face simultaneously. Horrified, I put Joy in the car. After finally getting her inside, I struggled with what to do with Keyes. He was way too small to leave him unattended with a five-year-old.

"Fuck!" I cursed, and Joy looked at me with curled eyebrows. "Sorry," I immediately apologized. "I'm right here, honey, but I need to close the door." I closed it shut before she could say anything and held Keyes close to my chest as I cautiously approached Coop who was putting Jameel's face into the concrete. Blood was splattering everywhere. A small crowd of funeral attendees had gathered around, looking on in disgust and disbelief as Coop tried to destroy the man with his bare hands.

"Coop!" I shrieked as I pulled on his suit jacket.

Jameel deserved this ass whooping, but these kids needed Coop. Not just Keyes. Joy needed him too. She had grown attached to Coop in the last few months. "Coop! Please?"

Angel ran up with Russell close behind her. I was relieved, thinking she could stop Coop until she saw what was happening and froze with a pleased look on her face.

My attempt to grab Coop was unsuccessful. He didn't even feel me. Every man watching in astonishment as he violently beat Jameel looked like they wanted to stop him but were too afraid because of Coop's massive strength.

And, then, as if True was coming down from the heavens and helping a sistah out, Keyes started crying. Coop stopped his attack and swung around as if he were afraid that his attack had hurt Keyes.

He rushed towards me with wide, fearful eyes.

"He's okay," I assured Coop as he huddled over me and Keyes. "But you gotta stop, Coop. You need to be here for these kids. And I..." I had to pause to keep myself from adding that I needed him as well.

When True first passed, I felt like I had not only lost her, but I had lost him too. Beyond our attraction to each other, we had developed a friendship that I feared would end once True's funeral was over.

Once the casket of a loved one dropped, so many things changed for the ones closest to the dead, and I feared that Coop realizing that I was just a moment in time would be one of those things.

I swallowed hard and instead told Coop, "You have to be here for these kids, not in prison. And you want to be able to see True get put into the ground, right?"

Like the Incredible Hulk turning back into Dr. David Banner, Coop's anger subsided, and he was back to reality as he looked at his crying son.

I rocked to soothe Keyes as I told Coop, "Get in the car."

He looked into my eyes and realized I wasn't asking him. I was *telling* him.

He looked back as Jameel lay moaning on the concrete.

"You ain't gettin' shit," Coop shouted seething at Jameel. "Not your daughter...not nothing, motherfucker," he barked. "On everything I'ma make damn sure of that."

I worried that my stern order had gone unnoticed until Coop took Keyes from me, tore the passenger's door open, and climbed in, still fuming.

≈

By eight that evening, I was stripping my clothes off in my house with relief. It had been the longest day. At the end of so much grief and sadness, I had been able to end it with a hot plate of comforting soul food at True's repast. Now, I had the itis as thoughts of True's wonderful homegoing replayed in my head. It was a sad occasion, but True's efforts to make us smile instead of cry with upbeat music and happy memories had worked. Tears were still sliding down the faces of the attendees, but often, the tears were accompanied with a smile.

A hot bath with lavender scented bubbles was running, and I was dying to get in it. Since True's passing, I had been on vacation from work, but the next night I had a new patient, so I had to get my mind ready to go back to work.

I was now down to my bra and panties, staring at myself in the full-length mirror on my bathroom wall. I would usually complain about what I saw, but Angel's tears as True took her last breath had replayed in my mind every day like the soundtrack to a heartbreaking symphony. I remember how Coop had loved on True, even when disease had taken her body so much that she didn't even resemble herself anymore. I touched my curves, now, not hating them but realizing that someone would love them eventually. And if they never did, then I always would.

Realizing that the water had risen to my desired level, I reached over and turned it off.

I grabbed my phone, swiping to my Amazon music app so I could play something soothing to calm my nerves from such a hectic day. As the sounds of SZA filled the bathroom, I took a deep breath and thanked True once again for changing my way of thinking.

As soon as I started to get rid of my bra, my doorbell rang. Curiously, I left the bathroom. On my way out of my bedroom, I grabbed the robe that hung on my door. I wrapped it tightly around my body as I headed for the door. I peered through the peephole and was deeply irritated when I saw Banks standing on the other side.

I tore the door open, spewing, "What?!"

Shocked at my anger, he backed up a bit. "Whoa, what's your problem?"

Seething, I spat, "What the fuck do you want, Banks?"

"I want *you*, baby. Where you been? Why haven't you answered my calls?"

I used to look at him and see my world beginning at his command and ending if he'd ever left. I used to equate my worth by his existence. But, now, today, I realized that life was so much more than me begging some ain't-shit nigga to stand beside me because I felt like his presence brought value to my worth. I was alive. I was breathing. And that deserved sincere happiness from me, whether I had some man lying next to me and dicking me down or not.

"*Now* you want me?" I taunted him with a smirk. "Now that your perfect Barbie has played you, you wanna come back to me?"

He tried to come towards me, but I backed up into the house. He stopped his approach, insisting, "It's not like—"

"Fuck you," I growled. "You don't deserve me. Go back to that bitch you chose. Good luck." And then I did what I had never done to him before; I slammed the door in his face. Finally, I was done with him and *not* the other way around.

21

ANGEL

Two days after True's funeral, my tears were still flowing. After her death and all the way up until her funeral, there had been floods of calls and text messages of support. My front door was revolving with family members and friends who wanted to surround me to ensure that I kept myself together. Those close to me feared for my sanity because I had already barely survived the death of my husband. They weren't sure if I could survive burying my daughter. So, they'd all clung to me until the moment I put True in the ground.

But after the fried chicken and sides had been eaten at True's repast, and everyone had said their goodbyes, all of that support had stopped, and I was left to deal with my suffering grief on my own.

Russell had tried his best to stay by my side every minute of every day, but since he had to get back to his life after a week of putting it on pause for me after True passed, he was having a hard time juggling babysitting me and taking care of his responsibilities. I could see the struggle in his eyes as he weighed the options of making sure that I didn't hang myself and making sure that he went to work so he could pay his mortgage.

"Urrgh!" I growled as I ignored Jameel's one-hundredth call. I tossed the phone on the couch and collapsed in Russell's lap. "I wish he'd stop fucking calling me."

"I can stop him from calling you." I knew exactly what Russell's tone meant.

"No," I instantly refused. "*Hell* no. I need you here with me, not fighting a murder charge."

He deeply chuckled, but I could hear the menace in his laugh.

"Russell," I whispered and sighed as I sat up from his lap and wiped my eyes. "You can go home."

He reached up and ran his fingers softly over my unkempt cut. "No," he refused, sweetly. Just then, his phone rang for the umpteenth time since he'd awakened that morning in bed next to me. As he had done every time, he silenced it without answering.

"You've been here all day. Your phone keeps ringing," I pushed.

He shrugged. "So."

"I know you have business to take care of. I'll be okay by myself," I insisted.

He smiled at my weak attempt at bravery. He lovingly rubbed my shoulder as he said, "No, you won't."

"I know," I admitted with a pout. "But I have to try. I have to get used to the fact that she..." I struggled. "That she's gone." My voice cracked as tears pooled in my eyes.

Russell's large arm reached for me and pulled me under him. "You know how we can fix all of this?" he asked.

"How?"

"You and Joy can move in with me."

I pushed back in order to look Russell in the eyes. "What?"

"Move in with me. Let me take care of you...you and Joy. You've spent the last two years taking care of True and Joy. Let somebody take care of you now."

I opened my mouth, unsure of what I was about to say. Then Joy's piercing scream cut through the air. I jumped to my feet and ran to my bedroom where I had left her taking her afternoon nap. I could feel Russell on my heels as I jogged up the hall.

"Mommyyyyyyyy!" Joy screamed.

"Grandma's coming, baby," I called out to her.

Finally, I entered the room. Joy was sitting up in bed, screaming in tears. "Mommy! I want my mommy!"

I ran towards the bed, jumped in, and crawled towards her. When I wrapped my arms around her, she started to fight her way out of my arms.

Since True's death, Joy had been asking for her. I had tried to explain that she had gone to heaven. Yet, her young mind still could not wrap around her mother being here one minute and then suddenly vanishing.

I was an adult, and, still, I couldn't understand it either.

"No! I want my mommy! Where is my mommy?!" she cried.

I held her in a tight bear hug, accepting her struggle as she cried into my chest. I watched as Russell walked towards the bed and sat. I began to rock Joy soothingly back and forth. She finally stopped struggling to get out of my arms and cried silently.

With tears in my eyes, I looked at Russell. A small, sarcastic laugh left my throat as I asked him, "You still want us to live with you?"

Placing a hand on my leg, he replied, "Yes."

"I'm scared," I admitted.

Russell's eyes squinted questionably. "Scared of what?"

Tears streamed down my face. "Of you leaving me too."

COOP

For the last two days, I had been pouring myself into work and Keyes. I was at the rec center making sure the staff that Rakim had hired in my absence the week True had passed were legit and knew what they were doing.

"I can do that for you, if you want."

I looked up to see Tamika, the front-desk receptionist, standing in the doorway of my office as I fed Keyes.

"Naw, I got it," I told her.

She smiled. "You sure?"

I nodded. "Positive, shorty."

She shrugged. "Okay. Well, I'm here if you need me."

I ignored the lustful twinkle in her eyes as she turned and walked away.

I instantly glared at Rakim who was leaning back in a chair breaking his neck to watch her walk away. Shorty did have a phat ass. She was a gorgeous, chocolate girl wearing long lemonade braids that reached her ass. Her body was tight and her ass was round. Her thighs didn't match her ass, so she had definitely gotten some ass shots. She was only twenty years old and thirstier than a motherfucker.

She was child support payments and drama waiting to happen to a nigga.

"I should fuck you up for hiring her young ass," I growled at Rakim.

"Why? She young and didn't want that much pay. I'm saving you money."

"And you're ensuring yourself some ass. You ain't slick. You hired her because she's pretty and got a phat ass."

Rakim nodded with a smile. "She can answer phones too."

I shook my head, giving my attention back to Keyes. I didn't trust anybody watching my son except Angel. But Angel had enough to deal with at the time. I wasn't trying to put my son on her. Besides, being a single father was something I needed to adjust to quickly. For the last week, I had been feeling what every single mother felt. Trying to juggle work, responsibilities, and Keyes had been unbelievably hard. I had a newfound respect for women, single mothers in particular, that I'd never had before.

As Keyes finished his bottle, I smiled down on my little man. He looked just like me, but I hoped that he would grow into looking like his mother because I craved to see her face again in something other than a picture.

With a heavy heart, I lifted Keyes to my shoulder to burp him. Trying to push the constant sorrow of True out of my heart and mind, I asked Rakim, "What's up with those NBA players coming to the basketball camp this summer?"

As Rakim filled me in on the details, my mind still drifted to True, the last few weeks in my life in particular. It had been a whirlwind of emotions that I had never felt before, especially mourning True while she was still alive. And I had gained more special people in my life.

True wasn't the only person I was missing. Angel and Joy had gained a special place in my heart. Yet, I felt like it would be too hard to manage the grief while looking in Joy or Angel's face, so I hadn't been by to see them yet. Hearing her tears during and since True's death had been torture enough, so I couldn't bear to call Angel either. Diving into my work to avoid the pain had led me to avoiding Angel as well. So, as Rakim talked, I took out my phone and sent her a text message, asking her how she was doing. I thought about Remi as well. I wanted to know how she was doing. I wanted to talk to her and make sure she was okay. But my interest in checking up on Remi was different than my interest in Angel.

I felt guilty thinking of Remi in the last two days almost as much as I had been thinking of True. I missed Remi too. She had become a part of my everyday life. When she'd become True's nurse, she had become mine too. She had taken care of True physically, but she had taken care of me emotionally. I had been there for True and Angel while Remi had been there for me. Rakim had tried, but he wasn't caring enough. He'd tried to fix my grief with jokes, drugs, and alcohol. He had also tried to put my mind on other bitches when the only women on my mind were either dead or forbidden.

Every time I thought of Remi, I felt guilty as if I was doing something wrong. So, I closed the phone and just hoped shorty was okay.

22

REMI

True and her family had spoiled me. For the last two months, I had been with a loving family that had pulled me into their tribe. Now, I had an old, white terminally ill patient that looked as if he barely wanted me to touch him. His wife was even worse.

"If that's all you need, then I'll be leaving for the day." A fake, professional smile was plastered on my face as I waited for Mrs. Crowe to relieve me. She sat at the kitchen table with her face balled into an unhappy, prude mess as she kept her eyes on the eggs Benedict a chef had prepared for her.

"That'll be all. Thank you," she replied curtly.

Snarling at her, I turned on my Crocs and headed towards the front door fast. I groaned, missing True, Angel, and Coop so much. I even missed the kids. True was more than a patient, and her family and Coop were more than merely my patient's family. They had in some way become even more than friends. They were my family as well. I had been there to take care of True, but she and Coop had taken care of me as well in my time of need. I had been a wreck before meeting them. Now, I felt brand new. I felt free of burdens and heartbreak. They had unknowingly fixed me, and I missed them all.

Finally outside of that stale home, I took a deep breath of the clean, warm, May-morning air. The Crowes' home was in Naperville, Illinois, so that air just smelled different. It smelled clean, unpolluted, and not like bullets and crack heads in the city air.

Walking towards my car, I admired how the sun was shining. It was the perfect day to get cute, put on a maxi dress, and walk on the beach. But I didn't want to look like a loser because I was alone. At this point in my life, I had no friends. I only spoke to my sister, Gigi, and that was rare, because she had a new boyfriend. My mother wasn't the company I wanted either. Honestly, I wanted *Coop*. I missed his company. But every time I reached for my phone to call or text him, I put the phone down. He and I had leaned on each other for comfort the week after True passed. Now, I feared that if he were around me, and True was not there to distract me, I wouldn't be able to control my attraction to him. So, as I sat in the driver's seat, I sighed, staring at his contact information in my phone. Glaring at the message icon, I chose not to defy True's memory by gushing over her man. So, I closed the app.

Suddenly, while still in my hand, my phone started to ring, scaring the shit outta me. When I saw it was Angel, I answered quickly, "Hi, Angel."

I eagerly waited to hear how she would sound. I had been messaging her every other day to see how she and the kids were doing.

She sounded as if she was holding up, but I knew better. "Hi, Remi. Did I catch you at a bad time?"

"No, I'm just leaving work. What's going on?" She had only called my phone when I was working for True and while I was helping with the funeral arrangements. I hadn't heard her voice since the funeral, so I was happy to hear that she actually sounded like there was a little happiness in it.

"I need you to come by the house this afternoon. Are you available?"

I was happy for the chance to see Angel, but I wondered what she wanted that she couldn't talk to me about over the phone. "Yes," I answered slowly. "Is everything okay?"

"Yes, everything is fine," she assured me. "I just need to talk to you."

She used that assertive tone that told me that even though she wasn't my mother, I still had no choice but to do whatever she said and not ask any more questions. "Umm... Ooookay."

"Come around two o'clock, okay?"

My face was still contorted with confusion as I turned the engine. "Okay."

"See you later."

She hung up with questions still lingering in my mind as I backed out of the driveway.

COOP

A week after True's funeral, I found the courage to take Keyes to see his grandmother and big sister. I needed to maintain every connection to True that I still had, so I intended on Angel and Joy remaining a part of my life, as well as in Keyes'.

"How are you managing, Coop?" Angel asked me as she cradled Keyes.

I looked up at her from the floor. Joy was sitting down with me. I was helping her with her homework packet while Grandma got some me time with Keyes.

As my eyes took in Angel, I was glad to see that she finally looked as if she was putting some care into herself. The days approaching True's death and afterward, Angel was an understandable mess. Her hair was always unkempt. her clothes were always disheveled, and her face was always weary.

Now, she had obviously taken the time to comb her hair and put a little makeup on. She was wearing a leisure short set, sandals, and a smile as she looked down on her gift from True.

"I'm managing okay," I answered.

She smiled at me. "Being a single father isn't easy, is it?"

"Hell nah," I grunted with a shake of my head.

"Look, Coop! I did it!" Joy beamed as she pointed at her home-work sheet with her pencil.

I looked down at Joy's attempt to write out three-letter sight words. "Good job. Now finish the rest."

She nodded. "Okay!"

"He's a good baby, though," I told Angel.

"Yes, he *is*," Angel cooed as she smiled into Keyes' face.

Looking around the living room, I noticed some moving boxes tied together and lying against the wall. "What's with the moving boxes?" I suddenly got nervous that she was running away from the bad memories in Chicago and moving away.

Finally, I saw a genuine smile on Angel's face. "Joy and I are moving in with Russell."

Relieved, I smiled. "Word?"

She nodded lovingly. "Yep."

"That's what's up."

"It is. I'm happy to have him. He's so good to me."

"Good for you. Have you heard from Jameel?"

Angel's eyes rolled. "On my voicemail," she grunted. "He's been demanding that I hand Joy over to him. I'm just waiting for the moment that he shows up at my front door to take her away from me. Luckily, I'll be moved out soon, and he doesn't know where Russell lives. I just pray to God that I win custody at court."

"I can handle that for you."

Angel looked at me for a long time. As she gave me that stern look, I saw so much of my baby, True, in her face. She and True were not twins, but they did share similar features and made the same facial expressions. Instead of sadness, I felt like True was finally in the room with me, and it felt good.

Angel sighed long and deeply as she tore her eyes away from mine. She knew I was a street nigga, so she was aware of how I intended on handling Jameel had she even looked like she wanted me to. "No," she said, but I heard the reluctance in her voice. "I don't need you to handle Jameel. Don't go back anywhere near him, Coop. Do you hear me?"

She looked back at me, and I was too much of a man to lie to a grieving mother, so I said nothing.

"*Coop*," she fussed. "I'm serious. You're lucky you didn't end up in jail for damn near beating him to death. I'm still waiting on the cops to show up over that shit."

I shrugged nonchalantly. "They can show up. That's a case I'll be glad to fight."

"*No*. The last thing Keyes needs is to lose another parent for any reason. You no longer have permission to do anything that will land you in jail or the grave. Do you hear me?"

Still, I didn't have any answer, so she sat up on the edge of the couch as mothers do whenever they wanted to be taken seriously. She leaned towards me with a tight jaw. "Coop."

I chuckled. "Okay."

"Promise me you won't touch him," she insisted.

"I won't."

Despite me giving in, she went on, "You have a rec center now. You're supposed to be an example now."

I laughed at the way she fussed with her eyebrows curled. I had never had a mother figure, and it was funny to me to have such a tiny woman calling herself telling me what to do. "Okay, okay."

Watching my smile, she sighed with relief and went back to admiring Keyes. As I watched her, I realized that although Keyes had lost his mother, he still had a mother figure. And even Joy would have a father figure because I didn't plan on going anywhere.

Just then, Angel's doorbell rang, and a smile crept on her face.

"Be right back," she told me as she stood.

Carrying Keyes with her, she disappeared out of the living room towards the front door. Because of her smile, I assumed that Russell was ringing the doorbell. I looked around at all the moving boxes with a grin. I was happy Angel had found Russell and now, she had someone to look after her. I would always look after her too, but being the man in her life, Russell would look after her in a way she had needed years before that day.

But as I heard a familiar, feminine, sweet voice enter the house, I knew it wasn't Russell. I could feel her. I could smell her. Goose-bumps covered my dark skin against my will. I suddenly got nervous. I looked up towards the hallway as her voice came nearer, antici-pating seeing her again. I was holding my breath until she appeared in the doorway, and I finally, *finally* exhaled. I felt like I had been holding my breath since that last time I'd seen her, and finally, just now, I was breathing again. She was beautiful. She was wearing the best foundation all over her body; her natural, glowing brown skin. If I were to hang her picture in heaven, so many angels would hide their faces in envy. And even though her beauty captured me, it was her amazing soul that left me speechless.

It had only been a week and a half that I had been avoiding her, but in that moment, I realized it felt like an eternity.

REMI

"C-Coop," I stuttered. And then to avoid the way his eyes were burning a hole into my soul, I whipped my head around to Angel's smiling face. "You didn't tell me that Coop was going to be here. What's going on?"

Angel placed a hand on my shoulder. "Have a seat on the couch, Remi."

With interrogating eyes, I slowly walked towards the couch. I nervously avoided looking at Coop. I was unbelievably happy to be in his presence again. *Too* happy. My attraction to him was overwhelming me, and guilt was suffocating me.

I suddenly felt so vulnerable. I was wearing a pair of yellow, cotton Bermuda shorts and a matching cropped tank. But I suddenly felt naked sitting across from Coop as he sat on the floor, adorably helping Joy with homework.

We weren't speaking or looking at one another, which was odd. We had gone from spending every day together to having no words between us. The tension between was thick. The sexual tension was impenetrable. Yet, the guilt was smothering.

I heard a giggle and looked up to see Angel shaking her head. "Okay," she finally spoke. "I have something for both of you."

She walked over to an end table and picked up a folded piece of paper. She then told Coop, "Get up and sit next to Remi."

His eyes held as many questions as mine did as he did what he had been told. As he sat next to me, I felt so much energy between us. That same intensity had been between us as we spent so many late nights comforting one another and forcing ourselves to ignore our mutual attraction.

"Now, I want you both to please keep an open mind," Angel instructed.

Coop and I stared at her intensely, waiting for her to cure our curiosities. She handed me the letter, and I took it from her slowly, staring into her eyes blankly.

"You all should read it together," she told us. "It's from True."

Hearing that, I starting to unfold it quickly, as Angel sat on the chaise. Coop quickly scooted closer to me. I leaned over into him so his eyes could read the words as well.

Dear Coop and Remi,

I knew you both would not be able to take heed to these words while I was alive, so I waited until after I was gone to tell them to you. Coop, I love the man that you became. I want you to be happy. I want you to have the love that you felt for me with a woman who can give you the happily ever after that I couldn't. You deserve a woman who can spend a lifetime with you, and my son deserves a mother who can spend a lifetime with him. I want you to permanently have that feeling that changed you into the man that you are today. I fear that if you don't, my son will have to watch you turn back into the man the streets once feared.

Remi, I did not have the opportunity to know you for very long. But I saw you care for my family and in particular, my children and Coop, in a way I hoped someone would come into their lives and love them once I was gone. It's only right that you finally get in return the unconditional love that you have shown so many in your work and personal life.

I was able to pass peacefully because I knew my mother had Russell, my kids had Coop and my mother, and that you two had each other. I was not too sick to see the chemistry between you two. I could feel the attraction you shared. I know you both respected me too much to act on it, and I love you both even more for that. But I want you to know that you have my blessing. Not only do you have my blessing, but I am asking you to please be there for one another in the way that only two people in love can. Be with each other, take care of each other, and love on each other so that I can truly rest in peace.

With love,
    True

As I finished reading the letter, my hands shook. "W-what?" I had read it with my own eyes, but I was still in disbelief.

"Wait a minute." Coop snatched the letter from my trembling hands and began to reread it as if he had read it wrong.

Rocking Keyes with a satisfied smile on her face, Angel told me and Coop, "She wants you two to be together. Not just for her, but for each other."

I was speechless. Never had someone been so thoughtful. True was so selfless. Her words resonated in me and sparked tears. Admittedly, I felt some happiness. I felt relief that I could explore this attraction to Coop without the guilt. But, even though we had her permission and Angel's blessing, it still felt so wrong.

"Man, this is crazy," Coop grunted as he slammed the letter down on the couch.

He was obviously against this and, even though I understood why, I immediately felt the sting of rejection and disappointment.

"Why is it crazy?" Angel argued. "You're attracted to her, aren't you?" she challenged.

He couldn't even look at me. Frustration filled his expression. Rather than feel touched, like I was, True's words had left Coop angry.

"This is some bullshit," he growled as he jumped up.

As he began to storm off, Angel called after him. "Coop!"

He kept storming out of the living room. Angel jumped up to follow him, but stopped when I stood too.

Embarrassment left me stuttering. "I-I should go." Rejection was leading me to flee.

The sympathy in Angel's eyes made matters even worse for me. She called out for me as I headed out of the living room. "Remi, don't go."

She struggled with deciding to follow me or Coop as I ignored her. I lightly jogged towards the door, hoping that Coop hadn't run outside as well. Luckily, he hadn't. I raced out of the house, hearing Angel calling me and Coop.

Making it to my truck just as the tears began, I flung the door open, wondering why no man ever chose me. Even when it was right and made sense, no man *ever* chose me.

ANGEL

"Finish your homework, Joy. I'll be right back." I scurried towards the hall. First, I ran to the front door to see Remi peeling out of the driveway. Sucking my teeth, I closed the door and then rushed through the house looking for Coop.

"Coop! Boy, where are you?!" I called out.

Once in the kitchen, I saw that my back door was opened. I rushed towards it and through it to find Coop plopped down on the patio couch, pouting like a big baby.

"Boy, what the hell is wrong with you?" I fussed as I sat beside him.

He grunted as he threw his face in his hands.

I understood his shock, but I hadn't expected him to be so cold.

I couldn't believe it myself when I'd finally read True's letter that morning. However, as I thought about the times I'd seen Remi and Coop interacting, it was evident. I then remembered all the times True had forced them to be together alone. She had been orchestrating this shortly after meeting Remi. She must have seen their attraction to each other and their connection even though they had respected her enough to hide it.

Keyes started to squirm, so I rocked him as I berated Coop. "Why would you run out on that girl? You made her feel bad."

Coop's glaring eyes whipped towards me. "Exactly! Why would True put me in that position? She knew how I felt about getting involved with another woman. I'm not on that shit."

I shook my head at his stubbornness. True had been right. He was already turning back into his old self. "Why not?"

His jaw clenched as he replied, "Because I avoided that shit for a reason. I ended up falling for True, and she only proved that my reasons for staying away from feelings and love was right. I just wanna raise my son and make my money. I ain't trying to be involved in anything else that will take me off my focus from that."

"You sound like me." Coop sucked his teeth and turned away from me. I gently grabbed his chin and turned his eyes back to me. He respected my authority and gave me his attention. "I avoided men for years after my husband passed away. I had different reasons, but I felt strongly about it. But when I met Russell again, he changed my life. And I know you and True didn't work out, but maybe that was because meeting her was supposed to lead you to the *true* love of your life... who may possibly be Remi."

That's when he pulled his chin out of my grasp and stood up. "Maaaaan..."

"I saw the look in your eyes when she walked in earlier," I pushed. "I saw the relief. You have feelings for her."

He grimaced but didn't deny it. "That don't mean I have to be with her."

I sighed, saying, "Coop, don't be..."

I stopped as he bent down and pried Keyes out of my arms. "No disrespect, Angel, but I have to go."

I watched him in total shock of his temper tantrum as he walked away. He didn't even go back into the house. He cut through the grass and stomped towards the gate. I shook my head as he stormed off. True had been absolutely right. I only had known the loving and devoted Coop. But True had told me the type of man that he had changed from. I couldn't see it then, but it was undeniable now.

With a sigh, I went back into the house. My heart went out to both Coop and Remi. When my husband had passed, I had only hoped to have someone close to me to be there for me who understood my pain. My daughter was there for me, but there was nothing like the support of the person in love with you. That support is different and desperately needed. But I believed my late husband had sent me Russell. It had taken a few years, but I had gotten my happily ever after. Fortunately for Coop, he would get his, sooner than later, if only he would open up his heart to it.

I felt so bad, like I had failed at the task True had given me. But I didn't plan on giving up. Yet, I knew better than to push Coop or Remi at the moment. I had just laid something pretty heavy on them. Therefore, I planned on giving them a few days to think about it before I started to nag.

"I'm finished!" Joy announced as I entered the living room. She stood up and waved the homework sheet in my face.

"Good job, baby." I smiled as I looked it over. The tracings were sketchy, but for a five-year-old, that's all her kindergarten teacher was going to get.

Just as I got ready to ask Joy what she wanted for lunch, the doorbell rang. I raced for the door, hoping it was Remi, Coop, or better yet, *both*. But as I peered through the peephole, my hope was crushed, and my heart was broken. With shaky hands, I opened the door for the two police officers standing on the other side of my door.

"Angel Jenkins?" one of the officers asked me.

"That's her," Jameel's bitch ass confirmed behind them.

I trembled with fear, praying to God that this wasn't the moment that the last family member I had to hold on to would be taken from me. "May I help you?" I asked the officers.

Jameel ripped, "Yeah, you can stop holding my daughter hostage!"

The Black officer cringed as he turned and gritted, "Sir. Please."

The Hispanic officer spoke up, "I'm Officer Lopez, and this is my partner, Officer Brown. Do you have his daughter in your physical custody?"

I sighed deeply, contemplating what to do. I faulted myself for not going into hiding with Joy the moment True passed. I gritted, confessing, "Yes, but—"

"But nothing. I'm her father, and I have shared custody," Jameel interrupted.

My eyes narrowed as I glared behind the cops at Jameel's punk ass. "Which you never shared until you were tired of paying child support. You don't pay now. She's dead. You're free, so go!"

Officer Brown lifted a hand to stop my rambling. "Ma'am, *legally*, he has parental custody of the child."

"But—"

"If you feel as if you have a right to custody, you can file for it and fight it out in court. But as for today, you have to give the child to her biological and legal father or we can arrest you for kidnapping."

Tears stung my eyes and quickly began to flow. I stood firmly in the doorway holding the doorknob, refusing to budge.

With a slight step towards me, Officer Lopez urged, "Ma'am, please relinquish the child peacefully or we will arrest you and make this situation even harder. It's your choice."

Sucking my teeth, I lowered my head, feeling so defeated. "Okay," I whimpered.

Reluctantly, I left the doorway. I heard their footsteps following me, so I spun around. "That son of a bitch is *not* allowed in my house."

Laughing, Jameel shrugged. "Whatever." He stood in the doorway, taunting me with his grin.

"Fuck you!" I spat as Officer Brown stood between us. "You *would* wait until my daughter is dead to pull this shit, you scary motherfucker!"

As he continued to laugh, Officer Lopez walked towards him to quiet him as Officer Brown guided me away from Jameel and into the house. With tears streaming down my face, I walked into the living room. I wanted to appear like everything was okay so Joy wouldn't be scared, but I couldn't. My heart was broken for myself and her. Her mother had already been taken from us. Now, they were about to separate us all because that punk wanted to be vindictive. At that moment, I felt regret for not allowing Russell and Coop to kill that motherfucker.

"Joy, baby, your father is here for you." She looked up at me with confusion. I bent down, took her hand, and guided her to her feet.

"Daddy?" she questioned.

"Yes, do you remember your daddy?" I asked her.

"Yeeeah," she answered slowly.

I sat down on the loveseat with burdens so heavy that I could no longer stand. I looked into her eyes as I held her hands. "Do you want to spend some time with him?"

"Yeeeah." She shrugged and then gave me big, hopeful eyes. "But can I still live here with you?"

My heart went out to her confusion. I hated that I couldn't protect her from any of this. "Grandma is going to make sure that you come back, okay, baby?"

She nodded. "Okay."

My tears were making her visibly sad. I wiped my face as I sadly stood and walked her to the door. Officer Brown was behind me. The front door was still open, but through the closed screen door, I could see Officer Lopez and Jameel on the porch. I wanted to take off running. I wanted to take my only treasure from True and run. I would leave everything, even Russell, just to be with her. But I knew that in order to keep her forever, I had to do this right. I put on a strong front, not wanting to give Jameel the satisfaction of seeing my pain.

As we approached the door, I squatted and kissed Joy's cheek. "I love Grandma's baby."

"I love you too, Grandma."

I let her go, weeping as she walked towards her father. As soon as Officer Brown walked out, I slammed the door. Wailing, I slid down the door and collapsed on the floor.

I had lost everything.

23

COOP

- A MONTH LATER -

"Hey, Coop."

Hearing Tamika's voice, I cringed. I was so sick of this little girl buzzing around me every time I came to the office. I barely made eye contact with her as I asked, "What's up, Tamika?"

Her smile was full of so much thirst as she announced, "I'm going to lunch."

I shrugged at her simple ass. "Okay."

"You want something?" she pushed.

I shook my head and put my attention back on the contracts in front of me. "Nope."

"I do," Rakim chimed in.

She reluctantly gave him her attention. "I was talking to my boss."

"I hired you."

Tamika rolled her eyes. "Because he wasn't at work at the time. You're an employee just like me."

Rakim gruffed as he lay back on the couch in my office. "Well, fuck you then."

My eyes darted towards him, "Nigga," I warned.

He shrugged, looking at me. "What?"

Tamika sneered at Rakim before she switched away from the doorway. I shook my head, making a mental note to find a reason to fire that baby mama drama waiting to happen.

"This is a place of business. Be professional," I warned Rakim.

He chuckled. "That THOT ain't no professional."

I glared at him. "You hired her, though."

"Whenever I fuck her, I'm gon' fuck the shit outta her," he promised with a bite on his bottom lip. "I'mma take all these games she's playing out on that pussy."

"Whatever. What's up with the block? Them niggas making my money?"

As Rakim ran down how the block was running, I forced myself to listen. This was what my life was now; hustling, managing the rec center, and Keyes. But, a month after True's death, I was over managing the center. I was proud of what it had turned into. It was a success. Many of the boys in the neighborhood were taking advantage of the facility. Cops had told me that crime had even gone down a bit in the area. Many boys were even getting bussed to the center from different neighborhoods. I had completed the task. I didn't need to come in daily anymore. I was in the midst of hiring a manager so I could get back to the block.

I had made an effort to change my ways, but I needed something else to put my mind on and to take my frustrations out on. I needed the griminess of the streets, the dirt, and the filth.

"RonRon been flipping the work faster than a motherfucker. He wanna get fronted two more bricks," Rakim explained.

My eyebrows rose with the excitement of more money pouring in. "Word?"

"Yeah."

"He paid the money for the first brick I fronted him?" I asked.

"Damn near. Well, front him five more, if he promises to turn that shit around in a month."

Rakim nodded. "Bet."

Just then, Tamika walked slowly past the office door. Rakim was facing me, so he didn't see her. Her smile was lust-filled and seductive as she licked her glossed lips, gazing at me.

My dick jumped. I hadn't felt pussy in months, but my dick didn't harden. Pussy was the last thing on my brain. Women weren't even on my list of priorities. The only woman I talked to was Angel, who I saw frequently because we had agreed to share custody of Keyes.

Angel had stopped asking me about Remi weeks ago, after I had shut that shit down for the fifth time and threatened to never let her see Keyes again if she brought it up again. I understood what True had tried to do, but she had gone over my head on this. She knew I had no interest in being that close to another woman again. I felt bad that I had left Remi feeling rejected, but I'd had no other choice. There was no way that I would voluntarily put myself in the position to hurt and yearn for something again. I had done enough of that as a child.

However, I felt like I had not only lost True, but I had lost Remi's friendship too. Every time I mourned True, I also mourned the connection I had formed with Remi. But my feelings for her were what was keeping me away from her. My feelings for her were why I had to ignore her and focus on living without True the best way I could and raise my son. I couldn't put myself through love again. I had stayed away from women for a reason, and I was never going to allow myself to fall again.

REMI

The door to the den creaked open. I looked up from the book I was reading on my Kindle app. Frances' smiling face was peeking at me through a crack in the door.

"Are you sure you don't want something to eat?" she asked.

I smiled. "I'm sure."

Her head tilted to the side. "Okay now. I can cook, girl."

"I believe you. It smells good." It indeed did. The aroma of fried catfish had been swimming in my nose for the last hour.

Francis gave me an interrogating yet sweet look. "You on a diet or something? Looks like you've lost weight."

"I have, but I'm not on a diet unless *stress* is a diet."

She chuckled. "That's the best diet, girl. Makes you drop weight quick."

I chuckled halfheartedly. "You're right about that."

In the last month, I had lost a drastic twenty pounds. I was happy to see it finally coming off, but it wasn't how I wanted to lose it.

Francis sighed. "Well, I'll let you rest."

"Thanks. I'll be sure to turn Sidney in an hour."

"Thank you." Again, she gave me a sweet smile as she left the doorway.

A twinge of regret hit my heart. Francis had been trying so hard to show me kindness since I'd started working for her husband, Sidney, two weeks ago. But after my experience with True and her family, I felt it was best that I keep a strictly professional relationship with my patients and their families.

Getting back into the book, *Secrets of a Side Bitch*, I fought to keep my attention on this scandalous but page-turning, storyline, rather than that constant nagging feeling in the pit of my stomach.

It had been a month since I'd walked out of Angel's house; a long month of thinking of Coop. True's letter had only ignited a fire in me that I had been fighting to smother before I read it. She had been right. Those nights that Coop and I had spent together talking and supporting one another had shown me how good he and I could be together. Yet, despite True giving us her blessing, he could walk out on that chemistry and perfection. He ran away from it as if I were disgusting. He had spent so many nights telling me that Banks was an idiot for not choosing me. Yet, when he got the chance, he hadn't chosen me either.

I had lost everything: my man, my friends, and then I lost another set of friends and a man who I never got the chance to even experience. It was June. I was used to my summers being full of parties, drunken nights, and laughter. While reading that letter, I thought that maybe God was finally giving me a chance at a happily ever after.

But maybe a happily ever after just wasn't in the cards for me.

I wasn't going to dwell in the self-pity, however. I would wait out this tortuous feeling in the pit of my stomach and keep living. Coop's rejection had not made me forget what True had taught me.

I was broken, but at least I still had a life to be broken in.

24

ANGEL

"Calm down, baby." The ripping sound of tape tearing from the dispenser cut through the room. I could feel Russell staring at me as he stood over one of the boxes that was littering my living room. I was moving that next day, moving in with Russell. If moving wasn't stressful enough, I also had a court date for full custody of Joy. I had filed for an emergency court date with the help of a very expensive lawyer that Russell had retained for me.

"I can't calm down." I sighed. "I'm a nervous *fucking* wreck." I wrung my sweaty hands together as I paced back and forth.

"Come here."

I'd heard Russell's calming, soothing order, but I couldn't comply right then. I was so nervous that my stomach was turning. I started to argue with him, "Russell—"

"Come here." Being the alpha man that he was, he insisted.

I felt a soft tug on my elbow. I turned towards his smothering, yet consoling, alpha persona and allowed him to wrap me in his arms. His sexy, masculine aroma soothed me. His arms protected me from the evils of the world.

I soon felt a kiss on the top of my head. "Everything is going to work out," he assured me.

"I hope to God it will." I laughed. "Are you sure you want me to move in with you?"

He chuckled as if my question was silly. "Why wouldn't I?"

I pouted into his chest. "I've been dealing with so much drama since we got together. I feel like I'm only adding confusion and chaos into your life."

I felt him shrug. "So? Of course, I still want you to move in with me."

I looked up into his eyes, looking at him as if he was a unicorn. "Why?"

Russell smiled at my confusion with his sincerity. He bent down and kissed my forehead so soft and lovingly. "Because with you is where I am supposed to be."

I sighed with relief as we stared into one another's eyes.

Then, slowly, the most mischievous smile began to spread across his beard. His dimples were buried so deep that I wanted to make them my home. His eyes began to twinkle with happiness. I stopped gushing and began to wonder what he was smiling so hard about.

He stepped back, playfully biting his lip through his smile.

"What..." I stopped my interrogating as he reached into his pocket and dropped down to one knee in one smooth swoop. I looked on the floor to see what he could be down there for. I hadn't seen him drop anything. Like an idiot, I looked around and under me until he called for me.

"Baby."

I looked down at him and gasped. "Oh!" There he rested on his knee holding an open velvet ring box that held a white gold engagement ring with a princess center stone with a three-carat diamond.

My eyes instantaneously filled with tears. My shaky hands flew to my mouth. I assumed what he was doing, but until he said the words, I didn't have the courage to believe it.

"Angel Marie Jenkins, would you please do me the honor of being my wife?"

The awaiting tears slid down my face as I gasped for breath that I had been holding since he'd pulled the ring out of his pocket.

A year ago, I could not imagine my life without True. I could not see how I would go on without her. I knew that surviving for Joy would be the only motivation I would have to keep going. Many times, however, I even wondered if that would be enough.

But, then, Russell came like a knight in shining armor. It was breathtaking the way that his presence put my insecurities to sleep, the way that he starved all of my fears. He gave me another reason to keep pushing, to keep going, to keep believing in miracles and love.

"Well?" he pushed nervously.

Yet, I did not want to corrupt his calm and happy life with my drama, chaos, and sadness. He had given me so much more, so that is what he deserved.

REMI

A few days after trying to read my way into not thinking about Coop, I was done with the entire *Secrets of a Side Bitch* series, and I was *still* thinking about him. I was tired of wondering why he'd walked out on me and why he had been so rude. I was tired of being lonely and missing the kinship I had felt at True's home. I was missing something, and it was *him*. I knew I couldn't have True again. She was gone. But I refused to continue to avoid Angel in order to avoid Coop. And I refused to allow Coop to keep avoiding me. If he didn't want me romantically, fine, but we could at least be friends.

I nervously walked into the rec center. My knees quaked under my form-fitting, mauve tank dress. My legs were so weak with anxiety that I was nearly sliding against the slippery tile floor of the rec center in my strappy, gold heels.

"May I help you?"

I smiled at the older man sitting behind the reception desk. His smile was perverted as he looked my curves up and down.

"I'm looking for Coop. Is he here?" I probably should have called, but I knew his orneriness wouldn't answer a call or text message from me.

The old man nodded. "Yes, he's in the gym."

I remembered where it was from my tour, so I started heading that way.

"Um, would you like me to get him for you?" he asked.

"No, thank you," I said over my shoulder.

As I headed that way, I ran my hands through my long stresses to make sure my hair was tamed. I had recently gotten a sew-in with twenty-six inches of Malaysian hair. The hair stylist had layered it and cut a swooping Chinese bang and curled it in loose barrel curls.

"Good D, Terrell!" As soon as I heard Coop's gruff, smoky voice, I became even more nervous. "Hustle, Brandon! What the hell are you doin'?!"

I started to second guess myself, worried that he would embarrass me yet again, only now in front of a bigger audience. I stood there in the doorway of the gym, ready to make an about-face until some of the boys started to stare. Some of their little asses even started to catcall. So, I felt like I had no choice but to complete my mission.

I swallowed hard and continued towards the bleachers where I saw Coop sitting with his back to me until whatever everyone was staring at behind him caught his attention, and he turned around. I stopped dead in my tracks, waiting and hoping for a smile or some sign of relief when our eyes met, but his face remained as hard as stone. He turned back around, giving his attention back to the practice. Let down, I wondered for a few seconds if he would even make this easier and meet me halfway. I became disappointed when I realized he was still sitting. Embarrassment and nerves turned to anger as I then started to march towards his evil ass. But then he finally stood slowly, said something to the guy standing in front of him with a whistle in his mouth, and then began to amble towards me as if he didn't have a care in the world. It was as if he hadn't spent the last month missing me as much as I had missed him.

I took a deep breath as he came closer and closer. Many of the boys were still staring, holding inquisitive smirks, and mumbling to each other.

I couldn't think of what to do with my hands, so I folded my arms across my chest. I could feel my heart beating uncontrollably fast as

Coop finally was in arm's reach of me. I parted my lips to say something, even though I didn't know what exactly.

However, before I could say anything, he took my breath away and rendered me speechless, by coldly asking, "What are you doing here, Remi?"

He was so mean, so emotionless. It was astonishing to me. Even though he had been the same when I'd seen him last, I thought it was because of the shock of reading True's words. But, now, he'd had so much time to think, to exist without my friendship. But clearly, it hadn't affected him the same way it had me at all.

"I, um... I wanted to... Um..." The hostile glare in his eyes had me tongue-tied. "I just wanted to say hi."

When he grimaced, I felt that same embarrassment and disappointment I had a month ago. Only this time, it made me mad instead of ashamed. "You don't miss me at all?" I snapped.

I just couldn't believe he had the nerve to stand there and look right through me as if we hadn't spent the most emotional three months together, like I hadn't spent hours wiping his tears.

My eyes squinted as I stared at him, trying to see who he truly was. "You're that cold?" I asked. "You feel nothing? She wants us to—"

His nostrils flared as he bit his bottom lip and gritted. "Don't mention her."

But I pressed, "We owe her."

He continued to scowl, only this time he wouldn't even look at me. "Didn't I say don't fucking mention her?"

I recoiled. "You don't have anything to say?" My heart was beating fast and hard with disappointment and anger.

Finally, he looked at me, asking, "Would you please leave?"

It was a question that had come out so demanding that it offended me.

My eyes bucked slightly with shock. "Leave?"

He stood stern. "That's what I said."

I laughed hysterically. This felt so familiar. Clearly, I hadn't learned anything from Banks' betrayal. "You know what?" I asked, shaking my head. "Cool. Bet this is the last time that I beg a man to see me. You can believe that."

I turned on my heels and stormed out. I had no hope that he would follow me. Clearly, I no longer needed to hold on to what I'd felt back then because Coop had shown me twice how he felt now. He'd made it crystal clear that what I had seen or felt before True's death was in my head and nowhere in his heart.

COOP

"Damn, who was that?"

Shawn was still staring behind me at the entrance of the gym as if Remi was still there. But she was long gone. I had made sure of it.

"Nobody," I grumbled as I sat back on the bleachers.

"It didn't look like nobody."

I glared at him as he stood over me with a goofy grin on his face. "Well, it *was* no-fucking-body. Don't you have a practice to run, motherfucka?"

He lifted his hands in surrender. "Aye, man, I was just asking a question."

"Keep talking, and I'mma knock the shit outta you, dawg."

Shawn chuckled as if I was playing, but, lucky for him, he walked away and continued practice. I watched the boys' practice game. The rec center's basketball team was now a part of the city league. I had been excited about the upcoming season until Remi showed up.

No matter how hard I tried to block her out of my mind, as I watched the practice, she invaded my mind. Her beauty was still as breathtaking as it had been the last time I'd seen her. That left me enraged. I wanted not to want her, need her, or think about her. I didn't have it in me to put myself out there again. I didn't have any more love to give. True had sucked it out of me and worn it out.

This was ruining my life. I couldn't focus on anything but True and our connection... and how I had never felt that for anyone else except Remi.

ANGEL

"Your Honor, this shouldn't even be a discussion," Jameel's lawyer cockily stated. "My client is the legal and biological father. He had shared custody with the mother prior to her death. The fact that the grandmother is demanding full custody is preposterous."

"I beg to differ," my lawyer, Regina, cut in. "Your Honor, when a parent is deemed unfit, then the grandmother does indeed have rights to custody of the child."

Jameel whipped his head toward me and Regina right along with his lawyer.

"Unfit?" his lawyer questioned.

"Yes," Regina pressed. "Unfit. May I approach the bench, Your Honor?"

Judge Samuel nodded, and Regina and Jameel's lawyer quickly approached. I could feel Jameel staring at me, but I kept my eyes on Regina with a satisfying grin. I watched the lawyer's face as he read every derogatory text message that Jameel had ever sent True after they divorced where he voiced no interest in being a father to Joy. After getting my court date, I had gone through True's phone for evidence to prove that he was unfit, and I had found plenty.

Once the judge was done reading, Regina returned to our table, explaining, "I also have some recordings that I would like for you to hear, Your Honor."

Finally, I looked towards Jameel and smiled at him pleasingly as Regina pushed play on the recorder and put the audio on speaker. Soon Jameel's filth filled the air. There were voicemails that he'd left on True's phone starting from when they had divorced.

"If I have to pay all of this fucking money, you can parent your own damn daughter. Y'all don't need me... I thought the doctors gave you a year to live?" As it played, tears fell from my eyes. "Why are you still alive? Die bitch... I shouldn't have to pay you shit for you being a fucking mother. *You* asked for this life. You wanted to have a child, not me... You're still alive? Why? That tumor hasn't killed you yet?"

The derogatory messages went on and on, exposing Jameel's obscenity and refusal to be a father, until he figured it was financially beneficial if he were one full time.

"All right, all right, all right!" the judge cut in with a disgusted look on his face. "That's enough. Turn that off," he ordered.

Regina ended the recording, and I sat back feeling relief as I wiped my tears. Finally, my daughter's side had been heard.

However, clearly that had not been enough for the judge.

Jameel's lawyer pleaded, "Your Honor, my client's personal feelings towards the mother has nothing to do with how he will care for the child."

Regina laughed cynically. "It has *everything* to do with how he will care for the child and it proves how he felt about being a parent."

The judge banged his gavel. "That's enough!!" he snapped as his fingers frustratingly combed his forehead. "This a courtroom, not Jerry Springer."

Seeing his frustration, I jumped up. "Your Honor, please? As my daughter died, she begged me to make sure that I had custody of Joy because she knew that Joy would be better off with me. I will ensure that I give her a loving and nurturing home." Tears came to my eyes as I clung to the table, begging him, "Please? This is what True wanted."

Sighing, the judge lifted a hand to stop my pleas. "I understand completely, Ms. Dunlap, but unfortunately, what your daughter wants does not rule this courtroom."

25

REMI

♫Tell me whatcha say now?
Tell me whatcha say
Come again?
If you cannot stay down
Then you do not have to pretend
Like there is no way out
I shoulda never let you in
Cause you got me face down♫

I was laying across my ottoman staring up at the ceiling. A glass of Nightjar wine was in my hand. After fleeing the rec center and running to my car, I headed straight home and stripped down to my bra and panties. Then I called off work. I didn't have the energy to do anything but drink and waddle in my anger.

♫And don't take this personal
But you're the worst

You know what you've done to me
And although it hurts I know
I just can't keep runnin' away ♫

"*I DON'T NEED YOU, I don't need you,*" I sang along to Jhene Aiko. "*I don't need you, I don't need you. But I...*'Hate yo' ass, Coop!" I hissed at the ceiling so harsh as if his cocky ass was hoisted up there. "Fuck you! Who the fuck do you think you are any-fucking-way?"

I was swimming with anger. Banks had been an asshole, but I had never had a man be so cold to me to my face. Banks had at least pretended to care. Coop didn't have an ounce of that decency in a bone in his body.

"Urrrgh, who the fuck is this?" I groaned as the doorbell rang. "Fuck that."

I was drunk with anger, and I was on my way to being drunk off of the wine. I had finished two bottles and was already on my way to finishing the third. Whoever was at the door could suck my dick.

However, whoever was on the other side started to bang on it. So, I reached for my phone and turned the music up louder.

"*I don't mean to! I don't mean to! I don't mean to! I don't mean to! But I loooove...*" Startled, I sat straight up as the knocker started to hammer on my window, causing the glass to sound as if it were about to break.

"Who the fuck?!" I jumped up and rushed towards the door. I still had no intention of opening it. I was just going to curse out whoever was on the other side knocking on my door like they had lost their mind.

Standing on my tiptoes, I peered through the peephole and gasped. Suddenly, all my anger subsided, and I was like putty. Even with a face flooded with frustration, Coop was fascinating to lay eyes on.

But he was still an asshole! So, I whipped the door open, ready to read him for filth, but as he laid eyes on me, the sadness and sincerity in them had me speechless once again.

The closer he came, the more I couldn't breathe. The more I looked at him, his towering body, massive build, beautiful melanin, and gorgeous face, the more I realized I didn't want his friendship. Forget his friendship. I wanted *him*. I needed him. I wanted to help him heal from the hurt in his eyes. And I was so happy that True had been selfless enough to give us her blessing.

Stepping into me, he grabbed both of my hands, rested his forehead on top of my head, and admitted, "I need you."

COOP

I knew that showing up at Remi's crib was digging my own grave.

I had barely survived True. I was still recovering. But as I left the rec center that day, I couldn't get True or Remi out of my mind. I was tired of the two replaying over and over again in my head. I needed them both, but could only physically have Remi, and she would help me heal from losing True. True had been right. I needed Remi to make me better and whole again. I knew her address from seeing her ID so many times lying around True's house when Remi was working there. I showed up, ready to plead my case and shower her with my apologies.

However, when she opened the door, her exquisite body wrapped in nothing but panties and a bra, I had to admit that my fear of giving myself to another woman did not outweigh how much this woman meant to me and my survival.

As she stood there, "Mood" by dvsn started blaring inside the house like some cute joke that True was playing on us to set this insanely, sentimental gesture that I was reluctantly making.

I cringed inwardly as I let my stone wall down and walked towards my destiny.

As I held her hands, I remembered the support she had given me when I needed it the most. The comfort in her hands let me know I still needed it.

With my forehead on the top of her head, I admitted, "I need you."

I hated how I felt when I admitted that. I hated giving my fate to yet another woman, but it gave me relief that I was still able to do something to please True. I could still make her happy. And Remi had been right. I did owe True that.

I lifted my head to look into her eyes. She bit her bottom lip nervously and finally let her guard down. She moved out of the doorway and gave me space to come in.

Stepping into the doorway, I held her waist as I guided her inside and closed the door.

She reached back for one of my hands and led me to the couch. She reached for her phone on the ottoman and turned down the music.

She stared at me only the way a woman does when she's pissed at you but still loves you.

I cowered and peeked at her. "You mad at me?"

Snapping, she swung and punched me in the arm. "Yes!"

When Remi laughed, I was relieved. "I'm sorry. I didn't... This was... It was just too much for me."

"It was too much for me too, but damn, you didn't have to be mean to me. That hurt!"

I turned towards her and pulled her towards me. We sat sitting face to face on the couch.

"Look, I never wanted to be this close to any woman. When it happened with True, it was an accident that came out of nowhere and was the best and worst thing that ever happened to me. I never want to feel that type of pain again, so I ran from you."

Looking at me, I could see some relief that she had been at first too frightened to completely let show. "But?" she asked.

I smiled. "What you mean?"

With an adorable smile, she raised an eyebrow. "Is there a 'but' coming?"

I smiled harder and shook my head. Squeezing her hand, I answered, "No, there's an and... *And...* I'm done running from you."

She finally met my intense stare with her own. I could see that her breath was choppy as her chest heaved. "Soooo?" she asked slowly. "What is it that we're going to be?"

"What do you want us to be?"

Adorably, she shrugged. "I don't know."

I bit my lip with a teasing smile and leaned towards her, making her lie back on the couch. Her eyes were full of so much anxiety as my lips came closer to hers. "You don't know?" I dared her. But closing in on her space had left her speechless. "Huh, Remi?" I pressed. "You don't know?"

Before she could answer, I kissed her. I felt like a boy losing his virginity as I finally got the opportunity to taste her without feeling any guilt. At first, I enjoyed the taste of her lip gloss as I sucked her bottom lip. Then the beast in me took over. I hungrily tasted her mouth. Our kiss was long, throaty, and passionate.

I hadn't come over for this—the physical—but the way she breathed into my mouth told me she wanted it. Feeling as hard as my dick was, I needed to finally feel her.

I began to leave a trail of kisses down her neck. I took my time because, even though it felt like I already had her, I had a point to prove. I wanted her to realize I had been worth the wait and headache.

As I traveled south, I took a moment to taste each nipple, and she hissed lovingly. The way she sang along to the R&B soaring from her speaker made it hard to keep traveling, but I kept going. Once at her stomach, her hands were in the way, hiding it from me. Taking her by the wrists, I held them at her side as I tongue kissed every gentle curve.

The scent of her was already filling the air. It smelled like the sweet aroma of a meal I had been starving for. I left her stomach and traveled down to her dampness that was pulsating with need. I slid her panties off. Her legs opened for me as I threw the thongs to the floor. My tongue then grazed her bare, pink center. Her back arched as a sweet moan left her lips. I started to lash her clit with my tongue, and she started to cry out. I released her wrists and started to cup her soft breasts, squeezing and stimulating her nipples as I started to suck her throbbing clit.

"Mmmm!" she moaned above the music.

"Yeah, that's it," I spoke into her pussy. "Cum for me."

I wanted to taste her release. I began to suck more intensely until I felt her pouring into my mouth. Most of it ended up in my beard. I sat up, resting on my knees as I pulled my shorts down. I looked down on her as she heaved from the orgasm. I planted myself between her legs and brought my hard brass to her leaking opening. As I slowly pressed inside of her, she reached up, clawed at my shirt and brought me down to her, kissing me just as passionately as we'd done before. It made me harder as she tasted her own cum.

REMI

I cringed as I heard my cell phone blasting in my ear somewhere near me. My eyes pried open as they adjusted to the sudden light of the living room. I blinked rapidly, realizing where I was. The last thing that I remembered was Coop and I cumming together before he collapsed down next to me.

I had fallen asleep in his arms. Feeling them around me as I woke up had me smiling from ear to ear.

I reached for my phone and realized it wasn't mine that was ringing. I sat up as much as Coop's large arms would allow and picked his phone up from the floor.

I started to nudge him. "Coop... Coop." He groaned as I stuck the phone in his face. "Your phone is ringing."

Even coming out of a deep sleep, he was so beautiful. As he took the phone from me and answered, I wondered what I had fallen into. Coop was the kind of man who left a woman not thinking clearly. And now that I had had him physically, I was completely smitten. After Banks, I swore to myself that I would make better decisions when it came to men. I promised myself that I wouldn't jump into anything feelings first, and be more careful. Yet, Coop was far from that.

Looking at him felt like loving dangerously.

Hanging up, he began to detangle his body from mine and sit up. "We gotta go."

"*We?*" I asked curiously. "Where?"

He stood up, and I was in awe. As we had sex, he had finally taken off all of his clothes, but I hadn't had the chance to see him completely, as he lay on top of me, giving me continuous, earth-shattering orgasms. Yet, standing up now, I could finally lay eyes on him completely.

He was perfect.

He didn't even notice me gawking at him as he answered, "To Angel's."

"Why?"

He shrugged as he threw on his wife beater. "She didn't say."

I immediately shook my head. "Unt uh. I don't have the energy for another one of her emotional surprises."

Coop cocked his head and ordered me, "Girl, c'mon."

"Did she ask for me?" I pressed as I sat up, holding my heavy breasts.

"No, but I want you to go with me." He had said it with so much ease, as if me being with him was so natural.

"Coop."

He looked up from stepping into his shorts. "Yeah?"

"You never answered my question," I reminded him.

His bushy eyebrows curled. "What question?"

"What are we?"

I needed to know. I didn't want to be naïve again. We'd had sex, but that meant nothing to most men. I needed to hear him say it.

Coop pulled up his shorts, saddening me because his beautiful piece of steel was now hidden from me. He walked towards me and sat back down on the couch. He held my hand, answering, "We are *us*. You're mine, and I'm yours. We're going to do exactly what True wanted us to do. Like you said, we owe her."

COOP

Remi and I spent the ride to Angel's house catching up since we hadn't had a real conversation since True's funeral. Every time there was a pause in our conversation, our eyes wandered towards one another's, giving each other flirtatious and intense glances. I playfully squeezed her thighs. She couldn't keep her hands from clinging to my biceps and running her nails over my chest.

We had been forced apart because of loyalty and then fear. Now, we were finally in each other's arms, and we couldn't get enough of one another.

When we pulled up to Angel's house, Remi beamed when she saw Joy riding her bike up and down the driveway. Once I was in park, she happily jumped out my ride and ran towards Joy.

"Remi!" I heard Angel call from the porch. "I didn't know you were coming."

As I got out of the car, I heard Remi tease Angel. "Oh yeah? Don't feel good getting surprised, does it?"

Angel smirked as she walked towards Remi with her hands on her hips. She questionably stared back and forth between me and Remi as I met them in the driveway.

Remi ignored Angel's glaring eyes and gave her attention to Joy. "Hey, Joy!" Remi cooed as she bent down and hugged her.

Looking up from her bike ride, Joy squinted as the hot June sun beamed down on her as it set. "Hi, Remi!"

Remi kissed her cheek. "I missed you, honey."

"I missed you too!" she cooed.

I reached down and playfully pinched Joy's cheek. "You ain't speaking today?"

She giggled as she swatted my hand away. "Hi, Coop!"

"Hey, baby. Have you been good?" he asked her.

"Yep!" she promised with a nod.

"Good job." Looking down on her was sweet sorrow. She was the spitting image of her father, but I saw True so much in her smile that it hurt while making me smile at the same time.

As Joy took off on her bike down the driveway, I asked Angel, "What's going on?"

She had insisted that I come over right then, so I was eager to know what was going on. I had made sure that Remi came with me because now that I had her, I couldn't get enough of her. I finally felt whole again. Life finally felt right and like I was missing nothing except True. However, standing there with Angel, Joy, and Remi, I felt like True was still in my life to some extent.

"You tell me," Angel insisted as she continued to look between me and Remi with a smile.

I taunted her by ignoring her subliminal question with my usual crass attitude. "Maaan, why you call me over here?"

Suddenly, Angel's eyes filled with concern. "Where is Keyes?!"

"Chill," I insisted. "He's with Rakim."

"Oh *hell* no!" Angel snapped as she shook her head.

First, Angel gave me the middle finger. Then she started to beam as she announced, "I got custody of Joy."

Remi gasped and shrieked, "What?!"

Angel jumped a bit from the excitement. "Yes, *full* custody. The judge was going to give us shared custody, until I played him a tape of Jameel acting a fool in her house a few months ago."

"That's dope, Angel," I told her as I took her into my arms and hugged her. We rocked from side to side for a moment before I let her go.

"I'm so happy for you," Remi told her as Angel wiped a lone tear from her eye. "And... Oops!... Is that an engagement ring on your finger?"

Following Remi's eyesight, I peeped the phat-ass rock as well and grinned with pride, happy that True's wishes were coming true. Her mother was being taken care of.

Just then, Russell came out of her house, and she looked back at him with a smile. "Yes," she gushed. "He asked me to marry him yesterday, and I said yes!"

"Awwwww!" Remi squealed as she hugged Angel tight while Russell approached us.

Remi grabbed Angel's hand and checked out her ring, which she seemed to instantly envy. The ring *was* beautiful and sparkled blindly in the sunlight.

As Russell shook up with me, I told him, "Congratulations."

"Thanks." He grinned.

"Okay, soooo, enough of that," Angel pressed as she again looked between me and Remi. "What's going on with you two showing up here *together*?"

Remi lowered her head, blushing. I confidently held her hand as I replied, "This my baby."

It was time that I stopped fighting and running. Clearly, this was the path that I was supposed to take in my life. It had been a dangerously rough path that had led me to a place I didn't know I needed to be.

"Yes!" Angel shrieked as she brought Remi and me into a united hug.

"Good looking," Russell told me with a prideful smile.

As Angel released us, she told us both with tears in her eyes, "Thank you."

I shook my head. "No," I insisted. "I thank True for even giving me Remi. True was right. I need Remi. I love her."

Angel's eyes bucked as Remi's widened even more as she looked up at me. "You *love* me?" Remi asked.

I smiled down on her, admiring her as I put my arms around her, bringing her into the place where I always wanted her to be—under me. "Yes, I love you, baby." Then I looked around, realizing how complete I finally felt. "I love all of you. We went through something together that created a bond between us that will never go away. Angel, you, and Joy will forever be my family. I will always be here for you. I lost True. *We* lost True. But I realize now that I finally have the family I never had." Tears slid down Angel's face as she leaned into Russell. He put his arm around her as she clung to his waist, crying happy tears for once. Then, I looked down on Remi's joy-filled, tearful eyes with the same admiring, sincere look that she was giving me. "Remi, I will always love you. This love developed from something different and deeper. It wasn't from intimacy, but the bond and chemistry we have is stronger than lust. And I know it won't be long before I'm madly in love with you."

Grinning into my face, she stood on her tiptoes and kissed me on the lips slowly. "I love you too."

Squealing, Angel wrapped her arms around us both, bringing us into a bear hug once again. "I love y'all too!"

I grinned into their embrace, knowing that this was where I needed to be.

And True was there with us. She would always be there...with us.

True was now my angel that had saved me from my old self. Even after experiencing her untimely, traumatic death, I was like brand new. She had lost her life while giving me a new one.

Every once in a while, in the middle of chaos, life gives us a fairy tale.

The End!
#FUCKCANCER

If you would like to receive a text message when a book is released by Jessica N. Watkins, using your phone, send the keyword "Jessica" as a text message to 25827!

MORE BOOKS BY JESSICA N. WATKINS

Follow Jessica on social media:
Facebook: https://www.facebook.com/missauthor
Facebook Group: https://www.facebook.com/groups/femistryfans/
Instagram: https://www.instagram.com/authorjwatkins/Twitter:
https://twitter.com/authorjwatkins
Snapchat: @authorjwatkins

More books by Jessica N. Watkins:

SECRETS OF A SIDE BITCH SERIES (COMPLETE SERIES)
Secrets of a Side Bitch
Secrets of a Side Bitch 2
Secrets of a Side Bitch 3
Secrets of a Side Bitch – The Simone Story
Secrets of a Side Bitch 4

CAPONE AND CAPRI SERIES (COMPLETE SERIES)
Capone and Capri
Capone and Capri 2

A THUG'S LOVE SERIES (COMPLETE SERIES)
A Thug's Love
A Thug's Love 2
A Thug's Love 3
A Thug's Love 4
A Thug's Love 5

NIGGAS AIN'T SHIT (COMPLETE SERIES)
Niggas Ain't Shit
Niggas Ain't Shit 2

EVERY LOVE STORY IS BEAUTIFUL, BUT OURS IS HOOD
SERIES (COMPLETE SERIES)
Every Love Story Is Beautiful, But Ours Is Hood
Every Love Story Is Beautiful, But Ours Is Hood 2
Every Love Story Is Beautiful, But Ours Is Hood 3

WHEN THE SIDE NIGGA CATCH FEELINGS SERIES
(COMPLETE SERIES)
When The Side Nigga Catch Feelings
When the Side Nigga Catch Feelings 2

THE CAUSE AND CURE IS YOU SERIES (PARANORMAL
COMPLETE SERIES)
The Cause and Cure Is You
The Cause and Cure Is You 2

LOVE, SEX, LIES SERIES (COMPLETE SERIES)
Love, Sex, Lies
Love Hangover (Love, Sex, Lies 2)
Grand Hustle (Love, Sex, Lies 3)
Love Drug (Love, Sex, Lies 4)
Bang (Love, Sex, Lies 5)
Love Me Some Him (Love, Sex, Lies 6)
Good Girls Ain't No Fun (Love, Sex, Lies FINALE)

Don't miss another release from Jessica Watkins! Test the keyword "JWP" to 22828!

Jessica Watkins Presents is currently accepting submissions for the following genres: African American Romance, Urban Fiction, Women's Fiction, and BWWM Romance. If you are interested in becoming a best selling author and have a complete manuscript, please send the synopsis and the first three chapters to jwp.submissions@gmail.com.